PINK
DIAMONDS

Mikhaila Stettler

Creatrix Arts, Inc.
Santa Barbara, CA

Creatrix Arts, Inc.
133 E. De La Guerra, Ste. 51
Santa Barbara, CA 93101

Publisher's Note: This is a work of fiction. Names, characters, places, and incidents are a product of the author's imagination. Locales and public names are sometimes used for atmospheric purposes. Any resemblance to actual people, living or dead, or to businesses, companies, events, institutions, or locales is completely coincidental.

Cover Design: Emily Mahon
Author Photo: Kremer Johnson Photography

Ordering Information:
Quantity sales. Special discounts are available on quantity purchases by corporations, associations, and others. For details, contact the "Special Sales Department" at the address above.

PINK DIAMONDS/ Mikhaila Stettler. -- 1st ed.
ISBN 978-0-9981570-0-9

To Izaac, who always believed.

CHAPTER ONE

Daniel
My First Tangasm

It's been a few weeks since my first tangasm with Daniel. I stand in my closet assessing my wardrobe. I want to look hot and sexy but not slutty. My choices are limited — lots of business attire, casual clothes and yoga wear with a few cocktail dresses mixed in. The dresses are all at least ten years old and inappropriately short for a middle-aged peri-menopausal woman. Time to invest in a whole new wardrobe. I settle on a flowing low-cut top and a pair of skintight jeggings. It's a thing now, leggings that look like jeans. I have two pairs of shoes to choose from, both old and stretched out, a pair of salsa practice shoes from back in the day and a pair of hand-me-downs from Zhenya. This is going to be an expensive addiction, between a new tango wardrobe and made-for-tango-only shoes at two hundred bucks a pop. I take extra time with my makeup, apply a triple coat of mascara to my lashes, outline my mouth and shine my lips to a full pout. I check myself out. Not bad for 48. I give my hair a final fluff, blow a kiss to the mirror and head out.

My love affair with tango began with Daniel. I was still an ignorant novice. I had never stayed after class for social dancing before. My teacher, a dishy Ukrainian Jewess if there ever was one, kept encouraging me. "Alexis," she said, "The only way to get good at tango is to practice." But I felt insecure and intimidated. "I don't know, Zhenya," I said. I'd stayed late after class one time to watch. A group of experienced dancers frequented the *milonga* that followed class at this unlikely hotel bar near the Burbank airport. My corner seat by the DJ gave me an excellent vantage point to observe the ladies' footwork. It looked way beyond my meager technique. "I'm not really good enough yet," I said. What if I can't follow their lead? What if I start back-leading again? What if I make a fool of myself on the dance floor? What if no one wants to dance with me? I'm transported back to junior high, when my overriding concern was how to get boys to like me. "Maybe next week," I said.

Not one to give up, Zhenya suggested I take some private classes. I quickly improved. Back at the bar a few weeks later, I still felt tentative and uncomfortable. "What the hell," I thought, "If I want to get good at this, I'm going to have to bite the bullet and put myself out there." Class ended. I stayed. Marco invited me to dance. He was one of my favorite partners from class. We had good chemistry together, despite our height difference, he at six feet, me at five foot four. I liked Marco. He was kind and funny. I felt safe with him. He led me onto the dance floor. I was nervous, unsure. "Relax," Marco said and pulled me close. It was early still. There were only a few couples on the dance floor, some like us who had stayed after class and some early arrivals for the social dancing. His hand felt warm and comforting on my back. "Just listen to the music and let me lead you." I took a deep breath and tried to relax. I focused on feeling our connection and tried to sense his intention from his chest, the way Zhenya taught me. It worked! I was doing it, following him. Marco made it easy for me. He kept the steps basic, led me into a sequence we'd learned in class. I made it through the entire four-song set of the *tanda* with only a few stumbles.

Marco led me off the dance floor back to my stool near Zhenya's check-in table. "See, that wasn't so bad, was it?" she said. "No, I managed with Marco's help," I said and squeezed his hand. "Thank you for being so patient and kind, Marco." Marco squeezed my hand back and gave me a kiss on the cheek. "No problem, Alexis," he said, "You'll be a great dancer one day. Just keep practicing," More people had begun to trickle in now that class was over. The next *tanda* started up, a Nuevo Tango set. I like Nuevo Tango best, much more than traditional tango music. It's sexier, more dramatic. It speaks to me. I feel it in my body. It makes me want to dance. A man I had seen here the week before walked by and caught my eye. I nodded back, my confidence boosted by my first social dance experience.

He led me out onto the dance floor. "I'm Daniel. What's your name?" he said. "Alexis," I said, "But I should warn you I'm a beginner." Daniel smiled and held out his hand. "No worries," he said, "We'll take it easy." Daniel took me in his arms with gentle authority. He was tall, well built, about early-60's with greying hair. At first, he just stood holding me, breathing deep and shifting weight from left to right. It was easy to sync up with him. I liked the way he felt. Then he gave me a clear signal, a little lift, and the dance began. He walked me around the line of dance smooth and steady. I could feel him reading my energy. I'm a sucker for a man who can read energy. It felt like millions of tiny antennae caressing my field. The more I felt him feeling me, sensing me, attending to me, guiding me, taking care of me, the more I trusted him. God, he felt good!

The first song of the *tanda* ended. Daniel took a step back. Wide-eyed, I looked up into his face. I watched him check me out and saw the appreciation in his eyes. I was glad I'd made the effort to dress up a little. Usually I wore casual workout clothes to class, but all the women who came to dance dressed up in sexy tango outfits. It was part of the scene— sexy clothes and the cult of the high-heeled tango shoe. The next song started before I could say anything.

Daniel pulled me into the close embrace. I took a deep breath and willed myself to relax and focus. I closed my eyes and laid my cheek on his chest, on the soft black silk of his shirt. His scent intoxicated me, something exotic with a spicy top note I'd never smelled before. How a man smells is so major, either a turn-on or a turn-off, and there's nothing you can do to change that reaction. I nestled my face into his neck and breathed him in. The voice of reason, or maybe my mother, piped up, "Jesus, Alexis, what the fuck are you doing? You don't even know this man and you're nuzzling and sniffing him like a wild animal." Daniel just squeezed my hand. No time to think. Just feel and respond to his lead.

As we circled the dance floor, I felt protected in his arms, totally taken care of. I felt alive, wildly present in the moment. With my eyes closed, all my other senses amplified. I could feel the heat of his body against mine, the collar of his shirt tickling my face, the melody and rhythm of the music billowing through me, my feet caressing the floor. My feminine energy began to open and radiate. I could feel all my womanliness respond to his male essence. My sense of presence heightened, both his and my own. Our connection was intense. I could feel everything. We became one with each other and with the music. Daniel guided me into some simple *ochos*, crosses and *ocho cortados*. Miraculously I was able to follow him, to respond to the signals of his intent coming through his chest and hands. He slowed down our steps to express the dramatic sexy song. I matched him step for step, attuned to the rhythm of the music. I could feel his hand moving energy up my spine, opening my chakras. I gasped and almost stumbled. Daniel just pulled me closer. My pussy began to tingle. Waves of pleasure rolled up and down my body. I pressed myself up against him, leaned into him, more than I should have for proper technique, but I couldn't help myself. Daniel didn't seem to mind. He held the strength and power of his chest steady. He pulled me even closer, lifted my right hand into the upturned palm of his left. His touch made me feel contained and free at the same time. It sent a thrill of heat and electricity through my chest and my belly, down to the delta between my thighs.

The second song in the *tanda* ended. I stood there stunned. What just happened? Who was this man? I was in a daze. My legs felt shaky. I clung to him. I didn't want to open my eyes. The third and final song in the *tanda* began. Nothing existed but this man, our connection, and the song that moved us. I let all my energy flow free. I stroked the back of his neck and the back of his heart. I pressed my face into the side of his neck. I melted all over him. Daniel kept us moving in the line of dance, but I was oblivious to anything outside the circle of our embrace. I could feel my body heating up, getting wet inside and out. I was so turned on. We breathed together, felt together, moved together. It was like making love right on the dance floor, so intimate, so present, so connected. I was flying high in ecstasy.

The song ended. Daniel stepped back and slid his hands down to hold mine. I didn't want to open my eyes and break the spell. I didn't think I could walk off the floor on my own power. Without him holding me up, my legs felt weak and shaky, as though he'd just fucked my brains out. "I think I need to sit down," I said. Daniel seemed to understand and guided me to the nearest seat in a booth along the back wall. He sat with me while I tried to gather my wits. "Have you had any training in martial arts, or energy healing or something?" I asked him. The way he moved, how his body felt, how he shared his presence, how he tracked my energy all reminded me of master martial artists. "Quite a bit actually," he said, "Why do you ask?" I was still holding onto one of his hands. I didn't want to let go of him. My thigh was pressed up against his. I could feel how wet my pussy was from dancing with him. I wanted to lean over and kiss him. I had to stop myself. A fast *milonga* was playing as couples swirled past us. The bar was dark, the decor cheap and dated. A few random blue collar guys sat at the bar, looking surprised to find themselves mixed in amongst the well-dressed tango crowd. The dance floor was filling up. "The way you move energy," I said. "It's amazing." I have a thing for martial artists, especially if they're experts in all the internal practices. Their power and strength excite me. Their fierceness and capacity for controlled violence scare me and turn me on. If they know how to read energy, how to build the charge, how to circulate it, how to focus it wherever they want, it makes them sensational lovers. Daniel stroked my hand as we watched the dancers slide by us. "Would you like something to drink?" he said. "Some mineral water, please." Daniel left to get our drinks. I sat there trying to figure out what just happened.

We finished our drinks and the next *tanda* started up, a romantic *tango vals*. Daniel looked at me and gestured to the dance floor. He guided me out into the line of dance, pulled me close and held me there, breathing with me and shifting our weight side to side. My cells lit up like they were plugged into an electric socket. I closed my eyes and gave myself over to him and to the music. Our connection was absolute heaven. Daniel guided me into moves I didn't even know I could do. I felt like I was coming right there on the dance floor, wave after wave of orgasmic pleasure. Light and sweat streamed from my pores. My panties were drenched. I could feel him moving energy up my spine again and I opened everything to him. My body felt like liquid light. I could smell his animal maleness beneath the spicy cologne. I had to restrain myself from leaping into his arms and wrapping my thighs around his waist. I felt him slide his hand down to my back of my waist, then down to my sacrum. I gasped and missed a beat, but he caught me and brought us to a pause. We breathed together, shifted our weight again. I was getting dizzy, lightheaded, weak in the knees.

The *tanda* came to an end and Daniel walked me back to my stool by the check-in table, thanked me for the *tanda*, smiled and squeezed my hand, then walked away. Zhenya saw me and came over. "Oh. My. God," I said, "That was incredible. I'm completely high. I can barely walk straight. It was like making love on the dance floor." Zhenya laughed. "I think you just got bit by the tango bug," she said. "I totally get it now," I said, still trying to catch my breath, "how people become completely obsessed with tango." I blathered on for a while until someone needed her attention and interrupted us. I just sat there, dazed and amazed, trying to process the experience. Another man caught my eye for a dance, but I didn't want to chance it. I didn't want to lose the high of dancing with Daniel. I sat there in an altered state, watching the dancers, until I got it together to leave. That night, my obsession began. I fell head over heels in love with tango. I didn't realize that my tangasm experience with Daniel was a rare phenomenon, elusive as a yeti sighting, but it was too late. Now I'm addicted, and like any addict, I've been chasing that original high ever since.

When I walk in to class tonight, Zhenya eyes me up and down. She gives me a big smile and knowing wink. "Hi Alexis," she says, and pulls me close for a big hug. A heady mix of fragrant warmth and voluptuousity envelops me. She smells like the tropics, ripe, juicy and sweet. I think I'm falling in love. Zhenya is married and neither of us are lesbians. These are insignificant details when faced with the wolf-eyed, raven-haired beauty before me. Who could resist the brilliance of an intellectual Soviet-trained concert pianist improbably grafted onto a she-wolf with an earthy sense of humor and a heart as big as the sky? "You look great," she says. "Thanks," I say, "I thought I'd make more of an effort." I'd been coming to class in workout wear and barely any makeup. Not exactly elegant or sexy.

Class takes forever. I'm impatient with my fellow students' fumbling leads and their awkward lack of musicality. I keep checking the clock and scanning the tables for Daniel. When it finally ends, I take a seat at the bar with a good view of the dance floor. The lights dim and the DJ starts a set of traditional tango music as the bar begins to fill up. Daniel comes in. He smiles when he sees me and walks over to say hello. "Hi, Alexis," he says. "How are you?" Daniel looks great tonight, casual but sophisticated, in a midnight blue heavy silk jacquard shirt and black trousers. He leans in to give me a kiss on the cheek and I catch his distinctive scent again. He orders a beer. I ask him how he's been, but before he can answer, some people come up to say hello to him. Every time I get his attention, some woman comes over to kiss him and he turns away. He heads off to the dance floor with one of them, a tall gorgeous blonde in a revealing halter top and clinging skirt with a thigh-high slit. I feel like I'm 16 at the school dance crushing on a boy. Why do I feel jealous?

I sit on my stool and wait for an invitation, feeling stupid and insecure. Since I'm new to the tango community, I don't really know anyone yet. Besides, I'm a beginner. I can't keep up with the good dancers. I wonder if this is how it felt to Doug during our marriage, never able to keep up with me, always lagging behind. To me it felt like he was always holding me back, dragging me down. He was so threatened by anything new I wanted to do. Zhenya has taught me the strict etiquette of traditional Argentine tango, a safe container for the intimate connection this form demands. The man invites the woman to dance with a *cabaceo* — he catches the woman's eye and gives a gesture with his head to indicate the invitation. If the woman doesn't want to dance, she avoids his glance or looks away. This convention prevents the awkwardness of a direct refusal. Marco comes to my rescue again. I like dancing with Marco. I relax into his embrace and let myself enjoy the feeling of a man holding me close in his arms. Ever since my divorce, I've thrown myself into my work. I put dating on the back-burner, but

I promised myself I would get out more once I got settled in Los Angeles. I decided to try tango because I love to dance, and I was in the mood for something more elegant and sophisticated than salsa. I figured I could meet some new friends and maybe even some eligible men. Marco and I share a *tanda* and I manage to keep up. After the fourth song ends, he walks me off the dance floor back to my barstool and heads off to find another partner.

I guess I must look pretty hot tonight. Despite my inexperience, several men catch my eye over the course of the evening. It's a challenge to follow them. I have to concentrate just to keep up with the steps. I try and focus on the embrace, on the connection, but I don't feel that electric charge with any of them. How come Daniel hasn't asked me to dance? I know it wasn't just me. I know we both felt the connection. I'm about to give up and head out when Daniel comes back to the bar. "Be cool," I tell myself and swing around on my barstool. "Having fun?" I say and give him a flirty smile. He's changed into a grey and black patterned shirt that goes perfectly with his grey eyes and his salt and pepper hair. "Always," he says, "How about you?" I lie and say, "Absolutely!" He drinks his beer and he introduces me to some of the people sitting next to us at the bar. The next *tanda* starts up with a super sexy Nuevo Tango song. I'm praying he asks me to dance. Daniel turns to me and inclines his head toward the dance floor. Finally! I slip off the barstool and he leads me out to the edge of the floor.

Daniel takes my hands, pulls me close, and we enter the tango embrace. A thrill of nervous excitement starts in the pit of my stomach and skitters up and down my body. I try to match my breath with his as he shifts our weight in time to the song. I tell myself to relax and focus on the music. I surrender into the embrace, close my eyes and lay my cheek against his chest. There it is, my chemical reaction to the crystal velvet of his scent and the feel of his body. It's as good as I remember. He may be older, but there's solid muscle under there. I can feel him reading my energy, like the sweep of a hand from my crown to my tail. I want to melt all over him. "Keep it together, Alexis," I tell myself. He starts us off with a simple tango walk at first. I put everything out of my mind, everything but the music and our connection. I may not have the technique, but I have the musicality. With a song like this, the music takes over and fills my body with pleasure. I have to remind myself to stay focused, to wait for his lead and not choreograph my own thing. The song ends and we stand there breathing together. I catch a glimpse of us in one of the mirrored pillars. We look good together in the low light of the dance floor. I pull back a bit to look up at him.

There's something fierce in Daniel's eyes. It's kind of a turn-on. All of a sudden, I see him astride a shaggy horse. He's wearing what looks to be medieval Chinese armor and a helmet with a red tassel on top. Superimposed over his features are narrow, almond eyes and a drooping mustache. His sword glints in the sun. I'm overcome with the smell of smoke and mud. The taste of copper fills my mouth. We're in trampled fields surrounding a walled city. All around me I hear the screams and grunts of men fighting, horses snorting. With a savage yank on the reins, the Daniel-warrior pulls his horse around. He raises his sword and swings it down toward me. I'm frozen in place. I hear a thwack followed by a scream of agony. Blood splashes in my face. A severed arm clutching a sword falls to the ground at my feet. I gasp and step back. "Alexis?" he says. What the fuck was that? The battle fades in and out. I try to bring the dance floor back into focus. I'm sweating. My heart is pounding. I can feel the adrenaline coursing through my body. "Are you OK?" I shake my head to clear my vision. I look up at him again. I see concern and kindness in his grey eyes. "That was weird," I say. "What happened?" he asks. The next song in the *tanda* starts up. "I'll tell you later." I step in again to take up the tango embrace. I take a deep breath and try to calm my racing heart. Did we have a past life together in China? Why would it bleed through on the dance floor? Who were we to each other?

There's no time to think about it. I try to put the vision out of my mind, re-establish our connection and just focus on the dance. I feel his strength and attention. I know he's checking me out to make sure I'm OK. Daniel runs a hand up my spine. It sends a rush of energy through my body, makes me feel safe and protected. I turn up the dial and open my field to receive his intention and register his lead. His male presence amplifies in response, brings out even more of my feminine energy. The warmth of his hands kindle comet trails, passing the torch in relay races, spirals up and down my body. I'm all woman in his arms. My pussy starts to swell and pulse. I'm consumed with desire. I lose my focus for a moment and miss a step.

Daniel holds us in place to steady me for a few bars. I sync my breath with his as he shifts our weight from side to side. There's so much charge between us, it's hard to pay attention to my feet. I just want to open everything to him and let go. "Jesus, Alexis! Get it together," I tell myself. "What the fuck are you doing? You don't even know this man." The song ends and I stand there trying to process the experience. For a moment, I smell the smoke and mud again, then it passes.

The DJ plays two more Nuevo Tango songs in the *tanda*. It takes every bit of focus I can muster to keep dancing as waves of pleasure roll through my body. All I want to do is jump on him and wrap my legs around him. My panties are getting wet. I know he must be able to smell me, but it feels too damn good to be embarrassed. My eyes are closed, so I have no idea if anyone notices, and I'm past caring anyway. I have to admire his concentration. I have to follow his lead, but he has to navigate us around the crowded dance floor. Daniel escorts me back to the bar at the end of the set. "That was wonderful," I say. "Thank you." Daniel looks me up and down and shakes his head. "No, thank you," he says. He squeezes my hands. My legs are shaky. My panties feel slick. I need to pull myself together. I grab my bag and head to the bathroom.

I wipe myself after peeing. I can feel how engorged I am. My panties are soaking wet. I stuff them in my purse. I stand at the sink running cold water over my wrists trying to collect myself. Between the over-heated chemistry of our connection and that battlefield vision,

I'm a wreck. I look in the mirror. My pupils are dilated and my face is all flushed. My mascara has run all under my eyes and I'm a sweaty mess. I look like I've just had my brains fucked out. I fix myself up as best I can and head outside into the cold night air. I sit on a bench in the hotel driveway. There's a faint stench of jet fuel in the air and the roar of planes taking off in the background. Daniel comes out and stands by the door, scanning the entrance. I can tell he's looking for me. He turns his head in my direction and sees me sitting there in the shadows. He walks over. "Everything OK, Alexis?" he asks and sits down on the bench next me. "Yeah," I say. "I just needed to get some fresh air. What time is it?" He looks at his watch. "12:30."

"I think I'll head home," I say.

"Let me walk you to your car." I'm still all hot and bothered and make small talk to cover it up. "So how long have you been dancing tango?" I ask him. The boulevard is nearly empty of cars and the streetlights cast a harsh glare. The moon is almost full in a cloudless sky. "Oh, I grew up with tango," he says. "My parents loved to dance. Tango, cha-cha, salsa, all of it. They had weekly dance parties at our home." It sounds like he misses those times. "Where did you grow up?" I ask. "In Istanbul," he tells me. He doesn't look Turkish, but what do I know? What if he's religious and a traditional Muslim? I could never be with a man who expects me to obey him, who would want to dominate and control me. I try to reconcile evenings of sexy partner dancing with traditional Islamic attitudes when he asks me, "What about you? Where are you from?"

"I grew up in Seattle," I say. "I just moved to LA last year."

"What brings you to Los Angeles?" he asks. "Work," I say, "and I wanted a change." I don't mention my divorce. "What kind of work do you?" he asks. "I'm in marketing," I say. I don't want to talk about work. I stop walking. "This is my car," I say.

Daniel starts to stroke my hands and arms as we stand there next to my car. It's making me shiver, or maybe I'm just getting chilled in my sweaty clothes. Daniel pulls me close and just holds me. I have to stop myself from hooking my leg around him and grinding my panty-less crotch up against his thigh. I step back and take a shaky breath. He looks me up and down. "You are so gorgeous, Alexis," he says. I smile up at him. I've finally learned to accept a compliment gracefully, a little gift that came with age. "Thank you, Daniel," I say. I open the passenger side door to put my shoe bag and purse in the car. I bend over to deposit my bags and to give him a good view of my ass up in the air in my skin-tight jeggings. "Mmm, mmm, mmm, Alexis," he says, "you are so damn hot."

"Actually, I'm cold," I say and walk around my car to get into the driver's seat. I leave the passenger door open. Daniel leans into the car. "Are you getting in?" I ask. He climbs in and shuts the door. I start the car and turn on the heat. The sexy Alabama Shakes song I was listening to on the way over starts up. I turn to face him. We just sit there looking at each other. Then he leans over and kisses me, a soft sweet kiss. He pulls back and looks in my eyes. His eyes are hooded and fierce again. He takes my head in his hands and pulls me in for another kiss, deeper and more demanding this time. I part my lips and he slips the tip of his tongue into my mouth. I feel a tug down in my pussy. I hear myself moan and feel myself getting wet again. Without thinking, I reach over and put my hand on his cock through his pants. He's already half-way hard. I can feel the swollen head and run my fingers along the ridge. When I squeeze it, his cock thickens and comes to rigid attention. I start to stroke him through his pants, running my hand all along his impressive length and girth. He groans.

I come to my senses. What the fuck am I doing? "Sorry. I didn't mean to do that," I say, "I have to go." I pull back and turn away. I'm embarrassed now. What is wrong with me? I don't even know this guy and I'm giving him a hand job in my car. "Thanks again for the fabulous *tandas*," I say, "I'll see you next week." Daniel sighs and adjusts himself. Then he leans over again, puts his hand on my cheek and turns my head to face him. He kisses me slow and deep again, etching our nerve endings with the promise of more to come. "It was wonderful to dance with you, Alexis," he says. Daniel opens the door, then turns back and says, "Be careful driving home. Text me when you get there so I know you got home safe?" I'm touched by his request. We exchange numbers before he gets out of the car. He shuts the door and I take off.

I drive in a daze, like I'm high and tripping, with scenes of the battlefield still flashing before my eyes. I drive embarrassed and shocked by my behavior, excited and appalled, turned-on and wet. I drive with the sensation of Daniel's mouth on mine and his hard cock in my hand. I text him when I get there and he texts back, "Sweet dreams, beautiful." I take a shower to wash off the sweat and clear my head. It takes me along time to fall asleep, even after I rub myself off, reliving our *tanda* together. I dream of our life together in medieval China. I wake up with images of us training at sword practice in the courtyards of a mountaintop Taoist monastery, as comrades riding shaggy horses down endless dusty roads, clattering through the gates of our general's gilded palace with its curved roof, walking the length of his red-pillared hall between rows of armed guards to bow before him.

I call Zhenya the next day. "I need your help," I tell her, "I danced with this guy last night and I seriously embarrassed myself." The gods smiled on me when they brought Zhenya into my life. I totally lucked out with this one. A combination of intuition and Google led me to my first tango class with her. I knew she was a kindred spirit right from the start. Not only did I score a great tango teacher but also my first real girlfriend in Los Angeles. "Why," she says, "What happened? Was it Daniel?" I get up to close my office door. I don't want anyone to hear this. "Yes, it was Daniel." I cringe as I tell her about practically orgasming on the dance floor with him. I can feel my face turn red when I tell her about the aborted hand job in the car after. "I'm so confused," I say, "I want to fuck this guy and I'm not even sure I want to date him!"

"Alexis, you have to be careful in the tango community," Zhenya tells me, "It's a small circle and you don't want to get a reputation." I wince. I love the way Zhenya teaches tango, so much more than mere steps or technique. She brings an element of consciousness and spirituality to the process that suits me just fine. "I'm gonna steer you straight," she tells me, "I was newly divorced when I first got into tango, too. I made plenty of mistakes. I didn't have anyone to advise me, but you do." I'm grateful to have the wise and generous Zhenya as my mentor. "First of all, you don't want to ruin a beautiful dance relationship," Zhenya says, "If you have sex with him and it's not good, it's going to be really awkward at the *milongas*. You'll be seeing each other all the time." Hmm, good point. It would be impossible to avoid him. And everyone knows him. "But Zhenya, we have the most incredible connection," I tell her. "That may be," she says, "but that's on the dance floor. It doesn't mean he's like that in bed. Believe me, I know. It doesn't necessarily translate." I find that hard to believe. I think back on Daniel's kisses and the feel of his big hard cock in my hand. "I'm telling you from personal experience. Ask any of the women who've been in the community for a while. They'll tell you the same thing," she says.

I think about this for a minute. Then I think about my dreams of our Chinese life as sworn comrades-in-arms. Do I want to date Daniel? I don't know. He's kind of old for me, but maybe he's the one. Maybe we were destined to meet again in this life. "What do you know about Daniel?" I ask her. "Does he have any money? Do you know what he does for a living?" I refuse to be with a man who doesn't have serious bank. My 18-year marriage was a financial disaster. Ever since Doug lost all our savings in his second failed business, I was the sole breadwinner. For ten long years. All I got out of that marriage was debt. Well, debt and our daughter, Laura. I'm never going to support a man like that again. I want a man who can take care of me next time. Not that I don't want to make my own money. I can support myself, but I want my man to be fully empowered in the world and that means he's got to have the money part handled. For sure, he has to make more money than me. "Not much," Zhenya says. "I know he's from Turkey. Oh, and he sells Oriental rugs."

"Sells, as in he's a dealer, or he owns his own business?" I ask her.

"No," Zhenya says, "I don't think so. I think he just works in a store." This is not promising. "Do you know how old he is?" I ask her. "Maybe 63 or 64," she says.

Arrgghh! Two deal-killers right off the bat, age and money. For the first time in my life, I want to be with a younger man. Not a lot younger, maybe five years or so, but definitely not someone on the verge of senior citizenship! All throughout my 20's and early 30's, I was always attracted to older men. They were more mature with more money, and besides, I was working out my Daddy issues. Now that I just got out of a sexless marriage, I want a younger, fit, hot guy who will fuck me good and hard on a regular basis. I may be middle-aged, about to turn 49 and approaching menopause, but I don't look it. My three times a week yoga practice keeps me strong and flexible. Everybody tells me I look ten years younger than I am. I don't really believe that. Let's split the difference and say I look five years younger.

"If you want my advice—" Zhenya says. "Yes, please," I say. "—Then keep it on the dance floor," she tells me. "You may have a great connection now, but as your dancing progresses, that can change. As you become a better dancer, you may no longer enjoy the partners you love dancing with now. It's pretty typical." I consider this for a minute. I'm still lying in bed. I was so charged up I couldn't get to sleep until two in the morning, so I slept in late. I see my wadded up panties on the floor by the hamper and flash back to our dance together last night, how it felt to be in his arms, to move together as one with the music, that super sexy song playing, the feeling of his body against mine, breathing in his exotic scent, his hand on my back moving the energy up my spine, caressing the back of my neck. Something in my pussy tugs and twangs again. "Really?" I say. "I don't know if that would happen with Daniel." I imagine that impressive cock all up inside me. "We have super intense chemistry together." Then again, do I really want to get involved with a man that old? There's always Viagra, I guess. "Even more reason to preserve your dance relationship, then," she says. I get what she's saying, but then I get a flash of our past life together. We're sitting in a pavilion by a fish pond. A beautiful woman in sumptuous embroidered robes kneels at the edge, playing the flute. I tell Zhenya about the dance floor vision of the battle scene and my dreams from last night. "That is so... bizarre, Alexis," she says. She clears her throat. "I get how that would make things more confusing for you, but this life is here and now. Think it over and decide what's more important to you — protecting your dance relationship or having sex with the guy. And remember, there's a lot of gossip in the tango community. Word gets around fast. You're new and I want to protect you. Maybe have lunch with him first and see if there's anything between you off the dance floor. Find out if you have anything in common." Excellent advice. I am so lucky to have her to guide me. "Zhenya, you are an angel," I tell her, "Thank you for helping a sister out."

After we hang up, I debate the pros and cons of going to bed with Daniel. Pros— it's been a long, lonely, dry spell. Daniel is the first guy I've felt desire for in at least a couple of years. He can track and move energy. He has a big cock and probably knows how to use it. Cons—first of all there's the age difference. Do I really want to get involved with a man at least fifteen years older than me, who probably doesn't have much money, who might harbor traditional sexist Islamic attitudes, who will demand obedience and expect to control me? And what about our past life connection? Is that a pro or a con? What does it mean for this life? The only thing I know for sure is that I love dancing with him. In the end, I decide to follow Zhenya's advice and vow not to date my dance partners. At least not until I'm sure they're boyfriend material! I jump up from my desk to sweep the stinky remains of my team's takeout Mexican lunch from the coffee table into the trash can. My computer dings as another urgent email joins the other half dozen awaiting my attention. Back to the salt mines.

I planned to talk with Daniel about my decision to protect our dance relationship after class tonight, but he never shows up. This Monday the bar is full of women on the other side of middle age, on the fast slide toward 60. It's not a bad looking bunch. They've made an effort to fix themselves up, but you can see where the years have gnawed at them and worn them down. Sagging and bulging, faded flowers trying too hard. It happens to the best of us. I know. It's happening to me. No one gets out alive.

We're all here to dance. The younger women are already out on the dance floor. Tango meets Darwinism at an airport hotel in the San Fernando Valley. I wait to be invited to dance. A wave of anxiety and insecurity washes over me. I'm back in junior high. Am I pretty enough, thin enough, young enough, a good enough dancer? I cringe inside. I feel old and invisible. I went through an ugly duckling phase in eighth grade, my childhood cuteness gone, braces on my teeth, while my face morphed into adult features. That first school dance, I stood alone the entire night watching my nemesis flirt with Jacob. Marcia was everything I wasn't — tall with straight blonde hair and popular. Not a single boy asked me to dance.

Marco rescues me. Now I'm out on the floor again, trying not to back-lead. He pulls me close. I mean, really close. Close enough that I can feel his erection against my thigh. What the fuck? This ain't no salsa club, dude. I pretend I don't feel it and adjust my posture to make a little space between me and his little man. I'm distracted thinking about it. Would I even want to sleep with him? I miss a step and stumble against him. There it is again. A Top 10 pop song marks the end of the three-song *tanda*. I thank him for the dance and walk off the floor.

I don't know anyone here. I'm still new to the tango scene. I'm not a good dancer yet. Zhenya keeps insisting I start showing up at these things to practice, says it's the only way to get good, but I don't like it. There's a snobby element. I feel intimidated by all the better dancers. I don't like the drive to get here, don't like being here by myself, like some sort of social reject. I don't like the slightly seedy vibe of this bar, and I'm not drinking tonight anyway. I don't like being shoved around by men who aren't very good leaders. I don't like feeling old and invisible.

An older Japanese man invites me to dance. I've seen him occasionally in class. He's short and intense. His body feels dry and brittle, his lead rigid and demanding. I try to connect with his energy and follow him but something tender and delicate inside me recoils. My skin pulls tight like it's trying to get away from him. I miss a cue and he scolds me. I don't think I can stand this for another two or three songs. He tries to lead me into some move I don't know. He tsk's and scolds me again when I don't get it right. His hands feel like crow claws. A dried up old crow gripping me in his sharp black talons, ready to peck my eyes out, ready to tear into my breast and stick his pointy black beak between my ribs, ready to tear out pieces of my heart, my tender little heart, a hummingbird fluttering madly, trapped in the black steel cage of his grip.

He grips me tighter and hisses, "No, no, no. Back *ocho*." His breath smells like mold. My stomach convulses. I want to run off the dance floor. It's a major tango faux pas. I don't care. I can't take it anymore. "Excuse me, but I don't feel well," I say and make my escape. I grab my bag and practically run to the bathroom. I wash him off my hands, splash cold water on my face and neck, make the mistake of looking in the mirror. The fluorescent lights are not kind. I don't recognize the face staring back at me. I will never be young again. My romantic tango fantasies shrivel up and slink off to join their cousins in the corner, rattling around in the shadows. I go back to the bar. The women sit sipping their drinks and sucking in their stomachs. I turn and walk out the door. I head to my car. My tango fantasies limp along behind me.

It's been several weeks and I still haven't gathered the courage to venture onto the scene again. Zhenya calls to find out where I've been. I tell her all about my misadventure with the Japanese man. "Aww, honey, that's awful," she says, "But don't let that turn you off to tango. Just don't dance with him again." Beads of condensation dot my martini glass. "It's more than that," I say. At 36 years old, can she really understand what I'm dealing with? "I don't want to be just another pathetic, middle-aged woman looking for romance on the dance floor," I tell her. The late afternoon sun floods my bedroom with a warm amber light. I'm home from a stressful day at the office, filled with missed deadlines, angry phone calls with the printers, and interminable meetings where nothing gets decided. I'm lying on my bed, sipping a cold dry martini. Across the room, my newly purchased silver tango shoes glitter their reproach in the slanting light. "Alexis, darling, you are the least pathetic woman I know," she tells me. "Don't be put off by that scene at the hotel. There are plenty of other places to dance." I am so overdue for a pedicure that I've ripped a hole in the toe of my stockings. I skipped yoga this afternoon and feel guilty about self-medicating with alcohol instead. "Come out with us tonight," Zhenya says. "It's a very friendly *milonga* with an international crowd of all ages. There's a great dance floor and a free class before. Plus, my favorite DJ is playing tonight." I'm reluctant to venture out, but what's more pathetic than staying home and drinking alone? "Come on, Alexis," she says, "It'll be fun. There's a group of us going so you won't be alone." It's almost impossible to resist Zhenya when she wants me to do something. I sigh and take a big gulp of my martini. "OK, fine. Text me the address and I'll meet you there."

I decide to go early to take the free class before the *milonga* since I haven't danced in while. Even though I'm spoiled by the fabulous Zhenya, I enjoy the class. The teacher Emilio is a short muscular man. He's funny and charming and from Peru, of all places. I'm flattered when he singles me out for special attention. By the time class ends, I'm feeling way more confident. The lights are dimmed. The *milonga* begins. People trickle in. It's still early for the tango crowd. Much to my surprise, Emilio invites me to dance. He's a wonderful lead. He makes me look good. I'm having fun. Zhenya shows up in a royal blue dress that brings out the electric blue of her eyes. A deep V-cut displays her double-D boobs. She comes over, gives me a kiss hello. Sylvie is with her. I recognize her. She's the tall blonde Daniel danced with at the hotel bar. Zhenya introduces us. We get some drinks and sit down. Zhenya and Sylvie seem to know everyone. A stream of people come over to the table to say hello. There's much kissing of cheeks. I feel like I'm at the best table in the lunch room with the popular girls. Sylvie is hysterical. I'm laughing so hard, I'm practically peeing in my pants.

Carried along in their jet stream, a number of Zhenya and Sylvie's friends invite me to dance. I'm still a beginner and my technique is minimal at best but, these men are kind and generous partners. They keep it simple for me. Back at the table for a rest, Zhenya asks me, "Aren't you glad you came out?" I pat the sweat off my face with a napkin and take a sip of my wine. "I am indeed," I say, "I'm having a marvelous time." I'm looking around the room, watching the dancers and chatting with Zhenya when I catch sight of Daniel in the line of dance. I feel a thrill of nervous excitement. I haven't seen or talked to him since that night in my car. The *tanda* ends and Sylvie comes back to the table. Daniel comes over to say hello to us. I think he's going to ask me to dance, but he invites Sylvie instead. I feel a pang of jealousy when I see him take her in his arms with the same intimate embrace he shared with me. I turn away and catch Zhenya watching me. "See, Alexis," Zhenya says, "He's like that with everyone. That's his thing." I'm embarrassed all over again about our make-out session and the abbreviated hand job in my car. Thank God I came to my senses before it went any further.

The *tanda* ends and Daniel escorts Sylvie back to the table. I can't believe how disappointed I feel when he walks away without inviting me to dance. "I've been telling Alexis to watch out for guys like Daniel," Zhenya says to Sylvie. "He swept her off her feet a few weeks back and she didn't know what hit her." They both laugh. "Did he do his special thing and give you a tangasm?" Sylvie asks. "A tangasm? So there's a name for it?" I say. "Oh yes, the rare and elusive tangasm," Sylvie says and cracks up again. "Hey," Zhenya says, "I'm just glad Alexis got to experience it, because it made her fall in love with tango." I feel myself blushing. "Does he do it with you?" I ask Sylvie. "I've had it happen a few times, but not with Daniel," she says. Zhenya nods and takes a sip of her wine. "When you get more experience and become a better dancer," she says, "it's all about the connection, not about sexual energy." I need to get out of here and process this. I need to figure out why I'm so pissed off. I need some air. I get up from the table. Sylvie says, "Don't feel bad about it, Alexis. Daniel's a good guy at heart. He just likes making women come on the dance floor." They crack up again.

I walk up and down the sidewalk and take big gulps of air. I don't know which pisses me off more — the fact that this is Daniel's "thing," as Sylvie put it, or that I have so little self-control. I hate how vulnerable my unmet needs have made me, my needs for love, for sex, for intimacy. I feel like an out-of-control, horny teenager with no boundaries and no self-respect. This takes me back to when I was a teenager and how my mother shamed me for my burgeoning sexuality. Like that time in tenth grade when Rick and I were parked in my driveway after a date, making out in the front seat. My mother had been watching and waiting for me to get home. She stormed out the front door to yank me out of the car and drag me into the house, calling me slut and a whore. When I protested that we just kissing, she slapped my face. She told me boys only wanted one thing from me. Then she grounded me for a month. Uptight frigid bitch.

Fuck this shit! I'm a grown woman and I refuse to be ashamed of my sexuality. I give myself a little pep talk about owning my power and claiming my sexuality and making conscious choices over how I express it, blah, blah-blah, blah-blah. I pull up my tits, smooth down my skirt and head back inside, determined to clear things up with Daniel.

I find him by the buffet table. He's standing there chatting with a poodle in a pink dress, eating chocolate truffles. "Excuse me," I say to him, "Can we talk for a minute? I have something I want to share with you." Daniel hesitates. He seems a little swizzled, nervous even, but maybe I'm just projecting. "Don't worry," I say, "It's nothing bad." I lead him back outside. "Things got a little out of control the other week," I say. He looks like cracked cement. I go on. "I love dancing with you, but if we get involved with each other and for whatever reason it doesn't work out, then it will be awkward seeing each other at *milongas* all the time. I don't want to take the chance and maybe lose my favorite dance partner." Daniel seems relieved. "So I want to protect our dance relationship and keep it to the dance floor." I stick my hand out. "Deal?" I say. He takes my hand, "Deal," he says. He cocks his head toward the door, inviting me to dance. I smile and take his arm. We walk back inside and Daniel guides me to the dance floor. Our timing is perfect. The *cortina* between sets is just coming to an end. A *tango vals* starts up. We assume the position. I am hyper-alert to his energy. His embrace is still delicious, just more contained. He still smells fantastic. I still feel the chemistry of our connection. I still want to fuck him. As he guides me around the dance floor, I can't help but test him. Just because I've set a boundary doesn't mean I don't want him to want me! In fact, contrary creature that I am, I want him to want me all the more now that he can't have me. I tap into the core of my feminine energy, reach into my womanly center, let it fill and flow through my entire being, let it radiate without letting it loose. "Let's see how you handle that," I think. I can feel his male response, but he manages to restrain it and get himself under control. Is it fucked up that his control turns me on even more? It's not a tangasm, but it's very nice just the same. The song ends. We stand there for a moment without moving. My eyes are closed. My face is pressed up against his cheek. I'm smiling, feeling very pleased with myself. Then we're off again, gliding into the next song.

CHAPTER TWO

Dario
I Become A Tango Cliché

After last night, it's official – I've become a walking, talking tango cliché. I'm such a cliché that I'm a cliché of a cliché. Seriously. No shit. It's embarrassing. The only thing left is to book a flight to Buenos Aires and begin a passionate love affair with some hunky Argentinian tango master. I'm not proud to admit I've joined the ranks of the tango-obsessed, sex-starved, middle-aged sluts. You'd think I'd know better, sheltered under the protection of my voluptuous tango goddess from Kiev. But no, I'm just another sucker like the rest of 'em. In my defense, I was done in by two consecutive nights of the most exquisite tango foreplay that had me teetering on the edge of tangasm for hours.

The fabled tangasm is a phenomenon characterized by the intense full body pleasure you feel in the arms of a partner with whom you have a uniquely intimate and alchemical connection. A tangasm is accompanied by an electric charge just beneath the skin that sensitizes all your nerve receptors and telegraphs urgent messages to your pussy. A tangasm leaves you weak in the knees and wet in your panties, like you just got well and thoroughly fucked. A tangasm can make you want to have sex with a man you don't even want to date. A tangasm stops time and alters reality. A tangasm led to my downfall. A tangasm, I come to find out, is an event as rare as a unicorn sighting. I've had half a dozen in my first 6 months of tango. So you see, it's not my fault. I couldn't help it. The tango made me do it. You'd think I'd have better control after my early experiences with Daniel, but no, not so much. Not when my molecules rouse themselves into a frenzied maenads' dance of desire.

So get this — I'm at the Music Center Downtown Dance event on the plaza under the summer solstice full moon, with about three hundred tango aficionados. There's a live orchestra. A man I haven't seen around before catches my eye to invite me to dance. His name is Dario. He's from Argentina. He's tall, dark and handsome. I know, right? Another cliché. As soon as he takes me in his arms, I can tell this is gonna be good. He just stands there at first, breathes with me, gently shifts my weight left to right to get us in sync. I relax into the embrace. It already feels amazing and we haven't even taken a step yet. His embrace is confidant, relaxed, sensitive yet firm. I sigh and lay my cheek against his chest. Then we begin. He doesn't lead me into any fancy moves, just simple tango walking and some basic steps. So why does it feel like heaven? I'm jelly in his arms.

After the *tanda* ends, Dario walks me back to the table. There's a boisterous international crowd, and every inch of the table is covered with bottles of wine and dishes from around the world — Greek, Persian, French, Japanese, Indian, you name it. I immediately excuse myself to find Carla and get the scoop on this guy. Carla and her husband Gerhard are fixtures in the tango scene. They know everyone. Turns out Dario is a friend of theirs and he's staying with them while he's traveling through the States. Carla tells me he's a colonel in the Argentine army from an influential family, recently retired and recently divorced. I know, classic Latin lover, right? Like I said, I'm a cliché. We dance two more *tandas* and it's all I can do to keep from swooning in his arms. We make plans to meet up at a *milonga* the following night. I drive home high. I have a hard time settling down to sleep, my body is so electrified.

The next night is even better. Dario holds me in close embrace the entire time we dance. He has that certain something I can't resist. I'm a total sucker for the macho confidence he combines with courtly attentiveness, for the power of his presence he casually cloaks under a laid-back demeanor. I feel safe and protected in his arms. I feel cared for and cherished. I feel beautiful and desired. I feel special. He could dance with any woman here, women who are much better dancers than I am. I relax and let myself soak up the sensations. I don't think I ever felt this way once in over twenty years of marriage. As Dario steers me around the line of the dance, I marvel at the chemistry of our connection. Our molecules carry on their own private dirty dancing party as my cells sing rounds of Hallelujah. I try to keep some semblance of technique in place, when really all I want is for him to ravish me until I can't take it anymore.

My downfall comes the third night, at another *milonga*. After our third *tanda*, we're both hot and sweaty and go outside to cool off. Dario pulls me into the shadows of the parking lot, takes me in his arms again and kisses me. Oh. My. God. He's got one hand on the back of my head and the other hand on my ass. I'm clinging to him because I don't trust my legs to hold me up. I'm afraid someone will see us and I don't want anyone to know what a tango cliché I've become. He's kissing me like he's fucking my mouth, with this relaxed command that's driving me crazy. It's got me moaning and rubbing my crotch against his thigh.

Somehow Dario maneuvers us into the back seat of my car. What the fuck am I doing? He's got my skirt up around my waist and he's grabbing my ass. The parking lot lights glare and bounce off the windshield. It's all in a hurry, urgent kisses, fumbling with clothes. Next thing I know I'm sucking his cock and he's rubbing his hands over my breasts and pinching my nipples. It's all moving along kind of fast. Then, somehow, I'm on my back with one foot braced up against the rear windshield, thighs parted, panties dangling off the headrest. He strokes my wet folds, parts them open and enters me. A few slow adjustment strokes, then he's pumping me hard and dirty, rock 'n rolling me, panting and moaning. The windows mist up. It softens the glare of the streetlights. I fumble around looking for a tissue. I can't believe I just did that! What is wrong with me? Have I lost my mind? I'm embarrassed, mortified really, and yet I still want more. Like I said, I've become a total tango cliché.

Dario wants to come home with me, but I just can't handle that. I suggest Sunday brunch the next day and drive home filled with remorse. Here I am approaching 50, and I'm acting like some stupid teenage girl who can't say no. Loose hips sink ships. Have I sunk so low that I'm having sex with a virtual stranger in the backseat of my car? We didn't even use a condom. I'm not worried about getting pregnant, although I suppose that's a remote possibility. But what about safe sex? Then again, maybe Dario is the one, the man I've been looking for. So what if he's geographically undesirable? In my fantasy we fall in love and I move to Argentina. I become the mistress of vast estates and cavort in the highest circles of Argentine society. We shall dine most nights at 10 PM, then it's off to tango until 3 AM, then back home to make love and finally fall asleep in his arms at dawn. Of course, we'll keep a place here in Southern California, since we'll be traveling back and forth frequently. I imagine our wedding and wonder if he'll insist on a church ceremony. Just as I form the image of him proposing to me in front of an enormous fireplace in the main house of his gazillion-acre ranch at the foot of the Andes, an enormous engagement ring in his outstretched hand, I drive past my exit. Damn! Back to Earth.

This morning, I'm filled with regret. Should I keep our lunch date? I call Cheryl for confession and advice. I've been friends with her since our kids were toddlers. I count on her to keep me honest. "Cheryl," I say, "I'm so embarrassed." The morning light floods through my bedroom windows to where I sit propped up in bed. "I can't believe I fucked this guy in the backseat of my car!" Clothes are strewn around the room. A mug of strong Darjeeling tea sits steaming on my bedside table. My crystal earrings from the night before lay glittering next to it. Cheryl consoles me at first. "Give yourself a break," she says, "You were primed by three nights of hot and heavy foreplay on the dance floor." I consider this and for a moment it makes me feel better about what I've done. "It did feel amazing to dance with him," I say. "He's so sensitive and strong. We have such an intense connection." Cheryl and I have been through a lot together — raising our kids, first her divorce, then mine. "So you fucked him," Cheryl says, "Big deal. You're a grown woman."

Then I tell her about my fantasies. Dario is the first man I've felt this attracted to in a long time. He could be the one. He's a man of substance, and from what Carla tells me, wealth. He's big and solid, yet sensitive. I like his relaxed, laid back vibe. I tell her the few details I know about Dario. Cheryl breaks in. "Alexis," she says, "No woman with four children divorces her husband unless he's some sort of monster." This is not at all what I want to hear. I don't want my fantasy bubble burst. I don't want to a strong dose of reality, not yet. Not before I get a proper fuck. "They're probably all grown up by now," I say. "Even so," she tells me, "It's something to think about.

Be careful." Now I feel rebellious. It's just lunch and I've already fucked him. I owe it to myself to find out more. Besides, that brief episode in the car only whetted my appetite for more. I have to see him again.

Now that we're seated at our table, I realize I'm testing Dario. I've picked an elegant, expensive restaurant. A real seen-and-be-seen sort of place where fashionable women actually wear hats and tiny elaborate fascinators perched upon their perfectly highlighted heads. Dario does not disappoint. He has the exquisite manners of a South American aristocrat, which of course he is. A real *suavecito*. When our waiter comes for our drink order, I ask for a glass of champagne, but Dario insists on ordering a prestige bottle of Taittinger instead. A $350 bottle of champagne? Holy shit! Way to make an impression. Now I feel a little less embarrassed about the night before.

"*Salud*," he says and we clink glasses. The champagne is delicious, golden and complex with the tiniest of bubbles. I've overcompensated for our adventure in the backseat with a long-sleeved high-necked grey dress, a useless attempt to counteract any impression he might have got that I'm a cheap slut. The fact that it's made of whisper-light silk jersey and cut on a curve-clinging bias is beside the point. Dario reaches over, takes my hand and brings it to his mouth for a kiss. He kisses the back of my hand, then turns it over and plants one in the center of my palm. He sends a shiver all through my body, from my heart down to my belly, landing at the mouth of my womb. I can't help but let out a little gasp. I feel tipsy already. I stare at his hand, still holding mine, watching as he strokes his thumb casually over the spot he just kissed. I have a thing about men's hands, how they look, how they move, how they feel, how they hold me, stroke me, pet me, take me. My acid test for long-term sexual chemistry is the way a man uses his hands on my body. I like a firm, but sensitive touch. I want him to pet the kitty. A lot. It makes me feel cherished and adored when my man gives me plenty of physical attention and affection. I like being rubbed and fondled casually throughout the day. In bed, I want him to handle me with an attitude of ownership and command, but attentive and adoring as well. Dario's hands are large and firm, on the fleshy side, with thick straight fingers. His nails are clean, smooth and lightly buffed. He could crush me with those hands and there'd be nothing I could do to stop him.

Lunch follows at a leisurely pace. Dario is not one to be hurried. This is a man used to command. He takes his time with his pleasures. I'm relieved to think last night's quickie in the car must have been the exception. Dario's English is somewhat limited, but he has little difficulty making himself understood. He speaks to me of his life post-retirement, of his world travels, of his love of beauty, adventure and wilderness. He fascinates me. I can't quite reconcile his obvious culture and sophistication with my sense of danger and violence hidden beneath the surface. I can't imagine him a military man, though he's spent his entire career in the Argentine Army and comes from a family of generals. I can't think he's old enough to have been a junior officer during the military dictatorship in the 70's and early 80's. I wonder about his family's role during the "Dirty War" reign of terror.

I'm so attracted to this man. I sit at our fine table, amongst the china, crystal and flowers, ticking off ideal-man criteria in my head. Stature, strength, dark hair, dark skinned, power in the world, big time sexual chemistry, smart, interesting. Check. Check. Check. And check. I want to trust him. His sensitivity to me hooked me from the first tango embrace. It makes my heart want to open to him. He's a little overweight, but I don't mind, because underneath is the body of a stallion thick with heavy muscles, a body that moves with a smooth and smoldering grace on the dance floor. Besides, he's charmed me, sitting there across the table, completely at ease, with his open face and the mischievous glint in his dark brown eyes. What's not to like?

"Alexis," Dario says as he takes my hand, "Let us go from here so we can be close together." It doesn't even sound corny the way he says it. I consider playing hard to get in a vain attempt to rewind the clock and reestablish some sense of...well, what exactly I don't know. Maybe chasteness or respectability? Which is ridiculous given the man's already drunk the milk so why does he need to buy the cow, as my mother would say. He strokes my hand and wrist, sends a thrill up my arm, down to the bottom of my belly, below my navel. I'm a little tipsy, on champagne and seduction. I look around the mirrors, imagine us the best stilettos, flying private linen down to the tropics. We may have the order backwards, but Dario has wined and dined me with the graciousness of a prince, showered his charm and attention all over me. I can't find a single reason I want to resist. Afternoon delight? Why deny myself?

Back at my place, Dario takes his time with me. He lies down on my bed, pulls me into his arms and just breathes with me for a bit. We start kissing — long, slow, deep kisses. He cups my breasts through the thin fabric of my dress and pinches my nipples till they harden erect. I sit up to pull my dress over my head while he gets out of his shirt and pants. He stands in front of me at the edge of my bed. His cock is already bulging through his briefs. Impatient to see it, I pull his briefs down and take hold of him. Dario's cock is large, thick and long, with a somewhat conical head. I slide my hand up and down the shaft. He groans when I squeeze under the ridge below the head and then run my palm over the tip. A drop of pre-cum glistens at the opening. On my knees on the bed with my ass up in the air, I bend over to lick it. He tastes sweet. I take him into my mouth and start sucking him off. He's too big to fit all the way in so I use my hands to grip around the base, to cup and fondle his balls. Dario gets rock hard in my mouth and hands. He's groaning and murmuring something in Spanish. It turns me on even more. He slides his hands over my head, gathers my hair into one hand and pulls it hard to slow me down. He starts massaging my breasts and squeezing my nipples. Then he pulls me up, flicks off my bra, and lays me back down on the bed. I wriggle out of my panties.

Dario makes love to me like some Eastern potentate, a royal figure with all the time in the world, accustomed to taking his pleasure at leisure and with maximum enjoyment. He knows his way around a woman's body, that's for sure. He takes me with a deliberate, unwavering intensity that drives me wild. He's not greedy or rushed, but there will be nothing left behind when he's finished devouring me. He's planted himself between my thighs and parted the lips of my pussy like it's the best dish in the world, licking and sucking me, running his tongue up and down my folds, pulling my clitoris into his mouth. Then his hands are everywhere, pinching and pulling my nipples, squeezing my ass and hips, massaging my inner thighs. He wets a finger in his mouth and slowly slides it into me. Then he opens me wider with a second finger, stroking my G-spot, sucking my clit. I'm already coming. When he also opens my ass to add a finger there, I completely lose it.

Dario lifts me up as though I weigh nothing at all, moves us into a sitting position, face to face, with his back against the thick cushioned headboard of my bed. He positions me over his cock. Held suspended by my hips with my legs around his back, Dario slowly lowers me down onto him until he's planted up to the hilt and I can feel his balls. He does this with such sensitivity and steadiness that I can't help but open to him even more. I look into his eyes, hooded and gleaming. In a slow continuous motion, he begins to rock and roll me on his cock while penetrating my mouth with his tongue. His big strong hands are gripping my ass and hips, moving me up and down in a slow, circular, relentless rhythm, launching me into a spiraling wave of multiple orgasms. Everything in me opens wider to take him in. The honey and nectar pour down. I reach around and begin to stroke and cup his balls, wet and slippery from my juices. I pull on them gently. It drives him wild. He starts to thrust into me faster and harder until he buries himself as deep as he can go and cries out, "I come, I come! Oh God, I come!"

I get up to pee and grab a towel and warm washcloth. I come back to find him lounging in my bed flipping through his phone. I wipe him down, dry him off and toss the wet washcloth and hand towel on the floor. I snuggle into his arms and fall into a deep sleep as he strokes my head and runs his fingers through my hair. It's dark when I wake up, Dario is gone. He's a left a note on the pillow.

"Alexis,

Thank you for a most lovely afternoon. May I see you tomorrow? Dinner?

Besos,

Dario"

Today at work, I can barely concentrate. Flashbacks of Dario in my bed fill my head and make my pussy tingle. At noon, Cheryl calls to get the scoop. "So," she says, "How was it?" I'm sitting in my office, with a pile of untouched work on my desk. To my surprise, I don't want to tell her. "Fantastic," I say. She usually gets a full blow-by-blow report and analysis. I notice my wastebasket is overflowing. My mug of Sencha tea sits cold and half-drunk on a coaster. "Fantastic is good," she says. The whiteboard on the wall next to my desk is covered with multi-colored sticky notes. One of them, neon pink, has fallen to the floor "Hello?" Cheryl says, "Earth to Alexis.

Details, please." I don't want to answer any questions. I have to get off the phone. "Sorry, Cheryl," I say, "I can't talk now. I'll call you tomorrow. OK?" I like the rainbow-colored air in my fantasy Dario-bubble. The last thing I want is a cold, hard prick of premature reality. "No, call me tonight," she says. I can hear people laughing and talking out in the hall. "Not tonight," I say, "We're going out to dinner." I examine my cuticles. "Out to dinner?" Cheryl says, "Alexis, that's the fifth day in a row. Aren't you moving a little fast?" I love the bitch more than my own blood sister, but who does she think she is, my mother? Fucking cock-blocker. "Sorry, Cheryl," I say, "I really have to go. We'll talk tomorrow. Bye." I practically hang up on her.

I blow off the afternoon editorial meeting and leave work early for a bikini wax and pedicure. When I get home, there's a huge bouquet of peonies on my doorstep. Now how could he have possibly known peonies are my favorite flower? And where did he get them at this time of year? There are so many stems, a least two dozen blossoms, that I split them between a couple of vases. I run a bath, pour in a dozen drops of rose essential oil, put on my favorite sexy chill music mix, light a few scented candles and turn off the lights. I settle back on my bath pillow and take a long time luxuriating in the warm water. The master bathroom is the real reason I took this apartment. It's a girly-girl hedonist fantasy come true. There's a deep soaking tub big enough for two, a toilet with bidet, large double vanity, plenty of drawers and cabinet space, a heated towel bar, and a dream shower with a waterfall shower head. My newly waxed pussy feels soft and velvety. It's a little tender and puffy after the wax job. I've left a small trimmed triangle on the mons. I don't want to look like a prepubescent girl, after all. I admire my hot pink toenails in the candle light. I love tango but dancing for hours at a time in 3-inch heels sure does a number on a girl's feet. My fingers have turned pruney when I finally get out. I slather rose-scented coconut oil all over my body and wrap myself in a thick, fluffy bath sheet and walk into my closet.

I stand there considering my wardrobe. It's expanded quite a bit since those first few months of tango. I want to look sexy for sure, but also A-list elegant. I want to look delectable and irresistible. I want to look young and hip. I want to look thin. I want to look like second wife material. I try on a few things, but nothing is hitting the right note. I'm tired of black and want something more colorful. I settle on a flattering violet silk blouse with a low-cut draped neckline and narrow waist. I pair it with velvet skinny jeans in skin-tight silver and black that make my ass look fabulous. A pair of sky-high open-toed silver and black sandals finish it off. I take extra time with my make-up and decide on a subtle smoky eye and natural blush-pink lips. Back in the bedroom I stand in front of the full-length mirror. Sexy, but not slutty, definitely expensive looking, and the jeans and shoes add the young hip factor I'm going for.

The doorman rings up. Dario is here. I grab my bag and head out the door. When I step out of the elevator, I see Dario across the lobby, casually leaning up against the concierge counter. He greets me with a kiss on both cheeks. "*Hola*, beautiful, how was your day?" He looks like a page out of GQ in a perfectly cut black leather jacket and grey trousers. "Fine," I say. "The best part was coming home to those gorgeous flowers. I adore peonies." He escorts me out to a black chauffeured Mercedes SUV waiting curbside, its windows blacked out. "Where are we going?" I ask him. "One of my favorite LA restaurants," he says. I'm surprised when we pull up at Luques, a perennial hotspot for Mediterranean food. I'm impressed he got reservations on such short notice. Dario is obviously a connoisseur. He orders an array of dishes and three different bottles of wine, far more than we can finish, just to taste them. I find the contrast between Dario's laid back presence and his single-minded pursuit of pleasure a turn-on. During dinner, a leisurely production, I ask him about his family, but what I really want to know is why his marriage ended. He deflects my not-so-subtle questions and turns them back on me, but I don't want to talk about my marriage either. I switch gears and ask about his retirement, business interests and life in Buenos Aires. What I really want to know is whether my fantasies of his wealth and status in Argentinian society have any basis in reality. His manner is casual and relaxed, but there's a will of steel just beneath the surface. He's certainly not going to tell me anything he doesn't want me to know.

The conversation moves on to Dario's upcoming camping trip in the Colorado Rockies and the spiritual experiences he's had communing with nature. "We climbed up over a pass," he tells me, "and down below us was this great big field of wildflowers." He indicates the size of the field with his hands wide apart. "We walked down into the middle of the field. It was like a magic carpet of flowers. I lay on my back and didn't move for an hour." The image of Ferdinand the Bull amongst the blossoms makes me giggle. He ignores it and continues. "Then this wave of peace wash over me. I was in the presence of the Goddess." I cough into my napkin to keep from laughing. The presence of the Goddess? I don't want to insult Dario's reverence but it almost sounds rehearsed or something, like it was a line he picked up from a TV show about hippie tree-huggers. He looks off into the distance with an expression of soulful contemplation.

As dinner winds down, I excuse myself and head to the bathroom. I need a few moments to try and process what's going on, what I think I'm doing with this man. I am not the brief, casual affair type of woman, but what do I really imagine is possible between us? Given the geographic distance alone? I'm completely attracted to Dario, but I don't trust myself to distinguish fact from fantasy, not when it comes to him. While he comes off as open and easy-going, I don't imagine one rises to the rank of colonel without a significant amount of bad-assery. And if I'm completely honest with myself, his power and quiet command is a big part of the attraction. When I look back on it, Dario has had his way with me from the start. It would be useless now to try and resist his powerful body, his powerful mind, his powerful will or his powerful energy. I hear Cheryl's warning in my mind, how no woman with four children divorces her husband unless he's some sort of monster. He's been nothing but a gentleman with me, but I've only known him a few days. We've only really had two conversations, one at lunch yesterday and one at dinner tonight. The rest of the time was spent on the dance floor and in bed. I re-apply blush-pink gloss to my lips and head back to the table. Dario finishes his espresso and signals for the check. This was quite an expensive dinner, at least several hundred dollars between all the food he ordered and the three superb bottles of wine. When the check comes, Dario barely glances at it. He pulls out a wad of hundreds, casually peels a few off and tosses them in the folder. Dario turns to me and asks, "Shall we go?"

When we get outside, Dario's driver is waiting in front. On the way home, he runs his hand along my thigh and strokes my arm, igniting little flames of desire in his trail. He brings my hand up to his mouth and kisses the center of my palm. Then he takes my index finger into his mouth and sucks from base to tip. His mouth feels hot. I'm mesmerized. Then he does the same with my middle finger. His lips are soft as he sucks my middle finger in and out a few times. My head falls back and my mouth opens in a shuddery sigh. He pulls my hair back away from neck and kisses me along a line from my earlobe to my shoulder. He gently places his hand around my neck and slides it down to run his fingers over my collarbone. His hand slips into my blouse and cups my breast. I gasp when he pinches and pulls my nipple hard. Then we're kissing, long slow deep. Dario takes my hand and places it on his bulging cock. I grab it through his pants and squeeze the head. He pulls on the loose folds of my low-cut blouse to expose my breasts and bends his head to take them into his mouth, first one, then the other. He frees them from my lacy demi bra and sucks and bites my nipples. I moan with pleasure. I glance up and see his driver watching us. Our eyes meet in the rear-view mirror and he leers at me. His gold front tooth glints in a passing headlight. "Dario," I whisper, "The driver." I push him off me, adjust my breasts back into my bra and pull my top up. "He doesn't mind," Dario says, "Do you Hector?" They grin at each other. "No, Señor," Hector says. I flush with embarrassment and irritation. "But I do mind," I snap back. Dario seems amused but behaves himself the rest of the way back to my apartment, and confines himself to stroking my thigh.

Once inside, I dim the lights, put on some downtempo electronic music and run around lighting candles. Dario takes his jacket off and plants himself on my living room sofa. "Alexis," he says, "Come over here." I walk over and stand in front of him. He leans forward, pushes my breasts together and buries his face in my cleavage, kissing and sucking on my breasts. Then he pulls my blouse off, unhooks my bra and takes them into his hands. He's rubbing and squeezing them, sucking and biting on my nipples, and it's making me so hot I can barely keep my balance in my heels. Then he sits back, unzips his pants and pulls his cock out. It's obvious what he wants. I put a pillow on the floor and get down on my knees between his legs. I may be here a while and I want to be comfortable. I take my time and begin by kissing and biting where his inner thighs meet his groin. Dario spreads his legs wider. I kiss all along the shaft from the base to the ridge. Then I lick all around the head and run my tongue down the shaft to his balls. I run my hands up his body and lightly roll his nipples between my fingers. By this point, Dario is murmuring to me in Spanish. I have no idea what he's saying, but it sounds sexy, probably dirty. I wrap one hand around the base of his cock and slowly take him into my mouth. As I slide my mouth down his cock as far as I can go, I pinch his nipples with my other hand. Then I slide my mouth up the shaft again and suck on the head. He moans. I begin to suck him off in earnest.

I actually like giving blow jobs. I know a lot of women don't, but I think they just don't like sex or are too hung up or something. Sure, there's some technical difficulty involved and if you have a hyper-sensitive gag reflex, it's a problem, but guys love it. There's nothing like a skillful and enthusiastic blowjob to make a guy grateful and grateful guys return the favor. After all, I don't want a guy to go down on me as a reluctant duty. I want it to feel like an act of worshipful service. Besides, the sexual power I feel when I'm driving my man crazy sucking him off is a total turn on. I love it when I've got him at my mercy. I can tease and torture him as long as I want, bringing him to the edge and backing off again until he begs for it. There's only one thing I don't like when giving a blowjob. I don't like it when a man takes hold of my head and tries to control the action. I don't like it when he tries to fuck me in the mouth. It freaks me out. It makes me panic. It feels like I can't breathe. It makes me feel violated. It scares me. I'm totally fine with him holding my hair back and stroking my head, but not what Dario's doing now. His got one hand on each side of my head, pumping me up and down on his cock. It's making me gag and choke. I can't breathe. I try to pull my head away, to come up for air, but he's not responding. I'm starting to panic. Maybe he's about to come. I don't know him well enough to gauge how close he is, whether I can finish him off quick. I put a hand on his balls to feel if they're tightening up and decide to try to get him to come as fast as possible. I wrap both hands around his shaft, one on top of the other, to create some space for myself. Then I work the shaft in a sliding, wringing motion, suck the head and run my tongue along the ridge and across the spot where his foreskin attaches. Thank God it works and within another minute he yells out something in Spanish and comes hard in my mouth.

As soon as he lets go of my head, I jump up and run to the bathroom. I spit his ejaculate into the sink and rinse my mouth out. I'm shaking. I look in the mirror. My mascara has run all under my eyes. My hair looks like I just came through a wind storm. I'm pissed off and a little frightened. I take some deep breaths and try to calm down. What the fuck was that? Did he just get a little carried away in the heat of the moment or do I have a scary dangerous dude I know nothing about in my living room? "Don't over-react," I tell myself. Up till now, he's been a generous and delightful partner, on and off the dance floor, in and out of bed. Wouldn't Carla have warned me if Dario was abusive? Then again, she might not know anything about his sexual tastes or how he is with women. She might not have thought to answer my casual questions with this kind of personal detail about a friend. I don't know her very well. We're not really friends, so she would have no reason to be looking out for me. I hear Cheryl's voice of caution in my head again. I review our time together. Dario has given me no reason not to trust him. I decide to give him the benefit of the doubt. "Girl," I tell myself, "Grow the fuck up. Put on your big girl panties and go out there and communicate." Ask questions, get information about where he's coming from, set a boundary, all that kind of grown up stuff where I take responsibility for my sexual experiences. I clean up my face and run a brush through my hair. I'm about to leave the bathroom when I realize I'm naked from the waist up. I grab a robe from the back of the door and slip it on.

I head back out to the living room, but he's not there. What the fuck? "Dario," I call out. He's not in the kitchen, or the guest bathroom. I walk back into my bedroom and find him propped up naked in my bed. He's lit the candles in here. "Alexis," he says, "Come to bed." From the doorway, I can see his reflection in the mirror next to the bed. I have a minotaur in my bed. He's drooling and snorting. His horns are enormous. He looks at me through red-rimmed eyes, black, cold and ruthless as death. He throws the covers back and I catch a whiff of rank barnyard smell. A tail swishes lazily back and forth between his legs. The bushy tip wafts the stink of beast around my bedroom. *"Cariño,* come," the Dario-minotaur says. I see my reflection in the background. I look small and pale. I close my eyes and take a deep breath. When I open them, there's only a large, charming, tall dark and handsome Argentinian man in my bed. I study the image in the mirror. No minotaur, only the man who just mouth-raped me a little.

"Dario," I say, "Will you come out into the living room for a minute? I need to check something out with you." I walk back out to the living room. I turn the lights up a little bit and sit down in the arm chair. He comes out in his briefs. "Alexis," he says, "What is it?" He looks relaxed, at ease, sure of himself. He's sitting there on my living room sofa smiling at me in his charming way. And aren't those the very qualities that attracted me in the first place? I stare at the pillow still on the floor. "For me, there are two essential requirements for good sex," I say. I'm glad to see this gets his attention. "First is chemistry. Without it, nothing works." A super sexy song comes on. The timing feels too coincidental. "Would you agree?" I ask him. "Sí, sí," Dario says, "chemistry is very important." I take a deep breath and will myself to act calm and confident. "The second is communication. Do you agree with that?" I say. I can feel the anxious knot in the pit of my stomach tighten. "Of course," he says, "Communication is also important." I shift around in my chair and adjust my robe, thinking how to phrase this next piece. "I want you to know I enjoy taking you in my mouth," I say. "But I don't at all like getting fucked in the mouth." I can't say it any clearer than that. Everything hinges on what he says and does next. For a moment I think I see a flash of ice in Dario's eyes, but then his expression changes. "Ah, *cariño*, I understand," he says, "Forgive me if I got too excited before." I realize I've been holding my breath. "You just turn me on so much," he says. He smiles with the most mischievous look. He comes over to the chair and reaches his hand out to me. "Come, let's dance," he says. I can't seem to resist him. I let him pull me up, but before I step into his arms I say, "Don't do it again." He murmurs in my ear, "Never," and kisses a spot under my earlobe.

Dancing with Dario is what got me into this situation in the first place. He's doing that thing I love, just holding me with an easy confidence, breathing slowly and deeply, shifting our weight side to side. He holds me with consideration and authority. It takes me a minute to relax in his arms. We begin to dance. I start to let go into the music. I feel his courtly attentiveness, drop my resistance and open to him once again. He dances us into the bedroom, over to my bed, bends his face down to mine and kisses me like he adores me. Then he lifts me up, lays me in the bed and removes all my clothes. He's totally shifted the vibe. Dario begins to worship my body, beginning at my feet. He rubs and strokes and kisses his way up my legs, skips over my naked pussy, to my hips and waist. I'm completely turned onto him again. I need his lips and tongue on me, his fingers inside me. I guide his head between my thighs and press my pussy against his mouth. He licks me from my clit to my ass, back and forth, sucking and pulling my clit into his mouth, flicking his tongue along the bottom of it. His hands spread me wide from stem to stern, squeezing my ass and pulling me open. It's driving me crazy and I'm off on an orgasmic spiral.

I'm still coming when he flips me over onto my stomach and props me up with pillows, on my knees with my ass up in the air. He positions himself behind me. Then he pulls my swollen lips apart and rubs the head of his cock into the wetness pouring out of me. He begins to enter me in slow rolling thrusts, shallow at first, then each one deeper and deeper. Once he's in up to the hilt, he pulls out so only the head is inside and begins to ratchet his way back into my depths. When he reaches around to pinch and pull my nipples, I start coming again. I'm moaning and wailing now, rolling my hips around. This seems to set something loose in him, something wild and dark. He grabs me by my hips and starts slamming into me hard. Then he's slapping my ass — much too hard. It hurts. I try to pull away. "Ow," I say, "Dario that's too hard. That hurts." But he ignores me. I try to pull away again but he grabs me by my hair and pulls hard to hold me in place. "Dario," I yell, "Stop! You're hurting me." But he doesn't stop. He lets go of my hair to spank my ass and pull my hips closer to him. In the mirror I see I've been mounted by a minotaur. His head is huge and shaggy with large black-tipped horns. His breath blasts over me, hot and foul. His strength is unbelievable. I'm crying as he slams into me, over and over and over again. I try to get away but he grabs my hair and yanks my head back. He laughs as he pounds into me, whacking my ass with his other hand. It goes on forever. With a roar, he finally comes. After a last fierce thrust, he rolls off me onto his back. I curl up into a ball sobbing. After a moment, Dario rolls over and puts his arm around me, "*Cariño*, was I too rough again?" he says, "It's only because you get me so excited."

I jump up from my bed, grab my robe and head to the bathroom. "Keep it together. Keep it together," I tell myself. "Keep it together and get him out of here." I want to scrub him off me, but first I have to pee. It stings and burns. The toilet paper is tinged pink when I wipe. I splash water on my face. I make the mistake of looking in the mirror. I'm all red and splotchy. I turn around to look at my ass. I can already see bruises in a fingerprint pattern on my hips. My ass is dark red. I'm desperately trying to get my mind in gear so I can figure out how to get him out of my apartment. I blow my nose and tie the belt of my robe tighter around my waist. I take a deep breath and head back into my bedroom. Dario is laying back with one hand behind his head and checking his phone. He has a self-satisfied little smirk on his handsome face. I feel nauseous. I check the wall mirror. No minotaur. I go into the kitchen to get a glass of water. "Think, think think," I tell myself. I walk back to the bedroom and stand by the door.

"Dario, it's been quite an evening," I say. He smiles at me like he's proud of himself. "Yes, it has, Alexis." Adrenalin is coursing through my body and all my cells are screaming, "Danger, danger, danger! Run!" I know it's lame, but all I can think to say is, "I have an early breakfast meeting in the morning, so let's call it a night." Smooth as silk, he says, "But *cariño,* the night is young still." He's enjoying my attempt to disguise my fear and panic. The room fills with a barnyard smell again. "Not for me," I say, "I need to get some sleep." He throws back the covers again and pats the bed. "Come. Take a little sleep and we can make love again." I try to keep up the pretense that he didn't just violate me, that he's not a monster. "Not tonight," I say. As I turn to head back out into the living room, I catch a glimpse of the tip of his tail, still hanging over the side of my bed. "Keep it together," I chant to myself. In the living room, I blow out all the candles, turn off the music and turn the lights up. Eventually he comes sauntering out. I go stand by the front door and hold out his leather jacket. He hooks it with a finger and slings it over his shoulder. Then he wraps his other arm around me and pulls me into him. My body stiffens. He leans his head down for a kiss. I turn my cheek. But he grasps my jaw in his big hand, turns my face to his and kisses me hard on the mouth. He pulls back to look at me and the expression in his eyes makes my blood run cold. His monstrous black heart stares back at me. Then he smiles that amused, self-satisfied smirk again. "Good evening Alexis," he says, "I enjoyed you very much."

I lock the door behind him and take big gulps of air. My legs give way and I crumple to the floor sobbing, then suddenly I have to vomit. I run to the bathroom and heave up dinner. I take a long shower and practically scrub my skin off. When I shampoo my hair, my scalp hurts. I catch sight of my face in the mirror when I brush my teeth. My eyes look huge, empty, haunted. I strip the bed and change the sheets, but the smell still sticks to my bed. I strip it again and change out the mattress pad, stuff my comforter and pillows into trash bags and stack them by the front door. They all reek. I'll have to take them to a laundromat with industrial size machines. I can't sleep. I review every single minute of our time together, looking for signs I missed of the monster inside. I have no way to process the minotaur. I dismiss it as some sort of projection my mind produced to warn me of the pleasure he takes in violence. When I finally fall asleep, Dario invades my dreams. I'm in a vast bed in some dark cavern, where a giant minotaur violates me over and over again in every orifice.

In the morning, I call in sick. I feel like one giant, raw, exposed nerve. I stand naked in the bright morning sunlight and examine my body in the full-length mirror. I have purple-green circles on my hips, four on each side, with two thumbprints on the back. My ass-cheeks are beginning to turn the same color. I keep catching a faint scent of rank animal in rut. I open every window in my apartment to try and get the smell out, empty the vases and dump the peonies down the trash chute. I promise myself to take things slow in the future, to really get to know the man before we get physically intimate. I try not to feel punished for my sexuality. I try not to judge myself a slut who got what she deserved. I try to forgive myself for not recognizing a sociopath. I try to dismiss the image of that minotaur in my bed, mounting me, hitting me. I try not to fall apart.

At eleven, Cheryl calls. I almost don't answer, but I need my friend. "So, how did it go last night?" she asks. I burst into tears. "Alexis, sweetheart, what's the matter?" she asks. I tell her about my evening with the monster behind the charming mask. When I get to the part about the minotaur, she stops me. "Wait, what did you just say?" she asks. I repeat the part about seeing a minotaur in the mirror. "Hang on," she says, "Let's get onto Skype. I need to see you." I burst into tears again when I see her face. God I miss Cheryl. I wish she were here right now to give me a big hug. Cheryl gives the best hugs, just wraps you in her arms and envelops you in love. "Honey, let me see the bruises," she says. So I show her. "Did you call the police?" she asks. "I thought about it, but it wouldn't help." Even if I could get him arrested after I clearly had consensual sex with the man, what am I going to do? Try and get him extradited from Argentina for a trial?

"Alexis, he can't get away with this," Cheryl says. I'm sitting in the chaise in my bedroom. I feel like shit. Even though it's a hot day and I have all the windows open, I still feel cold bundled up in sweatpants and a sweater. "But he can get away with it," I say, "and he knows it." Then it hits me all at once. Dario is a true sociopath. This is his M.O. He travels around preying on women, charming them with his manners and money, with his power and prestige, with his dancing. Then he has his way with them, and when they've already given themselves to him, when they're primed and defenseless, then he enjoys violating them. He probably would have groomed me for a while longer before really unleashing on me, but the frenzy of my sexual response must've been unexpected. He let himself lose control a little early. I flash on that smirking face with his cold black heart staring out of those beautiful brown eyes. I shiver again. "Come back to Seattle for a few days," Cheryl says. But I can't leave town now. I'm already behind at work and taking today off is only going to make it worse. Before we hang up, Cheryl tells me, "Now don't blame yourself for not recognizing he's a sociopath." That's exactly what I've been thinking. I do blame myself. "How could I not see it? Was I just lost in a fantasy world of my own projections?" I shift around on my chaise. It hurts to sit. "That's the definition of a sociopath," Cheryl says. "They zero in on your vulnerabilities and manipulate you like a master puppeteer. You never see it until it's too late."

CHAPTER THREE

Rafael

The trauma of Dario leaves me self-doubting and confused. How could I have read the energy so wrong? We had that intense connection on the dance floor. The sex was super hot, right up until he became violent. I think about telling Zhenya, to warn women in the community about him, but he was only in Los Angeles for a visit. Besides, I'm ashamed and embarrassed. I don't want anyone to know. I don't want anyone to think of me as a tango slut or just another middle-aged cliché. I promise myself not to date anyone in the tango community ever again, to keep it on the dance floor. If there's an especially steamy connection with someone, I can enjoy it for that moment, and leave it there on the floor when the dance is over. That's what I tell myself.

For the next few weeks, I re-focus on work. I limit my tango dancing to private classes. I practice my technique and my dancing goes through a growth spurt. Tonight is my favorite monthly *milonga*. It has a great dance floor and friendly crowd. The DJ booked for this evening plays a gorgeous mix of traditional music and Nuevo Tango songs. I finally feel ready to venture out again. As I get ready, I give myself a little pep talk about leaving the dance connection on the floor. "You can enjoy the hell out of a great connection, just don't let it go any further," I tell myself. I haven't been on a date since that last evening with Dario. I don't trust myself. I try on a skin-tight black dress with red and silver fringe suspended from the neckline. "Chemistry on the dance floor is not the green light to jump into your next love affair," I tell myself. I twirl in the mirror and watch the fringe fly out, then turn around to check it out from the back. I lift up my arms in the tango embrace position. The hemline rises high up the back of my thighs. Too short. Too risqué. Not age-appropriate. Why did I ever buy it, anyway? "You can look sexy and elegant, without showing so much skin," I tell myself. I try on a couple of other outfits, but they all seem too slutty to me tonight. I settle on a slinky high-necked black silk jersey dress, sexy, but not obvious. I've layered it with multiple strands of pearls, going more for classy than seductive. I look like a hot, but conservative widow, in mourning for my lost innocence.

There's quite a crowd by the time I get there. I say hello to a number of people I know. I walk over to Zhenya's table to put my things down and change into tango shoes. When the *tanda* ends, Zhenya and Sylvie come back with Justin and Farzad. There's much hugging and kissing of cheeks. Everyone is dressed up. The men wear suits and ties. Sylvie is stunning in a black and silver lace affair, low cut in the back and slit high up the thigh.

It sets off her blonde hair and blue eyes to dramatic effect. Zhenya looks like a wet dream come true in flowing red and black chiffon that moves like air around her hips and thighs. A red crystal pendant dangles between her fabulous boobs.

Farzad invites me to dance. I don't know why, but the tango community in LA is full of Persians. Farzad and I have become tango friends and he's one of my favorite dance partners. He's good friends with Sylvie and Zhenya, so I see him often. There's nothing sexual between us, but we share a lovely connection. He's got a very clear and considerate lead and I feel safe with him. Farzad has great musicality, so it's always fun to dance together. He's on the short side, maybe five-foot-eight, so we're a good height match with me in my tango heels. He's a perfect partner for my warm-up *tanda* of the evening. My only complaint is that he wears too much cologne and I can smell it on my clothes after we dance. After the first song in the *tanda*, I relax and loosen up. I realize I'd been tense and anxious about coming tonight. "You're here to dance," I tell myself, "So just enjoy it." I take a deep breath and will myself to relax even more. I focus on the present moment, on the music, on the wordless physical communication between us. When the last song in the set ends, I give Farzad a big hug. I feel happy and alive again.

I'm having a marvelous time tonight. I've danced with some familiar partners and a few new ones, too. Sylvie is in fine form this evening. She has me in stitches with her hilarious tales of life in the world of top-tier corporate consulting. It never ceases to amaze me how often male executives underestimate the brain power she possesses. She sees right through them. She's soft-spoken and her blonde beauty fools them completely, right up until the moment they realize she's got them wrapped around her finger. I'm ready to dance again, so I turn around in my chair and scan the crowd for my next partner. I run my glance over a number of candidates. A man I've seen around but haven't danced with before catches my eye. He's short, with dark hair and dark skin, well dressed and looks to be somewhere in his mid-30's. He invites me to dance with an inclination of his head and a smile. I'm in such a good mood. Why not take a chance? Maybe he's a good dancer.

I smile and nod back. He walks over to the table and holds his hand out to me. It's warm and dry. I like the way it feels. He escorts me into the steamy heat of the crowded dance floor, full of sweating couples in close embrace. A Nuevo Tango set begins, seductive and dramatic. My new partner takes me in his arms. "What's your name?" I say. But what I'm really thinking is "Holy shit! You feel amazing!" Inside the secure container of his embrace, my body switches into high alert. Pheromones fly like carrier pigeons. "Rafael," he says. The women's jewelry glints in the low light of the antique crystal chandeliers in the ballroom of this turn-of-the century social club. Cream-colored walls, honey wood floors and handcrafted moldings give the high-ceilinged room a sense of warmth and graciousness. "What's yours?" he asks. His deep-set brown eyes smile at me. I can smell his cologne, something spicy with a musky woodsy undertone, and beneath that, the heady scent of his maleness. "I'm Alexis," I say. Our first *tanda* together begins.

Rafael's lead is strong and firm yet considerate and sensitive. Something about his touch grounds and calms me but excites me at the same time. I can feel my molecules stirring, my heart beating faster. I can feel the warmth of his hand in mine, the solid mass of his body up against me, igniting my senses. I can feel the clarity and confidence of his lead. I can feel his musicality and creativity. The elegance and style of his dancing surprises me.

As we glide and swirl around the floor in the line of dance, I give myself over to the moment. Nothing else exists but this intense attunement to the music and Rafael's body. I focus on feeling his energy, on collecting my feet together. His entire body speaks to me. His chest and hands steer me. My body trusts him. I feel safe. I can feel him feeling me, tracking my energy and movements. I close my eyes and lay my cheek against his. Low down in my belly, something tugs and then opens. My pussy convulses and begins to tingle. The sconce ends. We stand hot case, breathing together. Whoa! I step back and break the embrace. I need to get my bearings. I adjust my check-in table. It's all twisted around me. "Where are you from, Rafael?" I ask to distract myself from my unexpected physical response. "I grew up in the Philippines and Mexico," he says. "My mother is Filipino and my father is Mexican."

Another Nuevo Tango song starts up. Rafael shifts gears, ups the ante, tests my chops. No time to think, just feel and respond. Tricky moves and sudden shifts, I have to stay completely present. My recent investment in private classes pays off big time. O*chos, sacadas, ganchos,* pivot, collect, syncopated footwork, taps, kicks, crushing, commanding excitement, electrifying, scrumptious, testosterone kaleidoscope. The song ends. I'm turned on. Sweating. Panting. Completely alive. Who is this man? I look him in the eyes. He looks back. Deep and intense, then kind. He smiles. I laugh. The third and final song in the *tanda* begins.

Rafael pulls me into close embrace. I think I hear him growl. Something coils around my waist. Is that a tail? I'm in the arms of a jaguar man, black and shiny pelt, fierce and wild. I feel out of control and it scares me, especially after Dario. I don't even know this guy and I'm ready for him to take me right there on the crowded dance floor, to rip off my panties and ravish me. We slide across the floor, my skin hot under his touch. He's making me dizzy. I feel him stalking me and smell the damp jungle floor. My ruby toes wink in the dark, flashing gold pencil heels skim above the ground. I feel an urgent need to put my lips against his neck, so I do. I can't help it. I keep my eyes closed, splashes of doom, my mother shaming me, calling me a fucking whore.

As if he can hear my thoughts, Rafael shifts the energy. In his embrace, I feel a sweet protective gentleness. It makes my heart melt, along with my pussy. My body turns to liquid in his arms. The final song in the *tanda* ends and Rafael steers me off the dance floor. "Thank you for the *tanda*," he says and settles me into my chair. "It was beautiful to dance together."

I nod my head numbly. I'm in a curious altered state, in a strange daze yet all my senses are amplified. I'm shaken and excited, and embarrassed by my excitement all at once. I sit captivated, trembling, squeezing my thighs together, trying to control the quivering, sweating pulsations. I wasn't even attracted to this one at first. No way does my ideal man description include short, hairy and half-Filipino, half-Mexican, you know what I mean? But hey, the pussy has a mind of her own. I hate to admit it, but the truth is I like to be handled like that, with attentiveness and protective authority, with confident intimacy. I like it a lot, even though it makes me feel so vulnerable and needy. I don't want anyone, least of all some guy I just met on the dance floor, to know just how much I want his hands on me, all over me.

We dance one more *tanda* that night. Lucky for me it's a fast *milonga*. I have to focus to keep up and we're moving rapidly, in and out of open embrace, with syncopated footwork — less chance to succumb to my desires and melt into him. Rafael escorts me back to my table. "May I get you something to drink?" he asks me. "Why not?" I think. I'm thirsty and I want to know more about this elegant man. "Thank you," I say, "Some mineral water with lime would be great." When he comes back to the table with our drinks, Sylvie and Farzad are there, too. I make the introductions and we begin to chat. Somehow, he and Sylvie get onto the topic of favorite hotels around the world. It's quickly apparent Rafael is a well-traveled and highly cultured man, with a quirky sense of humor. The two of them banter and tease back and forth about the pros and cons of French versus British hotels.

A *tango vals* starts up and Farzad catches my eye. As we head out to the dance floor, I see Sylvie and Rafael get up to dance. I feel a little pang of jealousy and scold myself for being ridiculous. It turns out this *tango vals* is the last *tanda* of the evening. Back at the table, I'm changing out of my tango shoes when Rafael asks if he can walk me to my car. "Thank you," I say, "That's very thoughtful." Sylvie catches my eye and winks at me. We all head out. In the parking lot, Rafael takes me by the arm in a protective manner and steers us through the exodus of cars. Why does the feeling of his hand on my arm make me feel so safe and cared for? When we get to my car, Rafael asks, "Do you ever go to the downtown *milonga* on Thursday nights?" The night air is cool and fresh after the heat of the day. The moon is almost full. Rafael is standing so close to me that I catch a whiff of spice, musk and maleness. "No, I've never been," I say. "Why, what's it like?" God, he smells so good, even after a night of dancing. "I think you would like it," he says. "It's less formal and traditional. They play a lot of Nuevo Tango music." Hah! Just what I need — to meet up with this guy my pussy-meter already has the hots for and dance to the sexiest tango music there is. "We could meet there this Thursday, if you care to go," he says. "No dating in the tango community," I admonish myself. "Sure, I'll check it out with you," I say. "What time does it start?"

We make plans to meet at 9:00. "What are you doing, Alexis?" says the rule-keeper in my head. "It's just tango, not a date," I tell myself. But who do I think I'm fooling?

I stand inside my closet Thursday night, arguing with myself about what to wear. In the end, I decide on a boobalicious low-cut red top with metal chain accents and a pair of black skinny jeans. I hook a hanging jeweled chain from the belt loop on my back hip and make a tango pivot in the mirror to gauge the effect. It swings and jingles, catches the light. "Bad girl," I tell myself. I smile. I'm in a dangerous mood. I choose a cat-eye look and finish it off with a bright red lipstick. I grab my new pair of red tango shoes and head out the door. This Thursday *milonga* is at a large downtown dance studio. Parking's a bitch. I get there late. Once inside, I look around for Rafael. I see a couple people I know instead. Marco is there, and I give him a kiss hello. "You're looking hot tonight," he says. He's still one of my favorite partners and we dance well together. It's odd — I can dance so intimately with him, really let my feminine energy out, yet the pussy-meter doesn't ding at all. I scan the dance floor for Rafael and see him with a woman I don't know. She's younger than me and a better dancer. I feel a pang of insecurity. "Jesus, Alexis," I scold myself, "get ahold of yourself! What are you, 16? And this is not a date! Remember?" I change into my shoes. "Are those new?" Marco asks. They're red suede with gold metal chain embellishments. "Yeah, I just got them," I say. "Very nice," he says. Marco and I head onto the dance floor. I focus on the music and following his lead. By the time the *tanda* ends, I'm warmed up and enjoying myself.

During the *cortina* between *tandas*, I look for Rafael. He finds me first and walks over with a big smile. "Alexis," he says, "I'm so happy you made it." He's wearing a stylish dark blue shirt with embroidered red details and a pair of loose-cut grey trousers. When he leans in to kiss me on each cheek, I catch that spicy scent with the musky bottom note. "Sorry I'm late," I say, "I had a hard time parking." Normally I don't care for musk at all, but on him it's a turn-on. "Yes, that's a problem with this *milonga*," he says, "but I thought you would like the music." The next *tanda* starts up and it's one of my favorites. "I love this song," I say. Rafael gestures to the dance floor. I take his hand, he opens his arms and I step into a close embrace. We stand there breathing with each other for a few bars as he shifts our weight left to right. Then we're off.

I love the way Rafael expresses the music with his lead. He matches my impulses exactly. We enter one of those rare perfect tango moments, when I become completely absorbed and alert to the present moment, in total oneness with my partner and the music. My entire being fills with joy. There's nothing like this combination of heightened awareness, deep meditative attention, creative expression, and sensual movement shared with another person. Well, except for sacred sex with the right partner. Rafael steers us into a sequence that expresses the melody and punctuates the rhythm to perfection. It's exquisite. I feel my face open into a wide smile. I am so happy in this moment. It's total bliss. We finish with a dramatic slide in perfect time to the end of the song. I stand there unmoving in his arms, feeling the pleasure course up and down my body. Then something shifts. I smell his man scent underneath his sexy cologne. It telegraphs an alarm code straight to the pussy-meter. Before I can get myself in hand, the next song starts up and we're dancing again.

Rafael leads me around the floor with a smooth feline grace. My body registers and responds without hesitation. I'm hyper-conscious of his body, of his warm, strong hands. His lead is delicious, clear and firm, but not overpowering or pushy. There's a quality of sensitivity, of consideration and attentiveness that feels like a protective container for me to dance within. It's like his body is telling me, "I got you. You're safe. Feel free. Be yourself." It makes me trust him and open my heart. I give myself over to the moment. There's so much charge running through my body, it's almost overwhelming. I have to take deep conscious breaths to expand enough and let it flow. It feels like I'm turning to liquid light in his arms. How am I ever going to resist a man who gives me tangasms? I catch myself making sounds, little sighs and moans of pleasure. How embarrassing! I shut up and lay my cheek against his. I think I hear a low rumbling growl and when I stumble, I feel a tail wrap around my waist to steady me. What just happened? Something about tango puts me into an altered state, or causes hallucinations or something. First the flashes of the past-life battle with Daniel, then the minotaur lounging in my bed, and now a big black jungle cat with Rafael. Well, the minotaur thing with Dario wasn't tango. I don't know was that was. I re-focus my attention on the music and the dance. It's the final song in the *tanda*. I can feel my little hip chain shimmy and bounce with each pivot. My senses heighten and shift up another octave. Like a jungle creature, I can hear and smell and feel everything — our hearts thumping, our blood coursing, our breath whooshing in and out. Currents of scent spreading tales of rose and spice, sweat and sex.

My condition must be broadcasting through the room, because men are lining up to dance with me like bees to nectar. Men who are much better dancers than me invite me onto the floor, men who are younger, men who I've never danced with before. I'm having a wonderful time, but they're not Rafael. They're lovely and all, but no tangasms. Which is just as well, given my history. I'm sitting down to cool off and rest a bit when Rafael walks over with two glasses of wine and a bottle of water under his arm. "I thought you might like something to drink," he says. He sits down and turns his chair towards me. "That is so thoughtful," I say, "Thank you." We begin to chat. After our experiences on the dance floor, I want to know who he really is. "What brought you to the States?" I ask him. "Music," he says, "I studied piano and composition at Juilliard." No wonder his dancing is so musical. "Do you perform and compose now?" I ask. "No," he says, "my mother insisted I take up the family business, so I went and got an MBA." I learn his mother comes from a Filipino family of bankers and industrialists, on his Mexican father's side it's politicians. Both families share a diplomatic connection. His parents met at an embassy party in Mexico City. He looks down at his hands like he's examining them for tremors or ragged cuticles, or maybe lost piano keys. I imagine those hands all over my body. It makes my pussy flutter. I squirm around in my chair. I want to find out more, but Rafael turns the conversation around and asks about my work and interests. When he hears I'm thinking about starting up my own branding agency, he says he may be able to help. Apparently he's an unofficial advisor to a number of companies here as well as in Mexico and the Philippines. He suggests we get together. It's as good an excuse as any.

We meet for coffee a few days later. Well, boba tea actually. Boba tea, aka bubble tea, is a cold, sweet milky tea with tapioca balls you suck up through an extra-wide straw. Rafael tells me it's hugely popular all throughout South East Asia and Asia, and it's caught on here, too. I've never tried it before. It sounds gross, but to my surprise, I like it. The tapioca balls are the treat. There's something addictive about their chewy texture, like gummy bears. The noisy downtown boba shop is crowded with 20-somethings. A young man shoves his way onto the communal bench where we're sitting and bumps into me. "Excuse, me," I snap at him. Typical LA millennial, he doesn't even apologize. Rafael puts his arm me around me protectively. I remind myself I'm here for business and attempt to make my interrogation sound casual as we slurp up tapioca balls. It turns out Rafael is quite the Renaissance man — he was Jesuit-educated in philosophy and the classics, speaks three languages fluently and another two passably, and he can read Homer and Ovid in the original Greek and Latin. To top it off, he had a brief career as a concert pianist and composer before joining the family business. As I listen to his impressive resume, I find myself attracted to the same calm, confident, considerate presence he brings to the dance floor. I'd like to stay and talk more, but I have a client meeting. "Rafael, this has been fun, but I have to go," I say. "So soon?" he says. "We didn't even get to talk about your plans for a new branding agency." He slurps up the last of his tapioca balls as I gather my things and stand up. Rafael takes my arm to escort me out to the sidewalk. Just the touch of his hand gets the pussy-meter purring. "I'd like to help you if I can," he says. "Let's continue our discussion over dinner." Some high-level international business introductions are the perfect excuse to override my solemn vow not to date anyone in the tango community. Well, that and the pussy-meter.

The guys you least suspect sure can surprise you, enough to make a woman break her rules. At dinner, we talk about the challenges of life in LA, the differences in business practices between the U.S., Mexico and the Philippines — nothing romantic. After dinner, he invites me back to his place. He lives in a modern, luxury apartment in Santa Monica with fabulous ocean views. It's the kind of building with ultra-high security, an Olympic-sized swimming pool, a full gym with saunas, and a row of luxury cars in the drive waiting for their owners. Rafael directs me to the valet in the driveway and drives his Acura SUV into the parking garage. I spot a couple of Teslas and a Maserati in front of me. The valet, an older

Hispanic man, comes over to open my door. I hand him my keys and walk into the massive lobby, where an imposing concierge asks my business. Rafael comes out of an elevator and saves me from having to sign in at the desk. My heels clack across the marble floor to the elevators. What am I doing here? Up in his apartment, we're on his sofa talking about my work when I find myself snuggling up to him. He smells so good I want to get closer. He puts his arm around me and I lay my head into the hollow of his shoulder. Just a friendly snuggle, that's all, nothing to freak out over. As per my strict post-Dario rules, I have absolutely no intention of going to bed with him, but the cells in my hive have other ideas. If I'm honest with myself, I'm the one who starts it. You know what they say about the best-laid plans of mice and men. He begins to stroke me, pet me really, as though we've been together for years, as though he knows my body, as though he's already claimed me, as though he knows exactly how to touch me, as though he knows what I want, as though he knows how to make me feel loved and safe, cherished and adored. With my cells all abuzz, I can't help myself. I tip my face up to be kissed.

Rafael kisses me with that combination of authority and sensitivity I love. He has me reeling. Damn my rules, I want him to do it again. I can't help myself. I climb onto his lap and straddle him. He takes my face in his hands and kisses me again. His lips are soft and full on mine. He slips the tip of his tongue between my lips, then sucks my lower lip into his mouth. I roll my hips around and feel his erection straining against his pants. I rise up on my knees and pull his face into my cleavage, take hold of his hands and place them on my ass. That lets loose the beast. Never bait a panther — once roused, there's no going back. Rafael begins to kiss and bite all over my face and neck and shoulders as he kneads my ass in his hands.

Did I mention his hands before? Rafael has beautiful hands. They're strong hands, well-shaped with long fingers, the agile hands of the concert pianist that he used to be. I don't want him to take his hands off my ass, so I help him out, pull my breasts free from my bra and hold them out for him. He devours them, first one, then the other, taking as much as he can into his mouth, kissing and biting them, pulling my nipples between his teeth. By this point I'm moaning and wet and beyond stopping, not that I want to stop. He takes hold of my hips, and in one smooth motion, stands up and carries me into the bedroom.

I wrap my legs around him and cling on, sighing. He carries me like I weigh nothing at all. I love to feel that strength and power in a man. It makes me crazy hot, takes me over the top. Rafael lays me down on the bed, takes hold of my ankles, lifts my legs up over one shoulder, pulls my thong off and tosses the damp slip of fabric behind him. He pulls my hips to the edge of the bed, still holding me up by the ankles. Then he separates my legs, kneels down on the floor between them and hooks a knee over each shoulder. He begins to kiss and bite my inner thighs as he works his way toward my pussy. I think I hear myself whimper. By the time Rafael puts his mouth on my clit, I'm practically coming. It doesn't him long to tip me over the edge, legs locked around his neck, hips rolling.

When the spasms taper off, I unlock my legs from around his head and pull him up for a kiss. I can taste my juices on his lips. Rafael gets up and pulls the covers back. He scoops me up and lays me back down with my head on the pillows. He pads out to the kitchen and brings me back a glass of water before washing his face and hands in the bathroom. Back in bed, he takes me in his arms and starts kissing me again. He's kind of hairy, but he keeps his chest and back man-groomed. There's no trace of the calm, soft-spoken man I met before. His hands are all over me now, stroking my breasts, pinching my nipples, squeezing my hips, running up and down my thighs, caressing my head and face. The way he's handling me is driving me wild. He's kissing me deeply, fiercely, in total control. I reach down and take hold of his cock. It's not that long, but it's thick with a little upturned curve. The head feels soft and velvety. It's well-defined, the way I like it. He groans that deep panther rumble as I stroke up and down his length, squeeze the head and run my fingers over his balls.

Rafael shifts position to kneel between my legs. He elevates my hips on a plump pillow. He lifts my legs around his waist, kisses each foot and sucks my toes. He reaches down and spreads my swollen lips wide. He lays the head of his cock up against the wet, open, pink mouth of my pussy. Then he leans over me, looks me in the eyes and mounts me. I take a long shuddering breath as Rafael enters me. Slowly, he begins to stroke in and out. The upturned curve of his cock rubs along my G-spot. I'm moaning and sighing, long drawn-out ahhhh's. He reaches one hand down to lightly stroke my clitoris and I open to him even more. "Yes, yes," I groan, "Take me! Please take me, I need you to take me!" And he does, shape-shifting over me, man, hawk, panther, clawed, fanged, furred and feathered. I'm taken by a warrior-scholar, relentless, primal, stripped bare, raw. I wail and he growls as he fucks me without mercy. I can't help but surrender, give myself over to the spiral waves of orgasm. I can feel him release into me as I come and come and come. I already know I want him to fuck me in the ass.

Rafael wants me to stay over, but there's no way I'm doing that. It's too much too soon and I have a lot to process. We never did talk about business. He calls down for my car, gets dressed and escorts me out through the lobby to the drive. The concierge, a different guy from before, barely looks up from his newspaper to say good evening. "Thank you for a beautiful night, Alexis," he says. The young valet driver is waiting with the car door open. I'm relieved to see they've changed shifts, because it's pretty obvious I've just gotten my brains fucked out — not that it's their business to comment on the comings and goings of residents and guests. Anyway, I'm glad he didn't see me on the way in. "So when can I see you again?" Rafael asks. What would be a decent interval? Not so long that his interest wanes, but not so soon as to look too eager. Who do I think I'm fooling here? The horses are already out of the barn. What good would come from shutting the barn doors now?

"How about this weekend?" I say. At this late hour, the driveway is empty. The other two young valets on duty pause their banter to focus on us. "I can't this weekend," Rafael says, "I have my children." Uh-oh. What am I getting into here? Laura is about to start her junior year in college. I'm done with all that. "You have children?" I ask. "Yes, twin girls and a son," he says. "Oh, how wonderful," I say, not meaning a word of it. "How old?" He smiles. "The girls are six and my son is eight." Shit, still in grade school. I'm finally at an age where I'm open to a younger man, but a man twelve years my junior? With three young children? And what about the ex-wife situation, assuming there is an ex-wife and he's not a widower? I stand there considering his situation while Rafael and the three valets await my answer. The night air this close to the ocean is damp and chilly. I notice I've buttoned my blouse wrong. There's a dime on the ground next to the valet's shoe. Rafael interrupts my paralysis, "Are you available for dinner next Monday?" I need to think about it. "I have to check my calendar," I say, "Can I let you know tomorrow?" I get into my car and fasten the seatbelt. "Of course, Alexis," he says, "Whatever works for you." Then he leans in, kisses me on each cheek, and whispers in my ear, "Just make it soon."

The next morning, I call Cheryl. I need someone I can trust, someone who will tell me the truth, someone who has my best interests at heart, someone who wants me to find true love, someone who won't judge me or shame me. I've been feeling so much shame about my sexuality since taking up tango. I keep hearing my mother's abusive, hateful voice in my head, calling me a slut and a whore. My recent impulsive behavior is so unlike me. Maybe I was just repressed during the last fifteen years of my marriage. Doug and I barely ever had sex, maybe a few times a year, and then it was white-bread missionary-style, boring and unsatisfying with zero foreplay. Tango unleashed all my previously inhibited wildness, like some hidden nymphomaniac has broken free. I have no control over her. Say what you will about her, but this wild, out-of-control "slut" has given me the most exciting, passionate, and satisfying sex of my life. OK, I could do without the violent part with Dario, but the rest of it has made me feel more alive, more connected with my feminine energy and more free than I've felt in years, since before my marriage, really.

I text Cheryl to get on Skype. I need to see her face for this. "Cheryl," I say, "I met someone very interesting." She's looking super cute this morning in her new haircut, short and edgy. She's gone a little darker with her blonde highlights. It makes her face look younger, more open. "Really?" she says. "Tell me about him." I start to fill her in, but she cuts me off. "Wait a second, didn't you tell me you weren't going to date anyone from the tango community anymore? You know, keep it on the dance floor?" Shit. Of course she's right, but what can I say? I can't resist a man who gives me tangasms. "I know, and I tried, but this one's special," I say. "I did at least wait until the second time seeing him off the dance floor." It sounds lame, even to my ears. She sighs. "Go on," she says. I tell her about him. "But there's a problem," I say. "He has three young kids, still in grade school." She frowns. "Really?" she asks. "How old is he?" I'm kind of embarrassed to tell her. "Thirty-six," I say. Cheryl laughs. "Seriously?" she says. "You're interested in a little brown man who's twelve years younger than you with three kids? What are you thinking?" That kind of pisses me off. "Hey, don't be racist," I say. "Or ageist." Cheryl's rolls her eyes and sighs. "It's not that. It's just very...outside your type."

"I don't think I have a type. And I certainly don't want another white-bread dickhead like Doug again. Besides, he's very cultured and sophisticated and all," I say. "Both his parents are from prominent families." I try to remember why I fell in love with Doug in the first place. I think his staid conventionality felt like safety to my frightened, insecure twenty-five-year-old self. "What's the ex-wife situation?" she asks. "I don't know. I didn't find out about the children till we were saying goodbye last night."

"If it gets serious, how do you feel about raising three young stepchildren at your age?" she asks. And that's really the issue. Do I want to take all that on again? Laura is basically gone, all grown up. She hasn't spent more than a few weeks at home since the summer of her freshman year. She and her boyfriend share a place in Santa Barbara, where she's an Environmental Studies major at UCSB. This is my time to focus on me, my career, and maybe a new relationship, not start over with motherhood and getting three kids out the door to college. "I don't know if it's a deal-breaker," I say. "I guess it depends on the specifics."

"What do you mean?" Cheryl asks.

"Well, what his relationship with the ex-wife is like," I say, "What the money situation is, you know, if there's more than enough for nannies, activities, household help, all that daily life stuff." Cheryl narrows her eyes and looks doubtful. "I hate to harp on it, but you really need to think about the age difference. "It might be fine now, but what about when you turn sixty and he's still in his forties?" It's so unfair that a man can be with a much younger woman and it's totally acceptable, but if a woman does it, she becomes an object of ridicule. The double standard pisses me off, but Cheryl is off on another tack. "Is Rafael close with his family?" she asks. I think for a second. I don't remember him saying anything about his family dynamics, just that his mother insisted he take up the family business. "I have no idea. Why?"

"Well think about it. Both Mexican and Filipino cultures are very Catholic, very family-oriented. And you said he comes from influential, powerful families. How do you think they'll feel about him getting involved with a woman from a modest background who's twelve years his senior?" I never even considered that. "But you're getting way ahead of yourself," she says. "It could just be a fun fling to get the taste of Dario out of your mouth." I flash back to the shape-shifting lover of last night and make my decision. I have to see him again. I have to be with him, have to have his hands on me, his mouth on me, his cock inside me again.

Tuesday night there's a *milonga* in Culver City. It's a casual affair. I'm taking a risk, I know, but I don't care. I want to dance with Rafael again. I can't think of any better foreplay. I call him to suggest dinner in downtown Culver City. We agree to meet up at a favorite Northern Italian spot a couple of blocks from the *milonga*. I lay down the ground rules once we're seated at our table. We enter the *milonga* separately. We dance no more than three *tandas* together. We leave separately. No kissing, except on the cheek. What I don't say is that I plan on having him in my bed tonight. Rafael is amused. "It shall be as you command, *Jefita*," he says. I'm not sure what that means, but it sounds good. I study him across the table. Cheryl was right. Rafael is not my type. He's not unattractive, but certainly not what you'd call handsome. He has a kind, unassuming face, warm brown eyes and golden-brown skin. He's short, maybe five-foot-seven, but his body is solid and powerful. It's really his manner and presence that gets me, the intelligent humor and basic goodness that shines through his eyes. Well, that and his hands, and that panther thing. "Oh," I add, "If there are any Nuevo Tango *tandas*, we dance them together." I could maybe get used to this older woman deal. "Of course, *Jefita*," he says, "whatever you say. Now tell me, what's good here?"

We eat dinner sitting side by side in a booth. The proximity affords Rafael easy access to caress my thigh, stroke my arm, run a hand around the dip of my waist and over the curve of my hip. I love the casual, natural way he touches me. Holy shit! There goes the pussy-meter again. When he pets me like that, he sure gets her purring. I attempt to pinpoint the exact quality in his touch, what it is that makes me feel so protected and cared for, so safe and adored. I squirm around like I've got ants in my pants, only they're not ants, but a jungle cat stirring the honeypot. I can't help myself. I have to snuggle up next to him. I catch his scent again. I glance around the restaurant. It's a hip Culver City version of Milan. There's not much of a crowd on a Tuesday night at 8:30pm. I don't see anyone I recognize. No one is looking at us. I put my face close to his and breathe in. I touch my lips to the juncture of his neck and jaw, then trace little kisses along his jawline to the corner of his mouth. Rafael turns to face me, slides his fingers through my hair to cradle my head and puts his mouth on mine. He kisses me like I'm the desert course of our meal, the sweet at the end. I hear a low warning rumble and realize my hand is wrapped around his cock. It hardens as I grasp and squeeze it. "Oops," I say and take my hand off, "I didn't mean to do that. My hand just went there." He laughs and hugs me in to him. "For Chrissakes, Alexis," I tell myself, "You better keep it together at the *milonga*!"

We walk over to the *milonga*. I don't plan on us being here too long. I have a different agenda in mind. Dancing is just the warm up. There's such a relaxed vibe here that I even see a couple of younger women in shorts! I'm in a cute little wrap dress with a lot of swing to the skirt and a deep V that molds to my cleavage. Hey, I don't want to sit around waiting for dances. The third *tanda* after our arrival is a Nuevo Tango set. I scan the floor for Rafael.

Good man, he's already heading over. He gives me the classic *cabeceo* and I nod my head back. Out on the floor we come together, take each other's hand and step into the embrace. What is it about him that sparks this visceral response? Just standing there breathing together sets electrons racing, molecules singing, atomic bonds do-si-do-ing. I put my attention on becoming completely receptive and available to the lead he offers. He starts us off with a subtle lift of his energy. Witchfire sparks and flares all along my synapses. I send him a silent growl. In response, I feel his tail coil around my waist, then a sharp little thwack on my ass. Everything electrifies. My skin turns telepathic. Clouds of scent molecules cast their spell. Cheek to cheek, our embrace catalyzes the mating dances of invisible tachyons. God damn if he doesn't give me another tangasm all through the fourth and final song in the *tanda*!

The *cortina* starts but I don't want to break the connection, it's just too yummy. I toss aside another of my rules and say, "Let's do the next *tanda* together if I like the song." We're standing in each other's arms, sweating. Rafael steps back and looks at me. "Are you sure?" he says. "Two in a row? What will people think?" He laughs and mops his face with a handkerchief. He's the kind of man who carries handkerchiefs. "Go ahead and laugh," I say, "but you know how gossipy the LA tango community is. I prefer to keep my private business private." The next *tanda* starts with a lovely *tango vals*. I nod yes and step back into the embrace. We waltz around in the line of dance. Rafael keeps it simple, with some tasteful flourishes thrown in. I'm carried along by the beautiful music and Rafael's impeccable timing. I keep trying to analyze what it is about his touch that makes me feel so safe and secure, so cared for, and so turned on all at the same time. I can't put my finger on it. It's like how certain people have a magical ability with animals, like a horse whisperer or something. Well, he's got that ability with me, like my body is somehow his tamed pet. It's still wild, yet obedient and responsive to his touch. I love dancing with him, but I want to get him home into my bed before it gets too late. I have to be up in the morning for work. When the *tanda* ends, Rafael walks me off the floor. I give him a kiss on the cheek and whisper in his ear, "Thank you for the lovely *tandas*. Let's go back to my place. I'll text you my address."

Once inside my door, Rafael takes charge. I've barely put my things down when he has me up against the wall, kissing my face and neck, running his hands up and down my thighs, squeezing my ass. I'm wet and moaning in no time. He turns me around, flips up the skirt of my dress, and starts stroking the inside of my thighs. He's kissing and biting the back of my neck, whispering in my ear, "Alexis, you turn me on so much. I just want to take you, right here against this wall." He slides a finger inside my mouth to wet it, pulls my panties aside, and starts stroking my lips. When he feels how wet I am already, he dips his fingers in and uses my own slickness to gently rub along my clitoris. I'm already engorged. He takes hold of it between his fingers, pulls it gently and growls, "Tell me you want it. Tell me you want me to take you, to give it to you." The sensation of being held and controlled by my clit between his fingers makes me crazy hot. "Yes, yes, take me," I groan. "I need you to take me." He pulls my panties down and I step out of them. He's kissing and biting my neck again when I hear him unzip his pants. I'm using my hands against the wall to support my weight. I'm up on my toes, arching my back and pushing my ass back into him. He takes my ass cheeks in his hands and spreads me open. He rubs his hardness all along the wetness of my folds. I arch my ass back into him and moan. Then, in one smooth move he slides his cock into me. I gasp as the thickness of his cock opens and fills me.

He begins to fuck me in a slow relentless rhythm, pulling out on each stroke until just the head is inside, then steadily driving himself into me as far as he can go. This controlled rhythm is driving me absolutely wild. I start to buck and roll my hips. "Fuck me, fuck me! Please. I need you to fuck me!" He won't let me change the tempo. Instead, he hooks his arm under my left thigh, lifts it high to open me even wider, and leans his hand against the wall to get more leverage. Now he's stroking into me with a rocking and rolling motion. His lips trace along my neck and ear. "Open to me," he whispers, "Let me in, let me all the way in." I turn my head to kiss him and he starts fucking my mouth with his tongue in the same relentless rhythm. He reaches his hand up to pinch and pull my nipples. He hoists my thigh even higher and I begin to come in long shuddering waves. That sets him off. He growls again, takes my neck between his teeth, pins me to the wall and starts to fuck me harder and faster. The nectar pours out of me. I can barely keep my weight on my standing leg. When he feels that leg start to give way, he hoists me up by my other thigh and rolls me around his rock-hard cock as he pumps into me. I'm in the jaws and claws of a black jaguar mounting me, and I lose all control. I'm moaning and wailing, coming again in overlapping spasms that travel up and down his length. He's purring and making "Hunh, hunh, hunh," sounds. Something in me opens even wider and he plunges in, climaxing with a long, low roar.

Rafael turns me around and pulls me into his arms. He kisses me softly and sweetly. His tenderness touches some delicate spot in my heart. I want him in my bed, but first a shower together after our sweaty tango and even sweatier sex against the wall. I make us pomegranate spritzers in the kitchen and pile some grapes and slices of ripe papaya onto a plate. "Come," I say, "Let's take a shower." Rafael follows me into the bathroom. I light the candles and pin my hair up. We strip down and I soap him up under the rainfall shower head, running my hands up and down his hard body and between his thighs. He's got his hands all over me, those magic pussy-whispering hands. When I've got all the soap rinsed off, I squat down to take him in my mouth. He's ready to go again. Ah, the joys of being with a younger man. He gets rock-hard and I spread his legs apart to tip my head underneath, lick his balls and suck them into my mouth. That gets Rafael groaning and murmuring in Spanish. He pulls my clip out and rubs his hands through my hair. There's a brief moment of anxiety when his hands on my head trigger a flash of Dario mouth-raping me, but it passes when Rafael tenderly pulls my hair back out of my face. Even his hands on my head as I'm sucking him make me feel adored and cherished. I must be doing too good a job, because I hear him gasp and his cock gets even harder in my mouth. Rafael pulls away and lifts me back up to stand facing him. He takes me by the back of my head and pulls me into him for a deep kiss. "Enough in here," he says, "I want to lay with you." We dry off with my fluffy heated towels and head to my bedroom.

We lie in my bed, breathing together in each other's arms. So simple. So beautiful. Even after a shower, his spicy scent intoxicates. We begin to kiss, deep luscious kisses. Rafael starts to rub his hands all over my body, massaging my breasts, pinching and pulling my nipples, squeezing my hips and my ass cheeks, stroking the inside of my thighs. His touch leaves molten trails of liquid desire behind. My entire body is sensitized and electrified. He wets two fingers in his mouth, then slips them between my swollen cleft to lightly stroke along the edges of my inner lips and up along the side of my clitoris. I lift my leg over him and he moves closer in between my legs. I reach down and take his cock in my hand, wrap my hand around the shaft and milk it up and down a few times, then slide and twist my hand over the head. A little drop of pre-cum oozes out. He groans as I stroke and glide my hand up and down his shaft. Then he dips his head down and starts devouring my breasts, gently biting and sucking on my nipples. I'm getting hotter and wetter by the minute. He circles his thumb around my clit, slides a finger inside me and starts to stroke along my G-spot. I can feel the walls of my pussy rippling up and down. I'm moaning and sighing, rolling my hips around. I hear that low rumbling growling again as he grips my breast in his teeth.

I need him inside me now. I reach down to pull his hand away and replace it with his cock. I lay the head of it between my wet and swollen lips. He lifts his head away from my breast to lock eyes with me. I rub the head of his cock around my opening. I can feel it swelling up even bigger. We're gazing in each other's eyes as he thrusts all the way into me. On the backstroke, the upturned curve of his cock rubs my G-spot. Then Rafael takes hold of my ass cheeks and kisses me mercilessly as he pumps in and out. Each stroke ignites me, turns my entire body into liquid fire. I'm rolling my hips deliriously as he thrusts into me with his relentless intent. I feel his tail wrap around my waist, pulling me closer. He's got me making sounds I can't control as the orgasms spiral in waves up and down my body. My pussy turns into a wild thing. I can feel it rippling all over his hard cock. When the mouth of my womb begins to suck him in he finally loses control. He lets loose a roar and pumps into me harder, faster, deeper, using his hands and tail to pull me into him even tighter. He plunges in as deep as he can go and I feel him explode inside me.

"Alexis," he murmurs, rubbing his lips in my hair and along my neck, "Are you alright? I didn't hurt you did I?"

"No, my darling," I whisper back, "You've only given me pleasure. You've made me very happy." And it's true. I feel completely and utterly happy laying in his arms. I hate to break the spell, but I have to pee. In the bathroom, I brush my teeth and splash water on my face. I massage some night cream into my face and neck. I'm glowing. I look ten years younger. Back in the bedroom, Rafael takes me into his arms again. I snuggle in and sigh. He kisses my head and runs his hand up and down my back. In his arms, I fall into a deep sleep, a contented, well-fucked, well-loved woman.

I oversleep the next morning and have to rush off to work. Rafael's left a note on the kitchen counter,

"Alexis,
What a beautiful evening!
Call you later,
Besos,
Rafael"

People compliment me all day long, saying how good I look. Fleeting images and sense memories of our lovemaking keep popping into my mind. It's hard to focus on my work. I can't wait to see him again. He gives me a call to invite me over for an afternoon of swimming with his kids on Saturday. Whoa, that's moving a bit fast. Meeting his children? I don't know if I want to do that. We haven't even talked about their mother yet. Does he have them every weekend? That would certainly put a damper on romantic get-aways. Shit! My bliss-bubble pops and fizzles. Then the 'ole pussy-meter pipes up. It gives a flutter and I hear myself accepting.

It's Saturday and I'm debating whether or not to cancel. I inventory my bathing suit collection. Pretty slim pickings. Stretched out bikini bottoms and tops too small to wear anymore at my age, especially in front of children not my own. Shit. Now I have to go buy a new bathing suit, unless I sacrifice sexiness for propriety and wear an old one-piece. I try it on. It's actually a flattering fit. Fuck it. Either Rafael is into me or he's not. I refuse to go shopping to impress a pair of spoiled first graders! I head over to Santa Monica, stopping to pick up a few containers of cut melon and pineapple on the way. The pool deck of his building is tricked out like a five-star resort. There's even a towel bar and pool boys to adjust your chair and your umbrella. Servers in white shirts and shorts carry trays of drinks to poolside loungers. I tug at the bottom of my suit and wish I'd gone shopping after all. Oh well. At least I've got a great hat and sexy cover-up. Rafael catches sight of me and jumps up to welcome me over. "Alexis," he says, with a kiss on each cheek, "I'm so glad you made it." He's wearing a pair of board shorts and a baseball cap. He really is a hairy guy. "Hi, Rafael," I say, "Thanks for inviting me." There's not a cloud in the sky. I can see the ocean in the distance. "What a gorgeous day," I say. "Yes," he says, "It's perfect. Come meet my niños." Rafael takes my arm and walks me over to their lounge chairs. Turns out his children are adorable, polite and well-behaved. They accept my presence without any questions. We have a great afternoon. Rafael is an attentive father, calm, loving and lots of fun.

I want to know about their mother, but I hesitate to ask while they're around. When they go off to play with some other children from the building, I take my opportunity. "Do you mind if I ask about their mother?" Rafael and I are relaxing side-by-side in lounge chairs. He's drinking a beer and I'm sipping ice tea. "Not at all," he says. "It's a bit complicated. Their mother is very difficult." Shit, shit, shit! Just then, the children come back so I don't get any details. It's late. We gather up our things. Rafael invites me to stay and have dinner with them. I'm tempted, but I decide one afternoon is enough to begin with.

Back home alone on a Saturday night, I try to sort through my feelings for Rafael. Slut that I am, I fucked him the second time I saw him outside of tango. I knew I was a goner from the first time he devoured me and drove me wild. Who knew behind that elegant manner and soft-spoken exterior beat the heart of a wild beast? In bed, he's a fierce and primal lover, with the sensitivity and creativity of an artist. Out of bed, he's a brilliant, thoughtful man with an engaging demeanor and exquisite manners. The more I get to know Rafael, the more he impresses me. He really is a Renaissance man. He's a musician, a tech guru and an entrepreneur with fingers in every pot. He's always flying somewhere to facilitate some business venture, close some complicated deal or come up with a game-changing sales strategy. He's your basic one-man think tank. In Rafael's world, everything is based on who you know. Need a tax attorney versed in international business? He's got two he can refer you to. Need to raise money for your start-up, hire an interim CEO to take your business to market, wrangle a herd of underperforming sales divas? He's your man. When we finally got to discuss my career situation and my ideas, he offered some very thoughtful suggestions. His knowledge of all things tech is au courant but in many ways, he's an anachronism, a throw-back to an earlier age, with the moral compass of a philosopher-prince.

On the other hand, there's the age difference, the young children, the difficult ex-wife and maybe even family complications to think about. Maybe I should end it now, before I get in too deep. But I've never responded to a man the way I respond to Rafael. I can't just let that go without giving the relationship a chance to develop. He is a rare and exceptional man, and I need to get to know him better before I decide what to do. "Just be careful, Alexis," Cheryl says on our next phone call, "Things are moving really fast between you. I don't want you to get hurt." I haven't seen or talked to Rafael in several days. He's texted me a couple of times, but he's been out of town. "I will," I say, "I'm not going into this blind. I know the risks." I tell her about our plans to go away this weekend, up the coast to some hot springs north of Santa Barbara. "I'll get more details about the ex-wife situation then," I say. Then we move on to talk about her new boyfriend, Paul. Cheryl's in love again, the first time since her divorce five years ago. She's so happy, and I'm happy for her. He's an adrenalin junkie like her. Leave it to Cheryl to find some super-rich, super-cool dude who's into all the outdoor activities she loves.

I'm so excited. I feel like a teenager again as I pack for the weekend. I'm planning on lots of sex and relaxation, so I stuff plenty of lingerie and loungewear into my bag.

Work has been a nightmare the past few weeks with difficult clients and projects overdue and over-budget. To make it even worse, my best copywriter and graphic artist are out sick. It's taken a toll. Plus, I haven't been dancing once since that Monday *milonga* in Culver City. We were planning to leave on Friday evening, but Rafael had to extend his trip another day, so we're leaving this morning instead.

I'm actually ready on time and waiting downstairs when Rafael arrives, a minor miracle. He takes me into his arms and kisses me once, twice, three times, then says, "All week long, sitting in those boring meetings, the only thing that kept me going was thinking about our weekend." God, it feels good to be in his arms again. I immediately feel more calm and grounded. "Me too," I say, "I've been looking forward to this all week." We hit the road and head out of town. Rafael made us a playlist for the drive, perfect cruising music. It's a beautiful day. There's hardly any traffic and I'm full of happy anticipation. We stop in Santa Barbara for lunch. I thought about trying to meet up with Laura, but I decided I'm not ready to introduce Rafael to anyone in my life. I need to be sure the relationship is going somewhere first. Besides, I'm greedy. I want him all to myself for now.

We get to the hot springs hotel mid-afternoon. Rafael has booked us a suite which comes with a fireplace and its own mineral water hot tub on the patio. After we settle in, we pick up a couple of bikes to explore the trails and head down to the beach. It feels so great to be out of LA. It's been ages since I've had a getaway. When we get back, we fill the tub with mineral water from the springs and get in to soak. I lay back in the hot mineral water and watch the leaves shimmer in the breeze. We're both quiet, enjoying the moment together. The late afternoon sunlight filters through the sycamore trees. I can feel the stress of the week gradually releasing. After soaking a while, I paddle over to Rafael, wrap my arms and legs around him and give him a soft kiss. "Thank you for bringing me here," I say. "It's a wonderful treat, just what the doctor ordered." He kisses me back and slides his hands around my hips to cup my ass. I can feel his cock beginning to get hard and bump up against my thighs. "You deserve it, Alexis. I'm happy it pleases you." We start kissing, slow, deep kisses. "Before we go any further," he says, "I have another surprise." I love surprises almost as much as I love to be pampered and spoiled. "You do?" I ask, "What is it." There's a knock at the door. I'm instantly annoyed by the interruption. Who could be bothering us? "Ah, that must be them," he says. Them? What the fuck is this going on? "Who?" I ask. Is Rafael into some sort of kinky swinger shit? I'm definitely not up for anything like that! "Your surprise," he says.

He gets out of the tub, wraps a towel around his waist and goes to answer the door. I take a sip of water and try to control my irritation. I feel like a total bitch when it turns out that Rafael's surprise is a couple's massage in our suite. Rafael walks back to the patio to help me out of the tub. He wraps me up in one of the hotel's thick terry spa robes. He may not fit the look of my ideal-man description, but he sure does act like it. "What a wonderful surprise," I say and give him a big, grateful hug and kiss. I'm already softened up by the mineral soak and soon drift off under the magical hands of my masseuse. The combination of the essential oils, the trance-like music, and her expert touch sends me floating away, cocooned inside a cloud. Afterwards, I'm so relaxed that I fall asleep for an hour. Rafael wakes me with a kiss. "It's time for dinner." I shower off the massage oil and get dressed for dinner. I pick out a flowing low-cut blouse in peacock blue that glorifies my boobs and makes my eyes pop. When he sees me come out, his eyes go wide. "Wow," he says, shaking his head, "You look beautiful!"

I finally get the full story about the ex-wife and the family at dinner. It's like something out of a telenovela. If it wasn't exactly an arranged marriage, it was close enough. Mirasol comes from an influential Filipino family with close business ties to his mother's family of bankers. According to Rafael, her beautiful face is the perfect camouflage for a devious, conniving sociopath. Apparently she's possessive, controlling and tyrannical, with an unquenchable thirst for money and power. When the marriage was over and divorce proceedings began, she manipulated the attorneys, court-assigned psychologists and the judge himself to challenge Rafael's custody rights. To top it off, she embezzled several million dollars' worth of marital assets in an audacious act of domestic theft. The money was impossible to recover. It was a brilliant achievement. The two of them are still embroiled in on-going custody battles over the children's residence. Mirasol wants them to live in her home in the Philippines, despite the fact she spends most of her time in the States. The children would essentially be raised by nannies. Family betrayals, failed businesses, and pressure from both sets of in-laws for the children to live in the Philippines further complicate the situation. I'm appalled. He's roused my protective instincts and I want to help him any way I can. I ignore the warning bells going off in my head.

"I'm sorry Alexis," Rafael says, "This is hardly romantic dinner conversation." He twists his mouth into a wry smile and pulls his napkin through his fingers. It's late. The restaurant is almost empty. Our table has been cleared. All that remains are the brandy glasses and Rafael's espresso cup. The flower arrangement in the center is just beginning to wilt in the heat of the candles. "No it's not," I say, "But I asked. I wanted to know." I reach over and take his hand. "I'm so sorry you're going through this. At least Laura was off to college when we divorced." I think of our age difference and feel the pit of my stomach clench. I don't want to think about any of this now. If anything, Rafael's story makes my heart open to him even more. Here we are, in this beautiful restaurant at this charming little hotel. He's planned everything so well for an idyllic romantic weekend away. He's pampered me, wined and dined me, and soon he'll make love to me again. We just need to change the mood, shift the energy. "Come on," I say, "let's get out of here," and give his hand a squeeze. We leave the restaurant and take a stroll around the gardens. The night-blooming jasmine fills the air with its heady scent. It's cooled off quite a bit and there's a chill in the air. I tell him a funny story to break the mood. A client's campaign went horribly wrong — the company was launching into the international market, but in one country, their slogan roughly translated as "eat shit." He laughs. Then I get an idea. "I have a little surprise for you, too," I say.

Back at the room, I ask him to light the fire and put on some music. "I'll be right back," I say, "I just need to prepare your little treat. Wait here." I head into the bedroom to change into some sexy lingerie — black lace stockings and a garter belt with a matching black lace demi bra and panties. I tie a sheer red silk robe over it and slip into some high black satin strappy heels. I brush my teeth in the bathroom, touch up my make-up, brush my hair out, and put on some bright red lipstick. Back in the bedroom, I dim the lights, pull down the bedcovers and light the candles. I grab my iPod on the way out to the living room and stop at the door. "OK, I'm coming out," I say, "Sit on the sofa and close your eyes." The fire casts an amber glow over the room. Candles flicker on the coffee table. "Are your eyes closed?" I ask. "No peeking." I plug my iPod into the dock and scroll to the playlist I've prepared: Sexy & Chill. I put on the second song, perfect for what I have in mind. I walk over to the fireplace. Rafael is sitting in the sofa across from me. "OK, you can open your eyes now." Rafael looks me up and down and gives a long wolf whistle. "Ay, *Chilosa*," he says. I begin to dance for him. I want to drive him crazy with desire. I really get into it, even make use of the wall and the fireplace mantle in lieu of a pole. By the time the next song comes on, I've removed the robe. I dance over to him and rub my breasts in his face. When he reaches his hands out to take hold of them, I smack them away. "No touching," I command. I turn around with my back to him, slowly remove my panties and bend over to give him a good look. I catch a furry black tail twitching back and forth out of the corner of my eye. I've done it again. I've roused the beast. A little thrill runs through me. I turn around and begin to give him a lap dance in earnest. I take off my bra, leaving only my garters, stockings and shoes. His eyes glow in the flickering light of the fireplace and the candles. I hear that low rumble again as I start to grind on him.

I rub myself all over him in time with the music, torturing him to the best of my ability. The next song starts up. Now I'm really going to give him a treat. I grab a pillow from the sofa and throw it on the floor between Rafael's feet. Then I get down on my knees, pull his hips forward to the edge of the sofa and unzip his pants. His cock is already hard and straining against his briefs. I pull it out and stroke it a few times to get it even harder. Then I place it between my breasts, squeeze them together and slide up and down on it. I dip my head down and open my mouth to suck the head in. He groans again and whispers sweet nothings in Spanish. He takes my head in his hands and runs his fingers through my hair, pulling it back out of my face. Some quality in his touch makes me feel so completely adored that I want to worship his manhood, give him pleasure, make up for all the pain and suffering his evil ex-wife caused him. I devote myself to his cock. My hands are everywhere, stroking and cupping his balls, gripping the base, sliding up and down the shaft, running up his chest and pinching his nipples, stroking his thighs. I suck the head, lick around the ridge and the tender spot under the frenulum. I suck him in as far as I can go, then slowly back out again. I change up the rhythm, driving him crazy and turning myself on at the same time. Rafael starts to massage my breasts and work my nipples. His touch makes me even more excited. I speed up and slide my mouth up and down, sucking and twirling my tongue around his cock. He's making that panther, "Hunh, hunh, hunh," grunting sound again. His balls tighten up. He's getting close. I try to take him in as deep as I can, to deep throat him, but I can't quite do it with that upturned curve of his. It doesn't matter. My expert enthusiasm reaches fever pitch and he comes with a low roar, spurting down my throat. With him, I actually swallow.

Rafael pulls me up onto his lap and kisses me with that pussy-melting combination of tenderness and command of his. I know he can taste himself in my mouth, but it doesn't seem to bother him. There's a bottle of water on the coffee table. I take a sip, then swish it around my mouth. I'm not particularly fond of the taste of sperm, though his is somewhat sweet and salty, with just a little pungent note. "Alexis," he whispers to me, "You're so beautiful, so hot, so amazing." I'm still in his lap as he strokes and pets me, nibbling on my neck and breasts. I can feel how wet my pussy is when it rubs up against his thigh. His touch makes me feel cherished, like he's in charge. He lifts me off his lap and sets me down on the sofa to stand up to take off his clothes. Then he scoops me up in his arms and carries me to the bedroom. I sigh and melt in his arms. "Oh, Rafael, I love it when you carry me like that," I whisper to him. "I love to feel your power and strength. It's such a turn on."

He lightly tosses me onto the bed and proceeds to devour me. A panther takes hold of me. He kisses and strokes my body in that way of his that makes me wild. What is it exactly? Some quality of possession and command, some sense of intimate knowledge, some primal male intent, some implacable untamable wildness? Whatever it is, I can't resist. While he feasts on my mouth, he's also rubbing my breasts, pinching and pulling my nipples, squeezing my inner thighs, grasping my hips. I writhe and moan. He gets down between my thighs and pulls my lips open wide to lick from top to bottom, plunging his tongue inside my opening. He starts to lick and bite my ass and I go crazy, which only spurs him on. He wets his fingers and slides them into my pussy, rubbing and stroking me from the inside while he works on my clit. He's got me on a coming jag, waves of orgasms, and my juices stream down. He slips his fingers out and begins to rub and massage around my asshole, still licking and sucking my clit. He slowly opens me and inserts first one, then two fingers, and I completely lose it. Some creature takes over, a raw primal thing. She grabs his head and rides it like her life depends on it, galloping harder and faster, howling as she crosses the finish line.

Now I want him to fuck me in the ass, but I'm too embarrassed to tell him. Thankfully, he figures it out on his own. He pauses for a moment to toss my shoes overboard and to hang the flag of my garter belt and stockings over the lamp. Then he climbs up the bed to take me in his arms and kiss me again. I'm practically delirious. He's whispering and murmuring in a combination of Spanish and English. I make out a few words, something about how sexy I am, how beautiful it is to make love to me. Then he whispers, "May I take you in your beautiful ass?" I nod my head. "Yes, please," I whisper back, "I want you to." I'm prepared. I grab the lube on the bedside table and hand it over. He rubs it on his cock, stroking it to get it hard again, then all around my anus. We lay on our sides with him behind me. He spreads my ass with one hand and lays the head of his penis up against me with the other. "Open to me," he commands, "Open your ass to me." I slip my hand between my thighs to rub my clit. Rafael takes his cue and reaches one hand under my thigh, lifting it up as he spreads my ass, and slides his hand down to take over for me. "Open to me, Alexis," he commands again. He presses himself into me slow and steady. I gasp as he stretches me open. The sensations are so intense as pleasure borders onto pain, but his work on my clit almost has me coming again. Once he's in all the way, he just holds still for a moment to give me time to relax around his thickness. Then he starts to slowly pull out to the ridge under the head and then press back into me again. With each round, he stretches me wider until he can bury his thickness all the way into my ass. Meanwhile he kisses and bites the back of my neck and shoulders, whispering encouragement into my ear. I can take his entire length and girth now as he rocks in out of me, rubbing my clit. I roll up onto my hands and knees, stick my ass up into the air and back up onto him. He takes hold of my hips with his hands and starts to pump into me. I'm moaning and wailing. He reaches one hand around to pinch and pull on my nipples, commanding me to open to him, to take him, to give myself to him. I'm bucking and rearing on him like a wild horse. I reach my hand back between my legs to rub my clit as he starts to smack my ass just right. "Yes, yes," I scream, "Fuck me! Fuck my ass! Fuck it good!" And he does, until I come so hard I collapse on my stomach and his cock slips out.

Rafael pulls me into his arms and just holds me, stroking my head. I'm kind of freaked out by how intense that was, how intimate, and how vulnerable I feel. I'm kind of ashamed how crazy nasty I got, but he's holding me so tenderly, whispering endearments to me, "my wild beauty" and *"amorcita."* I try to kick my mother out of my head and let myself relax into his loving embrace. I look up at his face in the flickering candle light. He smiles down at me and kisses my forehead. I burrow into his arms. After a few minutes, he gets up and heads into the bathroom. I hear the shower come on. I have to pee, and I should wash off anyway. I follow him into the bathroom and after I pee, Rafael holds open the shower door. "Come join me," he says. Rafael washes me like he's gentling a spooked animal. Once again, his magic touch has a calming, grounding effect. I figure, fuck it! I didn't do anything wrong. So what? I like anal sex, at least with this guy. He towels me off and wraps me in that fluffy spa robe again. I massage some serum and night cream into my face and neck, then walk back out. He's already taken care of the candles and the fire in the living room. He's left one candle burning on the bedside table. I drop the robe to slide into bed and into his arms. I kiss him, bringing all my appreciation, vulnerability and tenderness with it. He leans over to blow the candle out and I fall asleep in his arms.

CHAPTER FOUR

I Think I'm Falling In Love

I think I'm falling in love with Rafael. The early signs are there. I want to talk to him five times a day. I keep having flashbacks of moments in bed together. I plan sexy outfits to wear for him. My skin glows. My hair shines. I've dropped a few pounds. I wake up happy. I'm inspired, filled with creative energy. I come up with a concept for a new client's product launch that is total genius, if I do say so myself. I'm on fire when I pitch it and the clients eat it up. I lobby my boss Ben to let me bring in a hot young director I've had my eye on to shoot the spots. I've been working on the business plan for my own agency and it's all coming together. I've even had a couple of encouraging meetings with potential investors.

My favorite monthly *milonga* is on for tonight and I plan to meet up with my girls. I won't be seeing Rafael. He has his kids. I've hung out with them all a few times, even cooked everyone dinner. The twin girls are sweet and precocious and the little boy is a budding genius. I've been trying on the energy of stepmother, feeling out if I'd be willing to take that on. I haven't been dancing as much the past few weeks and I miss it. I figure it's better I'm going solo tonight. I'm not ready for people to know we're dating yet, not until I'm more sure of our relationship. It's still early days.

I'm in a naughty mood. I pick out a slinky red dress that hugs my curves and swings around my thighs when I move. I pair it with my red swede tango shoes, the ones with the gold chains. On the drive over, I play some sultry Neo-Soul music, which has me feeling even sexier. When I get when I get to the *milonga,* Zhenya and Sylvie aren't here yet. I see a number of tango friends, with the usual fanfare of hugs and kisses. I've no sooner finished buckling my shoes when Daniel walks by and catches my eye. I haven't seen him in a long time. He's the perfect partner for a warm-up *tanda*. The DJ's playing a dramatic song from a famous modern tango orchestra. Daniel leads me out to the dance floor and holds his arms open. I step into the embrace and catch that exotic scent of his again. Daniel's embrace is as delicious as ever. We stand breathing and shifting weight together. He gives a little lift and we move into the line of dance. The chemistry between us is as strong as ever. I'm a little surprised. All my sexual energy is focused on Rafael these days, but maybe getting laid on a regular basis has everything charged up and turned on inside me. I haven't danced much lately, but my body takes over and I'm pleased to discover my technique hasn't deteriorated. If anything, I'm dancing better than ever.

I feel happy and free by the end of the first song. I smile up at Daniel. "You're looking gorgeous tonight, Alexis," he says, "I've missed dancing with you." I love dancing in this gracious old room, with its high ceilings and the flattering light of its antique crystal chandeliers. "Thank you, Daniel," I say, "It has been a while." The next song begins. I lose myself in the moment, in the embrace, in the music, in the flow of the dance, in the connection between us. Daniel tracks my energy, caressing me with his energy antennae like he did in the beginning, when he gave me my first tangasm. I'm feeling my feminine power big time tonight and I let it unfurl in his arms. All my juicy sensuality radiates off me in rose-scented waves. I surrender to the embrace, to Daniel's male essence. I can feel the warrior respond within him. Fragmented scenes from our Chinese life flash behind my eyes — kaleidoscope images of sword practice in walled enclosures, silky pillows, smoky spirals of incense, and small cups of pale green tea, the porcelain so thin it's almost translucent. In the mood I'm in, it doesn't even phase me. I just open my senses even more, ascending into a state of multidimensional awareness, no thought, no time, just spontaneous action in the moment, instantaneous response to the music and Daniel's intent. By the time the *tanda* ends, waves of pleasure pulse throughout my entire body. Daniel is out of breath. I can tell he's had to work to control his energy with me. It gives me a perverse thrill. "Wow, Alexis," he says, "You are in rare form tonight." I smirk. You bet I am, buster! "Why thank you, Daniel," I say. He walks me back to my table. I see Zhenya by the door and wave her over. "Thank you for the *tanda*, Alexis," he says. "Perhaps you'll give me another one tonight?" Why the hell not? "Sure," I say. That would be lovely." I give him a hug. He holds it a beat too long.

Zhenya comes over and gives me a kiss and a big hug hello. "Girl, where have you been?" she asks. I can't help it. "Oh, just busy," I say. I think of Rafael and our smoking hot sex and I can't help breaking into a big shit-eating grin. "You know how it goes." Zhenya studies me for a moment. "Oh really?" she says, "Who is he?" I feel like the cat who ate the canary, but I don't want to tell her yet. I'm saved by Sylvie's arrival. After more kisses and hugs hello, Sylvie says, "What's up with Alexis? She's positively glowing." I duck my head to hide my face. "She's met someone," Zhenya says. "Who?" Sylvie asks. "Yeah, come on, who is he?" Zhenya asks. I'm blushing like a virgin on her wedding night. "Ladies, please," I say, "it's too new. I don't know if it's going to be a thing." Sylvie puts her hands on hips and looks me up and down. "Well whoever he is," she says, "he must be taking care of business. You look fantastic." What can I say? It's absolutely true. My only complaint is that between Rafael's traveling and his parenting responsibilities, we don't see each other as often as I want.

All that feminine energy emanating off me must be telegraphing pheromones to the men at the *milonga*, because they jostle to dance with me at every *tanda*. I give myself permission to pick and choose. I'm not going to lay all that juicy energy on just any Tom, Dick or Harry. I take it as a sign of my new-found tango maturity. I'm growing up, no longer an indiscriminate tango slut. Tonight, I only want to dance with men who feel good to me. I go home happy and satisfied. I wish Rafael were here to massage my tired feet and make love to me.

I have a dream. Rafael's ex-wife Mirasol is chasing me. She starts off small with a China doll's features and long black hair that streams out like silk behind her. I'm running through dirty streets in what could be Manila. She's screaming at me, calling me a filthy gold digger, a dirty whore, a stinking cunt. "He'll never be yours," she bellows, then lunges at my eyes with her long crimson nails. I barely escape and duck into an alley, but it's a dead end. I turn around. She's right behind me. I'm trapped. She's growing bigger and taller, laughing at me. "I'll kill you before I'll let you have him," she screams. She turns into a monster, a red-eyed, bat-winged, black-fanged, crimson-clawed beast. Her hair is an inferno. Flaming red daggers rain down on me as she turns into a tornado and sweeps me into the blackness. I wake up in a sweat, heart pounding. I sit up, switch on the light, drink some water, and take some deep breaths to try and calm down. I lay back down and stare up at the ceiling for a while. It takes a long time to get back to sleep. I have to get up twice to check all the doors and windows. My back stings in my morning shower. When I dry off and look in the mirror, I can see half a dozen little red lines like razor cuts. I reach around to touch them, to make sure I'm not just imagining it, but I'm not. They're really there, some kind of Filipino voodoo shit. My heart starts to race. I call

Rafael, but he doesn't answer. I send him a text message instead: "Something strange happened last night. Need to ask you a question."

I can barely concentrate at work today. I review all of Rafael's horror stories about this woman. From what he's said, she can be one scary bitch. Like the time he came home to find all his suits slashed to ribbons because she thought he was having an affair with a colleague. Or the time she thought he was flirting with a woman at an embassy party and threw a drink in the woman's face, then deliberately crashed his new Mercedes into a tree on the way home. He finally calls in the late afternoon. "What's up, Alexis?" he asks. I've been wracking my brain trying to think of how to frame this question. What is it that I really want to know? I get up and go close my office door. I need some privacy. "Rafael, I had a strange dream last night," I start. "Mirasol was chasing me, throwing daggers and trying to kill me. Then she turned into a giant monster and swept me up into a tornado." My desk is a mess, with papers everywhere. Outside, it's a beautiful fall day in Los Angeles. "Have you or the children told her about me? Does she know who I am?" I notice a little red cut on my arm. I think I see a bat hanging from the corner of the ceiling. "I haven't told her anything, but the children might have mentioned you," he says. Shit! I don't want that crazy bitch knowing anything about me. "She's always been very jealous. She loves to create drama and talk a lot of shit, but it's usually just talk. She never really does anything." Shit, shit shit! My assistant knocks on my door. We have a production meeting scheduled. "Rafael, I have to go. I've got a meeting. But this is not good. I don't want to have anything to do with your crazy ex-wife."

I need someone to talk to about all this. I text Cheryl when I get home, but I don't recognize her surroundings when we get onto Skype. "Where are you?" I ask. She's sitting on a stool at a kitchen counter with a wall of glass doors behind her and water beyond. "I'm at Paul's house on Mercer Island." Wow. A house on the water on Mercer Island? "What's it like?" I ask. "It's fabulous. And huge. Like, ten thousand square feet," she says. "I'm in the downstairs family room. There's a second kitchen down here." She gives me a little tour with the laptop camera. There's a huge TV screen covering about seven feet of wall space, a giant sectional sofa, a pool table and a couple of video arcade games. When she turns the computer to face out through the glass, I can see a pool and green lawns rolling down to Lake Washington, a dock with a motor boat, jet skis and a yacht. "Holy shit, Cheryl," I say, "That's not a house, that's an estate!" We talk about her new relationship for a while. I haven't seen Cheryl this excited about a guy since, well, since ever. She's glowing and giddy as she tells me about their recent hang-gliding adventures. This is the first guy she's dated for more than a few weeks since her nightmare of a divorce five years ago. She deserves to be happy.

Jeff went into a two-year rage when Cheryl told him she wanted a divorce, a real scorched earth kind of fury. He sabotaged her at every turn, even hacked into her computer and wiped her hard drive clean. He got hold of her client files and almost ruined her design business. To add insult to injury, he waited until the final settlement to push for alimony. Cheryl agreed just to be done with him and move on. She did the numbers and ten years of alimony would have cost about the same in legal fees to fight him. I don't know how we both ended up with such loser husbands. Early on in my marriage the illusion of safety I projected onto Doug evaporated, and I had to face the reality of a controlling, conservative and hyper-cautious husband. It wasn't too bad in first few years when Laura was young, but once she hit her teens and I wanted to go back to work in marketing, he poured doubt on every move I made. I had to justify and defend my every decision. The better my career went, the more he tried to undermine me. And it wasn't as if he was making any money himself, planted for life in his low-paying, dead-end accounting job.

I watch her face, all animated, eyes bright and sparkling. She tells me about Paul and how much fun they have, how smart and generous he is, how their sexual chemistry is off the charts. "Do you have any pictures?" I ask. "I want to see what Paul looks like." Cheryl screen shares and pulls up a few photos. There's one of them laughing on jet skis. He's got rugged good looks with greying hair and Paul Newman-blue eyes. "It's getting serious," she tells me. "Like how serious? Move in together serious, or married serious?" Cheryl looks down for a second and nibbles the cuticle on her thumb. "Married serious."

"Cheryl, that's fantastic! I'm so happy for you!" Cheryl's eyes light up and she gives me a big smile. "Thanks,

Alexis," she says. "So, what is it you needed to talk about?"

I fill her in on everything that's happened between me and Rafael. "It sounds like things are moving really fast," Cheryl says. "I know," I tell her, "I think I'm falling in love." Cheryl raises an eyebrow and shakes her head at me. "And what about his kids?" she asks. "They're actually adorable," I tell her. I fidget with the cord of my laptop charger. "So how would you feel about becoming their stepmother if things progress that far?" A vase of white lilies has dusted my end table with burnt-orange pollen. Rafael sent them. They fill the room with their gorgeous scent. My new curtains shimmer in early evening breeze. "I'm not sure. I'm not categorically opposed to it, but there is a problem."

"What's that?" she asks. "Their mother." I tell her about Mirasol, their marital history and my nightmare. "I would take that as a warning," Cheryl says. "He's already told you she's a sociopath. She has both sets of parents on her side and she even manipulated the court. Don't get involved in the drama. It cannot end well." Of course she's right, but my heart rebels in the face of this sensible advice. I've never felt the way I feel in Rafael's arms, never had sex like this before, never felt so cherished by a man, never felt so safe. I never had this much intimacy, not even in my marriage. "I think it's too late," I say. "I'm already involved." Cheryl sighs. Then she leans forward and looks straight into the laptop camera. "Alexis, you've worked so hard to clear the toxic people out of your life and get back on track after your divorce. Don't blow it now. I don't want to see you get hurt." Cheryl is right on all counts, but the heart wants what it wants, and the pussy too. Cheryl gnaws on her cuticle again. I can see her thinking. Then she hits me with the zinger. "Alexis, I have a bad feeling about this. If this woman truly is a sociopath, you could be in danger." I flash back to the Mirasol monster. I examine the little cut on my arm and shift around in my chair. I can still feel the ones on my back, too. My blood runs cold at the memory of her murderous look, the hate and evil in her eyes. "But I think I love him." I sound like a whiny sixteen-year-old. "Alexis, I want you to listen to me. You need to understand the psyche of a sociopath. They'll always be willing to go further than you to get their way. They feed off chaos and destruction. She will stop at nothing to keep Rafael from having another serious relationship, I just know it. Those children and that man are her property. She will destroy you if she thinks you're going to replace her." I look down at my chipped toenail. I need a new pedicure. "But they're already divorced." I still sound like a whiny little bitch. "That's irrelevant to a sociopath. Either your inner self sent you that dream as a warning, or that Freddy Krueger bitch actually tried to murder you in your sleep. This can never work. Get out now before anything bad happens. I mean it!"

We hang up, and I find myself looping through the same circuit over and over. Some part of me knows Cheryl's advice is sound. I should take it, but our intimate times together have me looking for ways to rationalize and minimize. My feelings for Rafael trump all reason.

I've already opened my heart to him. I want to help him, protect him, save him from this crazy bitch. Fuck. What did I just hear myself thinking? I want to save him? Martyr myself? This is not good. Cheryl's right — I have worked my ass off to get rid of the chaos in my life. Do I really want to risk all I've built for this man and his children? This is supposed to be my time to focus on my dreams, not offer myself up as the sacrificial lamb on the altar of their fucked up relationship. I might as well wear a sign saying, "Open for business. Feed off my energy. All you can eat buffet. Open bar."

Even though I'm exhausted from last night's dream-induced insomnia, I lie awake for hours. When I finally fall asleep, I'm walking through a dappled sunlit forest. The path turns muddy and the forest becomes a jungle. It gets dark and murky. The path narrows. I have to push vines and branches aside to keep going. There are rustling and breathing noises all around me. I get caught in the mud and start to sink. The jungle closes in on me. It gets darker and darker. I hear laughing and cackling in the bush. Wings brush by me in the dark. I wake myself up screaming. My heart races. I'm icy cold. I get up, splash water on my face and take some melatonin, then put on a Tibetan singing bowl CD to calm me down. I fall back asleep and wake up groggy and hungover in the morning.

Rafael and I have dinner plans tonight. I try to put everything out of my mind. I'm cooking. I want to enjoy our intimate time together. When Rafael arrives, he wraps me in his arms and holds me close. His touch calms and grounds me. I make a simple but delicious meal of poached salmon with lemon dill sauce, green salad and roasted potatoes. For dessert, we have imported Italian gelato and ginger cookies. Rafael talks about taking me to the Philippines. He wants me to meet his family. He tells me about their beachfront compound on Cebu. He wants me to meet his family already? I don't know how to feel about this. On the one hand, it's touching. It warms my heart. The teenage girl inside me is sure this means he loves me, that I'm important to him, that he's serious about our relationship. On the other hand, it's not even three full months since we met, he's in the middle of a nasty custody battle, and his mother is siding with his ex-wife! Once he begins to kiss me, all thoughts fly out of my head and my body ignites with desire. He holds me in his arms and pets me with those magic pussy-whispering hands that make feel so safe and cherished, so wild and free. He picks me up in his arms and carries me to my bed.

Rafael undresses me slowly, kisses and strokes each exposed area as he goes. He begins at my feet, massaging them and sucking on my toes. He pulls off my pants and leaves on my thong, slides his hands up the inside of my thighs to the crease of my groin, then over my hips and down the backs of my legs. He unbuttons my blouse, kisses his way up my belly and between my breasts. Now that he's got me stripped down to my bra and panties, he stands up and gets naked. His cock springs up and he slides into bed, takes me in his arms so we're lying on our sides, facing each other. "Alexis," he whispers, looking deep into my eyes, "You are so beautiful. I'm so hot for you." I'm hot for him too. He undoes my bra and begins to massage my breasts, pulls and pinches my nipples, then dips his head down to feast on them. I hear that low rumble again and I know I'm in for it. He reaches a hand inside my thong. When he feels how wet I am, he says, "Ah, *Chilosa,* you're ready for me." We start kissing again and I reach down to take hold of his hardness, stroking and twisting my hand up and down his shaft, squeezing the head. He dips a finger into my wetness, running his finger along the side of my clit. I moan and roll my hips. "I want you inside me," I whisper, "I need you inside me. Take me." His eyes turn fierce. In one quick movement, he flips me over to face away from him, hooks his arm under my top thigh, lifts my leg up and spreads me open. With his other hand he lays his cock up to my opening. He thrusts into me, kissing and biting the back of my neck. "Ahh," I gasp as he opens and fills me. Then he starts fucking me in that relentless rocking rhythm while he rubs my clit. It feels intense and primal to get fucked like this. It drives all thought from my head. I buck and grind on him, making wailing noises as I feel his tail wrap around my waist and pull me closer, holding me in place. He uses the arm under my thigh to control my hips as he thrusts into me, rolling me around his cock, pumping me with that unyielding ferocity. Then he changes rhythm, alternates between shallow and deep thrusts, sending me over the edge. I start to orgasm on his thick cock, rearing back to get him inside me as deep as I can, setting loose the panther. He growls louder, pumping into me without mercy, until I'm screaming and coming like a banshee.

He climaxes with a roar, then turns me around to face him. I nestle into his arms. He holds me close, stroking my head, whispering in my ear. "Alexis, my beauty. I love being with you like this." I sigh with happiness. I'm contented as a cat in his arms. All thoughts of danger and drama drift far, far away. I hate to break the spell of the moment, but I have to pee. He comes into the bathroom after me. We wash up a bit, then get back into bed. We're sitting up, drinking some water when he says to me, "Alexis, darling, I have something important to ask you." I'm on instant alert. He better not be asking me to marry him! "What is it, Rafael?" I say. He smoothes his hair back, adjusts the top sheet. "You know what a hard time I've been having with Mirasol about custody of the children?" He tugs on his eyebrow and fusses with the sheet again. I notice a tear in the lace edging. What the fuck is coming? "Well, I'd like you to take them for a few days and keep them here with you. Just until I can get a court order," he says.

My heart lurches inside my chest. I can hear Cheryl's voice in my head like she's here in bed with me: "Are you fucking crazy?!" I'm confused, then panicked. My stomach clenches and sends my heart flying into my throat. I don't know how to refuse him, but even the love-struck teenager inside me knows this a bad idea. All I can manage is a weak, "I don't know Rafael. I need to think about it. When would it be and for how long?" The more he says, the more he freaks me out. He's basically asking me to become an accessory to kidnapping. I don't know what to say. There's a buzzing in my ears. I can hear him trying to explain this insane plan, but it's muffled, like I'm underwater. I watch his mouth moving, the desperate look on his face, the begging tone in his voice, but the words don't register. Finally, I interrupt him. "Rafael, I can't talk about this anymore tonight. I don't think it's a good idea and I don't really want to get involved. This is a private matter between you and Mirasol. I have nothing to do with it." He jerks his head back and looks surprised. Then his face crumples in disappointment, just for a moment, before a blank mask drops down. He gets out of bed and starts to get dressed.

"Are you leaving?" I ask. "At this hour? I thought you were going to stay over." The energy has completely shifted. He's withdrawn, disconnected. He's moving mechanically. "Don't be angry. This isn't some small thing you're asking. I need to think about it," I say. He's dressed now. He stands at the foot of the bed, looking at me. I can't read the expression on his face. Then he softens and comes over to give me a kiss goodbye. "Don't worry," he says. "Think about it and let me know. I have an early flight in the morning. I'll call you tomorrow night." He walks out.

Fuck! Here comes another sleepless night. Even though I'll be groggy in the morning, I take a hefty dose of melatonin and put on my Tibetan bowl CD. I sleep the sleep of the dead, or maybe the doomed, and wake up with the alarm chiming. I drag myself into the shower and alternate hot and ice cold water to get myself in gear. Although I rarely drink coffee, I pick up a double cappuccino on the way into the office. I'm determined not to think about Rafael's request or his psycho ex-wife or the relationship at all today. I force myself to focus on work, but by early afternoon, my attention wanders and my energy flags. Flashes of our lovemaking send shivers of desire through my body and make my pussy tingle. He has me in his thrall and I feel powerless to resist him. I can still hear that low rumbling growl, still feel his mouth on the back of neck, his tail wrapped around my waist, his fingers on my clit, that thick upturned cock pumping into me. Get ahold of yourself, you sex-obsessed little hussy! I get up to grab another coffee, even though I know it will make me all wired and jittery. By the end of the day, I've plowed through a mountain of work, cleaned out my inbox, delegated a dozen tasks, and roughed out two campaign budgets. It's almost seven o'clock when I wrap up and get ready to leave. Rafael never called. Just as well. I'm not ready to talk to him. I slip my heels back on and notice the state of my feet. The polish has chipped on the big toes and my cuticles look dry and ragged. I decide to get a pedicure. There's a place right around the corner from the office that's open late. I don't want to go home to my empty apartment and I figure a pedicure is a healthier choice than hitting the bar for a drink.

At the nail salon, I stand in front of the rack of polishes and debate colors. I see a crimson red the exact shade of Mirasol's claws in my dream. It sends a chill through my heart. Instead, I pick a bubblegum pink. Not my usual palette, but whatever. I'm catching up on my junk reading and the lives and times of the Kardashian clan when I notice a woman walking by on the sidewalk outside the salon. Something about her disturbs me. I don't know what made me look up. I only catch sight of her for a second before my nail lady asks me about the length of my nails. The woman is gone when I look up again. She was short, with black hair, wearing jeans and a sweatshirt, of indeterminate ethnicity — some mixture, but definitely not Caucasian. I have this unsettled feeling, this nervous flutter in my stomach, this hot prickle at the back of my neck. What was it about her that caught my attention? She was completely nondescript. I glance around the salon, trying to figure it out. All the nail technicians are Vietnamese. That's when it hits me. Could she have been Filipina? I dismiss my uneasiness and go back to my magazine.

I'm famished by the time my pedicure is over. With paper thongs on my feet, I shuffle back around the corner to the garage under our office building. I order take-out Thai from my favorite place on the way home and spread the cartons out on the coffee table, then settle in to eat and catch up on the newest season of Downton Abbey. That's when I notice the position of the family pictures on the bookshelves. The ones of me with Laura on a ski vacation and me with my brother and sister have been moved. Was it the housekeeper's day today? I binge-watch three episodes in a row. When I look at the time, it's after midnight. I'm tired and go get ready for bed, but something doesn't look right in the bathroom. I wash off my makeup, then realize my jar of night cream and bottle of serum aren't in their usual place. They've switched positions. What day is today? Maria usually comes on

Friday, but today is Thursday. Did she switch days? I don't remember her telling me.

I still haven't heard from Rafael by Friday evening. It's an annoying pattern of his. We'll have an amazing intimate time, and then he'll be unavailable for days. Maybe I'll get a few brief texts. It makes me feel insecure and abandoned. What do I expect from him? What exactly do I want with this man? I don't want to think about any of this right now. I still haven't told him I can't help him with the children. Maybe I'll go dancing tonight. There's a Friday night *milonga* I go to occasionally. It's not my favorite. The vibe is kind of snobby and the dance floor is small and cramped with two pillars that impede the line of dance, but what the hell. It will be good for me to get out of my head. I've improved enough that I can keep up with the men who frequent this *milonga*. I can always leave if I don't like it or if I'm not getting asked to dance enough. I stand in the closet contemplating my tango wardrobe. This is a more traditional *milonga*. I choose a mid-calf black dress with a drop waist cut on a bias, so there's lots of movement. There are lace inserts in the skirt and the neckline that give an extra bit of spice to an otherwise conservative dress. It's flattering but not obviously sexy. I'm not looking to meet anyone new. I grab my silver tango shoes and head out.

I'm happy to see some familiar faces when I get there. Farzad is here with a group of Persian friends. He gets up to kiss me hello. "Alexis, where have you been?" he asks me. "I haven't seen you in while. How are you?" The dance floor is full. It's really just an old studio the *milonga* takes over once a month. It attracts an older crowd. "I've been swamped at work," I say. I'm not going to tell him I've been missing tango to get my brains fucked out by a shape-shifting half-Mexican, half-Filipino panther man. "Are you here alone? Are you meeting anyone?" he asks. "No, I came by myself," I say. "Well then, you must join us." He introduces me to his friends. All the men are wearing impeccably tailored suits with ties. The women are glamorous, dark-haired exotic creatures, beautifully coiffed and made-up. They switch from Farsi to English when I sit down. This DJ only plays classic tango music, nothing new. The next *tanda* is a waltz. Farzad invites me to dance. He's an elegant man who leads with clarity and consideration. He's always conscious of his partner, always makes sure she's feeling comfortable and supported. That and his superb musicality makes for a lovely dance experience. I relax and begin to enjoy myself.

Between the third and fourth songs of the *tanda*, I notice an unfamiliar man watching me. He's skulking in the shadows near the refreshment tables, sectioned-off behind a low wall. At first I think he's watching me because Farzad makes me look so good out on the dance floor. But when he sees me looking at him, he turns away. Something about him makes me feel uneasy, like he doesn't belong here. Then the last song in the *tanda* starts up and Farzad leads me in a graceful garland of back *ochos* with fancy little crosses. When the song ends, I give him a big appreciative hug. "Thanks, Farzad," I tell him, "I needed that. I love dancing with you." He escorts me back to our table. A couple of Farzad's friends invite me to dance. They are all accomplished dancers and I'm having a great time in their arms. I don't feel that super-charged Rafael chemistry with any of them, which I tell myself is a good thing. I'm sitting at the table chatting with Bijan and Sohaila when I notice that man again. He's tall and thin, in a poorly fitting brown sport jacket and black trousers. I point him out to the table with a nod. "Do any of you know that man over there?" I ask. I haven't seen him on the dance floor all evening. Something about him doesn't fit. One of these things is not like the others. When he sees we're looking at him, he walks out of the *milonga*. It's getting late. Farzad and I dance one last tango. I say goodnight to everyone and leave. When I pull out of the parking lot, I think I see that same man parked on the side of the road. That's weird. Kind of creepy.

I spend Saturday running around doing a bunch of errands — dry cleaners, shoe repair, hardware store, groceries. All day I keep getting an uneasy feeling, like I'm being watched. When I go into the dry cleaners, I think I see the same guy from last night in the parking lot, but he's gone when I come back out. Either I'm being paranoid or I'm being followed. I forget something on my list at Trader Joe's, make a quick U-turn and surprise a short, dark-haired woman. "Oh excuse me," I say. She looks alarmed and turns on her heel to walk away as fast as she can. She has no basket, no shopping cart. Now that's really weird. Was that the woman outside the nail salon from a couple of days ago? I shake it off and finish my shopping. Back home, I throw open all the windows. It's a beautiful fall day, warm and sunny with Santa Ana breezes. I happen to glance down and there's that guy again, smoking a cigarette across the street. What the fuck? I'm not being paranoid. People are following me. I move away from the window.

Cheryl calls. We haven't talked in over a week. She has big news. "Paul asked me to marry him," she tells me. "Oh my God, Cheryl!" I scream. "That's fantastic! Tell me how it happened — wait, let's get on Skype. I have to see the ring." I sit in the chaise in my bedroom and power up my laptop. Out the window and across the street, the man is gone. When Cheryl's face comes up on my screen, she's absolutely beaming. "Show me, show me," I say. She holds her hand up to the camera. There's an enormous yellow diamond surrounded by emeralds. "Oh, Cheryl, it's gorgeous. Is that a yellow diamond?"

"Yes! Paul had it designed for me."

"How did it happen?"

"It was a little cheesy, but so romantic. Paul flew us to New York for the weekend. After lunch on Saturday, we went around Central Park in a horse drawn carriage. When we passed the pond, he proposed to me. I said yes of course, but he didn't have a ring and I was like, what the hell, how do you propose with no ring? But then he said, 'Because I have three rings,' and he had the driver drop us off at Harry Winston. He had three rings waiting for me to choose from. I liked this one best." She holds her hand out, admiring it and grinning from ear to ear. We talk a while about their plans. They're going to have a small destination wedding in Mui Ne, Vietnam — or small for Paul, anyway. They're flying a hundred so of their nearest and dearest over on a chartered jet. There's stellar windsurfing and sand dune buggy adventures, so it's perfect for them.

"So tell me what's been going with you," she says. "How are things with Rafael?" I tell her about his request to take the children for a few days.

"What! Is he crazy?" Cheryl practically screams. "Don't you dare get mixed up in their custody battle!"

"I'm not," I say. "I mean, I won't. I already decided against it."

"Do you realize you could be charged with kidnapping or accessory to kidnapping?"

"Don't worry, I told you, I'm not going to do it. I just haven't had a chance to tell him yet. We haven't talked since he asked me." I'm dreading that conversation. Cheryl frowns and narrows her eyes. "And when was that?" she asks. "Wednesday night," I say.

"How did he bring it up?"

"We were in bed at my place when he just straight out asked me to take them. He went out of town the next morning. He was supposed to call me that night, but I haven't heard from him since." Now that I hear myself saying it, I'm pissed. How can he ask me that, then just get up from bed, walk out my door, and go MIA? "There's something else," I say. "Don't tell me you had a confrontation with his ex." I run my finger over the tiny scab on my arm, then glance out the window and scan my bedroom. "No, but I think I'm being followed," I say, "I saw a strange guy at tango Saturday night. He wasn't there to dance. He was watching me. Then today, I saw the same guy standing across the street from my building. Oh, and there's a woman, too. I saw her when I was getting a pedicure the other day, and again at Trader Joe's this afternoon. She followed me into an aisle and when I turned around, she practically ran to get away from me." I twist the cord of my laptop through my fingers. "Plus, some stuff was moved around in my apartment." Cheryl looks freaked out. "I bet that psycho wife of his has you under surveillance. She might even have cameras and microphones in your apartment. You need to call someone in to do a sweep or something." I dart my eyes around my bedroom. I get that prickling in the back of my neck again. My body tightens up with a surge of adrenalin.

"What? No, why would she do that? And who would I call?"

"I'll ask Paul. He has security people. You need to protect yourself. I'm afraid for your safety."

"Don't you think you're blowing this out of proportion?" I try to dismiss that creepy feeling I've been having for the past three days, the nightmare of the Mirasol monster, those little cuts on my back and my arms.

"Alexis, you have to shake the sex fog off your brain and take a long, hard look at this relationship. You've only known this guy for three months. And what do you really know about him? You have no friends in common, no acquaintances, no associates. You only know what he's told you."

"Well, I've met his children and been to his apartment."

Cheryl looks at me like I'm a retard and shakes her head. I do sound lame. "I have a really bad feeling about this," she says. "And my intuition is never wrong. Be honest with yourself. You must be getting alarm signals, too."

The truth is, I've been feeling confused and conflicted about Rafael. In bed and on the dance floor, it's sizzling hot. Our chemistry is off the charts. I'm falling in love with him, or maybe I already have. I've opened my heart and everything else to him. I've been so vulnerable and exposed. He's been wonderful, but I cannot allow myself to get pulled into all this drama and darkness. Of course, anyone could get involved with a mentally ill person, only to discover the full extent of their illness after they're already married with children. But I'm beginning to consider him in a new light. It takes two to create that kind of drama. Maybe he's not the helpless victim here.

"I really think you should end it with him," Cheryl says. "There's no way it can work out, between the children, the age difference and the crazy ex-wife who's probably spying on you! She will stop at nothing to exact revenge on the woman who takes her place." I try to think of a way it could work out. I don't want to give him up. "You say he travels all the time. Who do you think is going to be taking care of the kids when he's out of town, dealing with all the after-school activities and sleep overs and whatnot? And that's just now. Don't forget about the teenage years. You'll be in your late fifties by then. And what about your career? What about your dream of building your own agency? What happens to that?"

I start to cry. The situation is impossible. I have to let him go. I see my bed, piled high with pillows, where I've had the best sex of my life with Rafael. There's a votive candle on the bedside table, a souvenir from our weekend at the hot springs.

"Oh honey, I'm sorry. I just can't stand by if I think you're in danger." I'm bawling now, tears and snot running down my face. Everything she's said is true. "Alexis, listen. First thing's first — I'm going to call Paul and he'll send someone over to find out if your apartment is bugged." I blow my nose hard and try to get myself under control. I take a couple of shaky breaths. "You call Rafael and tell him you're not going to be a party to kidnapping his children! If he really cares about you — if he's really the amazing brilliant Renaissance man you've described, who's supposedly so ethical and principled — he would never, ever have put you in this situation in the first place." Fuck, she's right. I never really looked at it like that.

After we hang up, I stomp around my apartment fuming. I tear it up looking for hidden cameras. I keep running over to the window to look down into the street and see if that creepy guy is there. When I finally run out of steam, it looks like a tornado hit. I'm exhausted, completely drained, and collapse on the chaise in my bedroom. Then I think about how much energy this drama is consuming and get pissed off all over again. I watch the sky darken as the day ends. I realize I'm famished. I have a fridge full of groceries, but I never did get lunch today. I make a huge salad and a grilled cheese sandwich which I pair with an ice cold bottle of Sauvignon Blanc. After dinner, I straighten up my apartment, then I draw a bath, light the candles and pour in a calming blend of essential oils. I get into bed and watch an episode of Downton Abbey. To my surprise, I have no problem falling asleep.

I wake up with a new clarity. I've made my decision. I'm not going to see Rafael anymore. I just need to tell him. My pussy is bereft. She sends a pang of regret, an arrow straight to my heart, but I'm resolute. I love our chemistry, love being with him, love making love with him, but I'm not going to abandon my dreams, deny my needs, betray my values or ignore my inner guidance, God damn it. I'm just not. I pick up the phone to call him, but the phone rings before I can dial his number. It's him. "Rafael, where have you been?" I say. I can hear the accusing tone in my voice. I force myself to take a deep breath and get centered. "I'm so sorry I've been out of touch," he begins, "I was gone longer than I planned and I needed to get some things handled with Mirasol."

"About that," I say, "I've made my decision."

"Never mind about the children," he interrupts, "I never should have asked you. Please forgive me for putting you in that position." That takes the edge off my righteous anger.

"No," I say, "You shouldn't have."

"The fact is," he adds, "It's not safe for you to have them."

"Why?" I sit up straight. "What do you mean?"

"I found out Mirasol hired investigators and had you followed." What. The. Fuck. Cheryl was right, as usual. I look around my bedroom, wondering where the cameras and microphone could be hiding. Then I realize she's probably listening to our call right now. I'm absolutely furious, from zero to sixty in nothing flat.

"Rafael, I need you to listen to me. I can't do this anymore. I don't want any part of this. I can't have my life and my privacy invaded by your psycho ex-wife. I'm not going to see you again."

"Please don't say that, Alexis," he says, "I can work it out. I'm in love with you. What we have is so beautiful." A pang of pure longing stabs through my chest. I can't breathe for a second. He loves me. He wants me. I love him too, but I have to let him go. "I'm sorry Rafael, but it's no use. It's not going to work. I wish you only the best, but I'm done. Don't call me again." I hang up before he can say anything else.

I call Cheryl, spitting mad. "That fucking bitch *has* been having me followed!" I shout. "Are you listening, bitch?"

"How do you know?" Cheryl asks. "Because Rafael just told me." Cheryl is quiet for a moment. "Did you just hear me?" I say. "Yes, I heard you," she says. "I'm texting Paul to get someone over to your apartment now." Then I start crying again. I feel like a basket case. God damn it, I refuse to fall apart over him!

"I broke up with him," I say.

"Good," Cheryl says, "It's the right thing to do." She heaves a sigh and sits silent for a moment. "You had to end it." I really had fallen in love with Rafael. Now it's over. "I know, but it still hurts." I'm brokenhearted. I'll never have those magic pussy-whispering hands on me again, never dance with him again, never be held in those arms, never be kissed by those lips, never have that thick upturned cock inside me, never have that tail wrapped around me. I'll never open like that again. "Darling, it hurts now, but you will get over this. Think about what he exposed you to. Even though you ended it, that doesn't mean she's done fucking with you." I hadn't thought about that. Am I still going to have to deal with her invading my privacy? Invading my dreams? "What will she want with me now that I've broken up with him?"

"I told you, Alexis, you don't understand the mind of a sociopath. What will she want? To hurt him. To punish you. To get her revenge. You're still not safe."

How do I get out of this nightmare? I feel sick. I think I'm going to throw up. "Cheryl, I'll call you right back." I hang up, rush to the bathroom and dry heave into the toilet. Only bitter sour bile comes out. I brush my teeth and splash water on my face. I look like hell. My eyes are all swollen and red. My face is blotchy. I make a cup of mint tea with honey and call Cheryl back. "Alexis, I want you to get out of there," she says. "Fly up and stay with me for a few days." I'd love to go back home to Seattle and be with Cheryl. It's just what I need, but I can't leave town now. "I can't," I tell her, "I have a big complicated shoot for a client this week and the launch of a major campaign."

"OK, fine, then I'm coming down to stay with you. I'll call you back with my flight info."

A wave of relief washes over me, but I'm still too freaked out to stay in my apartment. I throw on some clothes and go down to my car. Once I'm on the road, I calm down a bit. Maybe I'll go for a hike. Get some fresh air and exercise. Clear my head. Get out in nature. Get grounded. Then I reconsider. I don't want to be out on a trail by myself, not with Mirasol's people following me. I head to the beach instead. There's always people at the beach in Los Angeles. Cheryl texts me. Her flight gets in at 4 pm. Maybe I'll go see a movie. I pick up a sandwich and catch a matinee, but I can barely concentrate on the movie. I keep looking around for that tall thin man, or the short dark-haired woman. I slip out before it's over and get to the airport early. When I get to the airport, I buy a magazine and sit in a cafe to kill time until Cheryl lands.

When we get back to my apartment, two men are waiting for us in the lobby. One of them looks like a nerdy techie, but the other looks like an ex-Mossad agent or something. Cheryl calls Paul to confirm his men are there and we go up to my apartment. The nerdy guy has two big black cases on rolling wheels full of electronics. They find cameras and microphones in the bookshelves, in the living room, even the ceiling fan in my bedroom. My cell phone has been hacked. I go into my bedroom and sit on my chaise. I'm shaking, furious and frightened. Cheryl comes in with Paul on the phone. She puts him on speaker and we discuss my options. I want to get a restraining order and press charges, but there's no proof it was

Mirasol. Cheryl is afraid it will only antagonize her further, feed the drama and give her more reason to fuck with me. I feel so powerless and frustrated. Paul tells us he'll have Uri set up 24-hour security for the next few weeks. It turns out he actually is ex-Mossad. "Don't worry, Alexis," Paul says, "You'll be safe now. I'll make sure Rafael and Mirasol leave you alone." I can't believe this is really happening. It feels like I'm in a movie. The security team left a tiny piece of copper wire shining on the end table.

"How will you do that?" I ask. I glance up at the ceiling fan where one of her spy cameras was. My whole body squinches tight — she must have watched us have sex the other night. "I'm not going to get into the details," he says, "Mirasol will be neutralized. Just don't call Rafael or see him. Uri has blocked him on your phone and email so he can't contact you. Uri's people will take care of everything." When we walk back out to the living room, the nerdy guy hands me a new set of keys. My locks have been changed and there's a new high security deadbolt. Uri enters his number into our phones. "I'll have a team of people watching over you," he says, "If you see anything suspicious — if anything feels wrong — call me, any time, day or night."

The men leave and Cheryl settles in. I make up the pull-out bed in my home office for her and put out fresh towels. Cheryl makes dinner and we sit down to watch an episode of Downton Abbey. I'm an emotional wreck. I can't concentrate. I'm nervous and jumpy. I keep getting up to look out the window, but no one is there. No one I can see.

CHAPTER FIVE

Yellow Diamonds

"It's ridiculous, really," Cheryl tells me, "Writing is the only thing I want to do, but I can't make myself sit down and do it." I ignore her and focus on the rhythm of my knife slicing through the yellow flesh of the heirloom tomatoes. I'm sick of hearing Cheryl whine about her self-inflicted struggles with her creative process. Like I really give a shit. Write or don't write, but don't come whining to me about it. "I've become a world-class expert on procrastination," Cheryl says, "I actually cleaned out the filter on the vacuum cleaner the other day instead of sitting at my desk and working on the second draft of my play." It's been a few months since she came down to rescue me from Rafael's crazy ex-wife. She's back in LA, staying with me while she shops for a wedding gown. She's narrowed it down to Monique Lhuillier and Vera Wang, both based in Los Angeles.

"Cheryl, that's pathetic," I say. She's sitting on a stool at my kitchen island, drinking my best bottle of wine, a 2012 Pinot Noir from the Willamette Valley, scarfing down the tray of pâté, cheese and crackers. I can't help but notice the giant diamond engagement ring flashing on her finger. It's at least 6 carats, a rare yellow, surrounded by emeralds. I'm sure Paul shelled out a few hundred grand for that baby, minimum. Cheryl loves showing it off every chance she gets. I move on to chiffonade the basil.

"Tell me how you do it," she asks me.

"Do what?"

"Make yourself write. How do you do it?"

"I don't have much choice," I say, "I don't have a rich fiancé paying my bills while I spend my days going to yoga class, getting massages and trying on designer wedding gowns."

We both freeze. Jesus! I'm a fucking bitch. Cheryl looks like she's about to cry. I feel like shit. "Cheryl, I'm sorry. I didn't mean it," I say. "You know I love you and I'm happy for you, really." Cheryl puts her glass down. "You don't sound happy for me. You sound jealous," she says. I slice the basil faster, without mercy. "Oh yeah?" I say, eyes on the cutting board. "And maybe you sound like a spoiled brat. If I have to listen to one more complaint about your wedding planner or the latest episode in the never-ending construction saga of your Maui estate, I'm going to scream." She and Paul have changed their wedding plans. Instead of a small-ish destination wedding, they've decided on a big formal wedding up in Seattle. Then they'll fly a horde of their nearest and dearest to Vietnam, after which they'll have a private honeymoon in Thailand. "Well excuse me for talking about my life with my so-called best friend." Her voice cracks on "friend."

I start to slice the buffalo mozzarella. It's so soft I have to slow down and be careful not to tear it. It focuses me. Centers me. Cheryl's right. I am jealous. Jealous of her relationship with Paul, jealous of the money and security he provides, jealous she doesn't have to struggle to pay bills anymore, jealous she got out of middle-aged single woman hell, jealous of her new life and her new friends, jealous of her engagement ring, which really is gorgeous. I stop slicing. I look up at Cheryl. She's gulping her wine and fidgeting with her ring. She deserves to be happy. It's been a long hard dry spell for her. I put my knife down and walk around the island. "You're right. I am jealous. And I'm being a total bitch," I say and give her a hug. "I'm sorry." Cheryl hugs me back hard. I realize how much I've missed her. "My emotions are all over the place since that whole thing with Rafael and Mirasol," I say.

"Still?" Cheryl asks, "It's been six months."

"I know," I say, "I've been doing fine, but seeing how happy you are with Paul, hearing about your fairytale life together and how amazing he is? I don't know, it triggered all this unresolved stuff. I don't mean to be projecting all over you."

"You'll find someone again," she says.

"That's just it," I say, "I'm afraid to start dating again. After the double-whammy of Dario and Rafael, I don't even trust myself anymore." I set the knife down and look up at her. "Oh, honey," Cheryl says, "That's awful. I didn't realize." I can feel hot tears beginning to spill over. I don't want to cry.

"It completely traumatized me. I feel like I'm being punished for my sexuality or something, like all my mother's shaming and guilt-trips are being proven true, like I'm just some slut-whore who got what she deserved." Cheryl slams her hand on the kitchen island, sloshing the wine around in our glasses.

"Alexis, that is complete and utter bullshit!" Cheryl says. "No offense, but your mother is one fucked up, repressed bitch. You have got to get her toxic voice out of your head."

I arrange the tomatoes and mozzarella on a serving platter and sprinkle the basil chiffonade on top. I pour my premium balsamic vinegar over it, zigzagging the thick syrup in a looping pattern. I add a dollop of fresh-made pesto to each stack, then move on to pound the chicken breasts into thin paillards for the piccata. "I think you killed it good and dead," Cheryl says, laughing. I stop pounding and look at the cutting board. There's a mess of pulverized chicken in front of me. Bits of it are scattered all over the kitchen island. I put the mallet down and step back. I look up at Cheryl. She's trying not to laugh, but it's coming out anyway. I go to the sink and wash my hands, letting the warm water run over my hands to try and wash the rage away. I take some deep breaths to calm and center myself. I sit down on a stool across from Cheryl and fill my wine glass to the top and take a big gulp.

"Feeling better?" Cheryl asks. I shake my head. "I keep going over it all, again and again," I say. "How could I have been so clueless with Dario? What signs did I miss? I feel sick when I think about the fantasy world I created. I literally pictured us getting married, the huge engagement ring, our life together, here and in Argentina." I take another big gulp of my wine. "Like some dumb ignorant teenager."

Cheryl frowns and wags her finger at me. "Dario was a very specific case of a sociopath," she says. "The very definition of a sociopath is their uncanny ability to imitate real emotions and love to get what they want. You got in and out pretty damn fast, so I wouldn't beat yourself up over that one."

"Yeah, but what attracted that experience into my life. It has to be something inside me. Sociopaths target the vulnerable, right?" I say.

"As I recall, you met him on the dance floor, right?" Cheryl says. I nod. "So you were horny and spellbound by his dancing. I'm sure he's got that seduction technique down to a science." As usual, Cheryl is right. Dario does have a very specific modus operandi, preying on middle-aged American women looking for love and romance in the tango world.

"It was different with Rafael. I fell in love with him," I say. "OK," Cheryl says, "let's talk about Rafael! The deal-breakers were there from the beginning. You just chose to ignore them." She ticks them off one by one. "The twelve-year age difference. The young children. The psycho ex-wife. The drama."

I interrupt to protest, "I didn't know she was psycho in the beginning!"

She holds up her palm to cut me off. "But you did know there was drama over custody," Cheryl says. "And it wasn't too far in that you found out about her. Maybe not the degree of her crazy, but the fact of it, yes."

"Do you enjoy being right all the time?" I ask. Cheryl smirks and takes a sip of her wine. I can tell she's trying not to say, "I told you so." She goes on. "Besides, he wasn't truly available, was he?" That stops me in my tracks.

"What do you mean?" I say. "Well, think about it. There was a yo-yo pattern — first super-close intimacy, then absence and distance." I think back over our time together. How did I never see this before? Right again. "If you think about it," she says, "It's a perfect replica of your early childhood experiences in your family. Unpredictable, inconsistent, emotional deprivation, even physical abandonment at times. Then getting punished and shamed for needing love. It's amazing you turned out as normal as you have."

I pull back. Woah, where is this even coming from?

"Since when have you become the relationship expert?" I ask.

"Since I didn't want to fuck up my relationship with Paul," Cheryl says. "I went and saw someone for a while. I starting studying attachment theory and how it plays out in intimate relationships. Paul and I even did some preventive couples counseling."

I take another sip of wine and spread some pâté on a cracker. I pop it into my mouth. Not as good as my homemade version, but still delicious. I get up to clean off the cutting board and the chicken bits from the kitchen island. Then I go back to pounding out the chicken breasts again. "I feel like I'm stuck in this cycle of fantasy projection—" Wham goes my mallet! "Falling in love—" Wham! "Only to end up heartbroken and disappointed. I'm afraid I'll never find a man and I'll end up old and alone like my mother." Wham! I sound like a whiny victim. "And I hate feeling like a whiny victim!" Wham! Cheryl cuts a big slice of cheese, puts it on a cracker and holds it out to me. "Some cheese with that whine?" she asks. We both crack up.

Cheryl has given me a lot to think about. I need to take a good hard look at myself. My jealous outburst shocked me. I retreat to my bathroom for some self-soothing. I draw a bath, light the candles, pour in essential oils, put on some meditation music and settle in. I lie in the tub thinking about my patterns with men, about Cheryl and Paul's relationship, and it suddenly hits me. I have never let myself feel, really feel, or even admit how much I want and need this kind of love in my life. I've never let myself acknowledge how big my need is to flame and be flamed in return, to flame to my full capacity, to flame unconditionally, to give my whole heart to a relationship, deep and true. I've defended myself from this knowledge, from this tenderness. There is no defense in the face of this need. For once, I let my heart open to it. I feel so young and naked, so raw and exposed.

Then I realize something I never understood before. My need for love is exactly as big as my capacity. I think about that for a minute. My need and my capacity are two sides of the same coin. What I need, how much I need and what I am capable of giving mirror each other. When I let myself acknowledge my ability to love this big, something changes. I begin to feel a kind of strength, a sense of authority, a surge of power. I try it on out loud. "I want this kind of love." It reverberates around my skull and off the tile walls of the bathroom. It settles in my belly and coils around my spine. It takes root in my heart. It's a relief to admit it, to say it out loud. "I really want this love in my life." More power surges up. I go for it, let myself claim it. "And I can do it. I am made to give and receive love. Wholeheartedly. Unconditionally. Devotedly." I sink into my tub and let it soak in. I am the only common denominator in all my experiences with men. If I want something different, I'm the one who needs to change.

CHAPTER SIX

Change Is In The Air

I've been off my game. All that drama with Rafael and Mirasol did a number on my confidence. My shit hasn't been tight ever since. I don't trust myself anymore. I don't feel ready to jump ship and start my own agency. Not the best time to leap into the unknown without a safety net. On top of that, something is going down. Ben, the agency CEO, is acting all shady. There are closed door meetings in our open door offices. I need to find out what's happening. I don a focused, purposeful air and stride through the office on reconnaissance. Our offices are part of a modern eco-design movement, spread over fifteen thousand square feet of a converted mid-century industrial building. They're terminally hip, with light-filled atriums, walls of succulents, recycled wood and brick. Ergonomically-designed fabulosity abounds all around. I've timed my surveillance to coincide with Jackie's mid-morning caramel macchiato fix. As Ben's executive assistant, she orchestrates his calendar. I pause and pretend to sort through a stack of folders to synchronize my arrival at her desk within a small window — after she turns the corner, but before her computer screen switches to sleep mode.

Well I'll be dammed! Three meetings in two weeks with the top dogs from the Aquilo Group. Either they're our newest and biggest client, or we're getting acquired. Our agency has been growing in both size and reputation, in no small part thanks to my work here. Ben's office door swings open. I act nonchalant, like I have some legitimate reason to be standing behind Jackie's desk, scrolling through her computer. Ben doesn't see me yet. He's turned back into his office to say, "I'll set something up for tomorrow afternoon." Whew! He buys me just enough time to head off in the opposite direction.

As soon as I get back to my desk, I Google the Aquilo Group. What started off as a small telecom company has grown into a multi-billion-dollar behemoth. Next I Google its founder, Nicolo Aquilo. Dozens of news stories and profiles describe a visionary iconoclast. He's defied the odds and proven naysayers wrong time and time again. Only a few failures mar his long string of successes, but they're equally spectacular. I can't find much about his personal life — just a brief mention of an early marriage which produced no children, and a divorce over fifteen years ago. He must have a team of high priced PR flacks on retainer, paid to protect his privacy. He'd make for an interesting and challenging client — or a formidable new owner.

An email arrives from Ben, subject line: "CONFIDENTIAL." There are five of us cc'd, the entire executive team of the agency. It reads, "Please make yourself available for a confidential meeting tomorrow afternoon in the conference room. 5-6 PM. Important news about upcoming changes. Do not discuss." I immediately text Jessica, head of business development, "Drinks after work?" She texts back, "Where?" I chew on my nail and think about our local watering holes. Too risky. I Google "best bars for college students near Culver City," and text her back the location. She replies with an "LOL" and a smiley face. Jessica and I are work buddies, the two top women in a testosterone-driven shop. She's a Southern belle, former debutante, crazy-smart and sassy as a firecracker. Clients love her. I have huge respect for her. She heads up business development, so she'll probably know something if the Aquilo Group is coming in as a client.

It's hard to concentrate on work for the rest of the day. After lunch, I pull out my laptop and open the folder with all my agency start-up files. I review my business plan, my list of prospective investors, my picks for the launch team. I haven't mentioned anything to Jessica yet, but she's on that list. I feel a pang of guilt. Ben has been good to me. He took a chance on me. It was a big jump from Brand Strategist in a smaller agency in Seattle to Director of Strategy here in Los Angeles. But I've proven myself, delivered all I promised and more, including an award-winning campaign that put us on the map big-time. If we are being acquired, it would be better to make the move now, before the news leaks. I wish I could talk it out with Rafael, but I hate myself for even thinking that. The truth is, it would take a major balls-to-the-walls scramble to put my plans into motion this fast. I don't really have all my ducks in a row and I don't want to set myself up for failure. Then again, when is it ever the right time to betray a mentor? I know Ben would see it that way, even though he left a big agency himself to start this one eight years ago. Besides, if we are being acquired, how many of us will be gone?

When I get to the bar after work, it does not disappoint — as long as you're a frat boy looking to get shit-faced with your buddies at a Tuesday night happy hour. The sound system blasts hip-hop, the food is a greasy Shangri-La for food-borne pathogens, the women dress like white trash road kill, and a throng of red-faced white-boy rapper wannabes jostle around. I'm holed up at what passes for a quiet table in the corner when Jessica comes swanning in. She's wearing a classic Miss-Junior-League-dress, beige fuck-me-pumps, which is an oxymoron, but somehow she pulls it off. She's accessorized with a prim little purse and creamy lace gloves. I don't remember her wearing this outfit earlier. She must've changed just for the pleasure of fucking with our fellow drinkers, to see if she could get a reaction. I wouldn't put it past her. A couple of young ruffians knock into her, completely oblivious. Her hands dart out and she grabs each one by an ear. That gets their attention. "Pardon me, gentlemen," she says, smiling sweetly in her best Southern belle drawl, "But it's customary to apologize to a lady when you run her over." They stand there in shock until she gives their ears another tweak. One of them finally says, "Yes, ma'am.

Sorry, ma'am." I'm already laughing when she sits down.
"Why hello, Alexis!" she says. "Lovely to meet you here."
We both crack up. "Well," I say, "I figured there would be
no chance of running into anyone from work." We both
scan the room. "It would be grounds for instant
termination," she says. We can't help it, we crack up
again.

A beleaguered waitress in denim cut-offs and a tube
top comes over to our table. "What can I get you ladies?"
she asks as she eyes us up and down. She's obviously
wondering what a pair of well-dressed women in their
forties are doing sitting at one of her tables. She stares in
fascination as Jessica pulls a napkin out of the dispenser
and carefully wipes off the table top before setting down
her prim little purse. She pulls her gloves off one finger at
a time and drapes them over the top of her purse. I order
a double shot of their best tequila and a beer chaser. Hey,
when in Rome. Jessica orders a bourbon and soda. "Oh
for heaven's sake, Jessica," I say, "Don't make yourself
sick." But she ignores me and gets into a conversation
with the waitress about which brands of bourbon they
stock. In the end, Jessica slips a twenty-dollar bill on the
waitress' tray and gives her thousand-watt smile. "Now
honeychile," she says, "please make sure you get that
barkeep to open a brand new bottle for me." If I do go out
on my own, I want this woman with me.

I'm nervous waiting for our drinks. I still don't know if
I should even tell Jessica about my plans, much less ask
her to come with me. I think I can trust her, but
everything could backfire if I'm wrong. Jessica's looking

around, amused as all get out by the three-ring circus. The bar smells like beer and piss and testosterone-infused sweat. That twenty did the trick, though. Our drinks come in no time at all. Jessica lifts her glass, inspects the rim, then holds it out and says, "Mud in your eye." I down half my double shot in one swallow. It burns going down and I decide to just come right out with it. "Jessica, what do you know about the Aquilo Group?" She looks blank. "Nothing," she says, "What should I know?" I scrutinize her. I'm a poker player betting her last stack of chips. "Ben has had three top secret meetings with them in the past two weeks," I say. Now it's her turn to scrutinize me. "And this has something to do with our confidential pow-wow tomorrow, I assume?" I can see the wheels turning. She puts her drink down and looks me straight in the eye. She drops the Southern belle routine like a hot potato, "Why don't you get to the point and tell me what this is all about?" The first part is easy. "Well," I start, "either we've just landed a major new client or we're being acquired by the Aquilo Group." She doesn't blink. Just waits. "And since you know nothing about it," I go on, "I have to assume it's the latter." Jessica sits up straighter. She takes another sip of her bourbon and soda. "And you know this how?" she asks, raising an eyebrow. "I happened to walk by Ben's office today at the end of their meeting," I tell her. "I heard him say he would set something up for tomorrow. He sent out that email right after." Jessica takes her time. I can tell she's considering all the implications. She takes another sip of her drink. "Tell me, Alexis," she says, "Why exactly are we here?" I decide honesty is the best policy. I have to risk telling her about my plans. If she's going to play a pivotal role in my new agency, I have to trust her. I down the rest of my tequila.

"I did a little research on the Aquilo Group," I tell her. "They're a multi-billion-dollar company you never heard of with an appetite for expansion and a crazy maverick at the helm. If we get acquired, it's not unlikely we'll lose our jobs in the process." Jessica considers for a minute. "Possibly," she says, "but I don't think Ben would have structured a deal that doesn't keep his core executive team intact. Especially two people key to the company's revenues and reputation." It's now or never. I take a breath. "Here's the thing," I say, "I've been planning on starting my own agency. This acquisition would be the perfect time to do it. I'd like you to come with me." I hold my breath and jump into the deep end. "As a partner." Jessica's face is unreadable. Her honey blonde hair is swept back into a classic chignon and her porcelain skin is flawless, the blessing of good genes and expensive facials. I watch her study me like a prosecutor. Then she grins and says, "I always wanted my own shop one day. You are a dark horse, Miss Alexis. I thought you were Ben's girl all the way." A stab of guilt slices through my gut. "He's been very good to me," I say, "and I don't want to disappoint him, but this is what I've always wanted." I've finished my tequila, and I'm not much of a beer drinker. The double shot has made me bold. I need a little more liquid courage, stronger than this piss water. I wave the waitress over. "Two more, please," I tell her. She hurries off through the noisy jostling crowd. I make do with a few tentative sips of beer while we wait. Once our second round is served, Jessica toasts again. "To agency dreams," she says. Some voice of caution whispers in my ear, calls a timeout for a huddle. "Take it one step at a time," it says. I listen. "Jessica, here's how I'd like to handle this," I say. "Let's go to the meeting tomorrow and hear what they have planned. Then let's meet again privately. If we both want to move forward, I'll have an NDA and a letter of intent ready." We clink glasses and down the rest of our drinks.

I wake up this morning dreading the unavoidable. I have to tell Ben I'm going to leave and start my own agency, and I'm taking Jessica with me — if Jessica still wants to go after the super-secret, hush-hush meeting this afternoon. I'm consumed by doubts. I'm afraid of losing everything I've worked for. I've been successful here, but going out on my own is a huge step. What if my big accounts don't come with me? They may want to stay put if we're going to be part of the Aquilo Group, not take a chance on a small start-up agency. I feel paralyzed. I'm risking my entire career. Maybe I haven't thought this through enough, haven't laid the groundwork. Maybe it's precipitous, premature, or just plain foolhardy. Am I rushing into disaster in business, just like I've done romantically? I shudder to think of my missteps and lack of judgment, how I gave in to my passions and fantasies, how I let my horny teenager run the show. Look where that got me.

It turns out my angst is all for nothing. Ben announces the Aquilo Group is our new 500-pound gorilla of a client.

We all sit around the conference table processing while a jubilant Ben rushes on. "Sorry to keep you out of the loop, Jessica, but the client specifically requested confidentiality until certain details could be worked out." Jessica nudges me with her knee. "So we're not being acquired," she mutters, "At least not yet." Ben bounces up and down on his toes like a 5-year old as he fills us in. "Our task is to launch Nicolo Aquilo's newest pet project in eco-friendly low-cost building materials." Apparently the Aquilo Group's material sciences company has made a breakthrough in their never-ending search for lighter, faster, stronger materials, and they're ready to go to market. He waves his arms around as he tells us, "It's going to be huge, both in terms of billings and in prestige. They want us to develop their entire brand strategy along with all the marketing and advertising, first for the U.S. and then the international market." Ben's eyes are lit up like a kid on Christmas morning and he's grinning from ear to ear. He bounds over to my chair and says, "Alexis, you're lead on the account. The mandate is to create something unconventional and original, to convince the world they've the solved the problem of high performance, low-cost, energy-efficient construction materials." I just sit there with my mouth hanging open. Jessica has to kick me under the table. "Lead on the entire account?" I manage to stumble out. "Yes," Ben says, "by client request. Our team meets with their team tomorrow, including the boss man himself." Holy shit!

Jessica walks with me back to my office and throws herself onto the couch. "Well, it looks like the agency gods have showered us with their blessings," she says. "Congratulations on the lead. I don't quite see what my role will be, but you basically got your dream account dropped straight in your lap." She's looking very naughty schoolgirl today, in her tight plaid skirt and tailored white shirt. Her sky-high black patent leather Mary Jane Louboutins are propped up on my coffee table. The red soles glare at me lasciviously. "I don't know what to feel," I say, "I'm flattered of course. It really is a dream assignment and right up my alley." So why do I feel like I just got the wind knocked out of my sails? Like I'm up in a plane, parachute on, ready to make the most daring jump of my life, when the mission gets aborted? I'm relieved but disappointed. Then it hits me with a jolt — this could be the biggest break of my career. Now I'm excited, and the news spreads through the office like wildfire. A stream of people stops by to congratulate me. If only they knew I was just about to jump ship and take two of the agency's biggest accounts with me! "This does change everything," I say, "Obviously our plans to start our own shop are on indefinite hold." I'm not stupid. There's no way I would turn down this account for the vagaries of running my own shop.

I take extra time with my hair and makeup the next morning, peruse my closet and consider the image I want to convey. Power for sure, but not too conservative. They want original and unconventional. What do I have that says smart, powerful, hip and creative? I decide on a black pencil skirt that stops at my knees, pair it with a royal blue shirt with angular architectural details and cut-outs. I choose a crazy pair of color-block Jimmy Choo platform pumps in sky blue and fuchsia, add a pair of triangular black and gold enamel earrings and assess the finished look from all sides. Damn, not bad at all. Simple, striking, but not too trendy. Definitely woman-power-executive-looking.

Back at the office, we gather in the conference room. There's five of us from our side — Ben, CEO, me, head of strategy, Jessica, head of business development, Jeff, head of account management and Roger, the creative director. Then the Aquilo team arrives. Four men walk in wearing jeans and casual collared shirts. Not the corporate culture I was expecting. One of them is Nicolo Aquilo. He's an imposing figure in person — good-looking for sure, in a rugged former athlete sort of way, but it's his presence and charisma that dominate the room. He's a little over six feet tall, well-built and tanned with dark curly hair greying at the temples. I nudge Jessica under the table. She raises an eyebrow at me. Introductions are made and hands are shaken all around. When he comes to me, he says, "I've been looking forward to meeting you, Alexis." The touch of his hand sends an electric charge up my arm. The pussy-meter shakes herself awake. "Your work on the solar initiative was brilliant." I command myself not to blush, to accept the compliment gracefully. "Thank you, Mr. Aquilo," I say. "It's a cause I believe in." He's peering at me with a funny expression on his face, like he's trying to figure out where we've met before. "Call me Nico," he says. "Everybody does."

Without further ado, Nico powers up a slide deck with stats about the global construction industry and launches the meeting. He speaks with the eloquence of a Roman orator as he lays out his vision. "We are about to transform the built world. Our material sciences group has developed a radical new line of building materials. With this line, we can solve just about all the significant challenges to building green." He pauses to let that sink in and clicks to the next slide. He goes on to describe their breakthroughs with the passion of a preacher possessed by the Holy Spirit. "We set stringent criteria for waste-free, cradle-to-grave sustainable production. The end products are completely non-toxic. We've achieved unprecedented energy-efficiency ratings, at 20% lower costs than traditional construction materials." I look around the room. All eyes are on Nico. He's mesmerized us all. My imagination takes off and a dozen ideas pop into my mind. Then, as he goes on, and I start to grasp the sheer size and scope of the work to be done, I begin to feel intimidated and overwhelmed. It's a daunting prospect and an enormous responsibility. He switches into another gear to outline his mission to provide affordable, quality, low-cost housing to those in desperate need. He's going to demonstrate the feasibility of this plan at two test sites, one in the favelas of Rio de Janeiro and one in the slums of Mumbai. Audacious goals, to say the least. It's a bold vision. One solution to many problems. The size of the potential market is practically unlimited. It's genius, if their materials perform as promised. Thirty minutes later, he leaves the meeting for the rest of his team to finish up.

He's seduced us, inspired us, stroked our egos, made us feel like the chosen creative elite.

The meeting turns into a briefing, led by Timothy, a no-nonsense Brit who's head of operations. Timothy is tall, lean and pasty white. He breaks down the multi-year master plan in a clipped monotone. "The plan is to launch AquiloBuilt in the U.S and South-East Asian markets simultaneously. We will focus on the commercial construction market initially, then move on to the residential market." He goes on to describe the launch process and the roll-out plan. Then he looks straight at me when he says in a pissy tone of voice, "We expect to be closely involved with your work at every stage." He's obviously got some sort of issue, but I try to ignore it. "That's great," I tell him. "We prefer to work collaboratively, in a joint team effort." Jessica will be working closely with their sales team on the construction industry strategy. I'm glad I'll have her by my side on this. Roger, I'm not too sure about. He's a classic California surfer dude, a talented enough creative director, but I don't know that he has the chops to pull this off. He's certainly not known for his multicultural sensitivity. His foot-in-mouth disease could really be a problem, like that incident with the brand manager of a major body care line. We were strategizing how to better tap into the Hispanic market and Roger suggested they probably wouldn't buy soap too often. The entire room went silent. I pretended he was joking and had to work my ass off to keep from losing the account.

Tim and I rough out a calendar and set up weekly team meetings. By the time they leave, my nervous system is fried. Ben calls a company-wide party to celebrate the new account. Our agency is filled with ambitious, competitive young people, about 70% male, and the party gets boisterous fast. Jessica and I amuse ourselves with side bets on who's going to come kiss my ass next as they jockey and lobby for a place on the team. It's like shooting fish in a barrel, so we have to make it interesting. We start betting on how they'll approach, how long it'll take them to make their pitch, what adjectives they'll use to flatter me. An hour and a half later, I figure I can make a decent escape. Jessica has hustled me for all she's worth — I owe her two spa days, three lunches and a movie. I give silent thanks to all that is holy she's on my team, then slip away and head home.

I strip naked as soon as I walk in the door. I'm elated, exhausted, overwhelmed, terrified. I grab a glass of ice cold chardonnay and retreat to my bathroom to immerse my body in hot, scented water. I sit in the bath. I take deep breaths. I sip my wine. My mind is still racing. I order in Thai food and try to shut my mind off with the last two episodes of Downton Abbey, but I can't concentrate. I have a hard time getting to sleep, and I wake up at four in the morning from a series of vivid dreams.

I walk down stone stairs in the first dream into the blackness below. I enter a frigid stone chamber. The flicker of my clay lamp barely illuminates the raised limestone slab in the center. I shiver in my plain shift, more from fear than cold. My final initiation as a priestess of Anubis is about to begin. I lay back on the slab and press the linen of my shift smooth. I force myself to take soft even breaths to quiet my pounding heart and wait for my Master to come. I must leave my body for three full cycles of the sun, cross over into the Shadowland and face the trials of Anubis. If my will fails, I may never return to my body. I may be enslaved, forced to serve the evil one for eternity. I may come back with a broken mind to sit drooling in the courtyard, like Sekeeta, for the rest of my days. I pray to Anubis, "Guide and protect me in the Shadowland. Let me not fail my Master." I hear his soft shuffle coming down the stairs. He sets his lamp by my feet and begins the rituals. I love him with all my heart. I look up into his gold-flecked eyes. He looks at me. His wisdom and compassion shine down upon me. Then he leans over and touches his lips to my third eye, blesses me and leaves. I hear the heavy stone door roll closed, sealing me in. It sucks the air from the chamber and my little lamp almost flickers out. I lay in the dark. The cold seeps into my bones. If I fail, I will be lost in the Shadowlands for eternity. If I fail, this chamber will be my sarcophagus. If I fail, I will never see those shining eyes again. I must not fail. I gather my courage and pinch out the tiny flame. I stare up into the blackness. The last thing I see are my teacher's eyes smiling down at me.

I ride away under a cloudless blue sky into the next dream. I gulp the clean dry air as we leave the noise and the stench of the city behind us. My heart soars free out here, away from all the intrigue and danger of the palace.

It's never safe to be together in the city, surrounded by my father's spying eyes. My beloved rides beside me on the horse I gave him, a beautiful and temperamental beast, black as midnight, swift as the wind. My peregrine falcon shifts on my wrist. She's restless, impatient to hunt. I glance over at my lover's warrior profile, proud and fierce. His hooked nose and finely carved lips mirror the golden eagle perched on his gloved wrist. We stop to take off their hoods, then cast our birds together. They race each other across the sky and we race after them. His horse is faster than mine, but my bird is the fastest of all. It gets late. We turn toward the setting sun and ride for our camp, hidden in the reeds near the Tigris. I slide off the saddle into his arms and we stand kissing in the shadow of my mare. My vigilant heart relaxes and fills with love for my forbidden captain. We make a child that night, on the piles of rugs in our tent by the river, a child I can never allow to be born. The last thing I see are his shining amber eyes.

I hear the jingle of a carriage and the clop of horses in my third dream. I pull aside heavy velvet curtains to peer down into the street. Heartless moonlight reflects off the silver surface of the Neva into the room. He's coming. I make a quick check of the dining room and rush to hide my mother's letter, asking me to send money, asking me to leave the Imperial Ballet, asking me to return to our people. Maybe when the winter season is finished, I can get away. I pour two glasses of champagne and stand by the fireplace. I hear his boots on the stairs, then Vasily stalks into the room and stands there glaring at me. When he doesn't say anything, I flounce over to the table and ring the crystal bell for dinner to be served. I wait by my chair, but he doesn't pull it out for me. He just stands there, his eyes glittering ice, mouth tight. I can see his jaw clench and twitch. I huff and sit down, make a show of arranging my skirts. I drink my champagne and fiddle with my emerald necklace. He walks over to the table and stands behind his chair, grips the back so tight his knuckles go white. I ignore him. The butler and footman come in with dinner. They wait by the table for Vasily to sit down. Their eyes dart nervously back and forth between us. After a minute, Vasily jerks his chair out and sits stiffly on the edge, back ramrod straight. He's silent while they serve dinner. The butler stands waiting for him to help himself from the tray of sliced roast and potatoes. Vasily doesn't move. The butler looks at me with panic. I sigh, roll my eyes, and gesture with my hand to serve Vasily. The two servants wait by the table after all the food is served, shifting and fidgeting in the uncomfortable silence. "Get out," Vasily tells them. "Leave us alone." The door shuts behind them. "I forbid you to flirt like that from the stage," he tells me in a low clipped tone. "I do not flirt on stage," I snap back. I put on a heavy Ruska Roma accent, "I daaance a role." He narrows his eyes. His nostrils flare. I hate his domineering, controlling ways. I hate how he thinks he can tell me what to do. I hate that he thinks he owns me. I hate feeling indebted to him, dependent on him.

"Your infantile jealousy is becoming quite tiresome," I say. I dip two fingers into the silver bowl of caviar, scoop up a big gob and suck it off. That just adds fuel to Vasily's anger. "Why can't you eat like a lady instead of a Gypsy animal?" he hisses. "Because you love it when I eat with my fingers," I taunt him. I lick and suck the remaining eggs and their slime off my fingers. I look straight into his eyes. "And you love all my Gypsy ways in bed, don't you?" He's spellbound. "All the wild animal things I do to you that your precious wife would never dream of doing?" I toss back the rest of my champagne and hold out my glass for him to fill. "You are mine," he says, in that dangerous clipped tone, "and I will not have the entire officer corps thinking they can invite you to dine with them. And that popinjay count, hanging about your dressing room? You are never to speak to him again, do you hear me?" I force a brittle laugh. "Count Oupensky?" I say, "He's harmless." We glare at each other across the table. I refuse to be dominated. "The fact is, Vasily, I am not yours, and I never will be." I pause for a sip of champagne. "Until you divorce the Princess and marry me, I am a free woman." I play with my emerald necklace, worth a small fortune I'm sure, enough to feed my family for an entire year. I stick my thumb under the large central stone, pulling the necklace out from my chest. "You can buy me all the jewels and clothes and carriages you like, but you can never buy my heart." I take off the emerald necklace and throw it in the fire. He jumps up and grabs the poker to save it from the fire. "You ungrateful little bitch!" he yells.

I watch Vasily stride about the room, trying to get himself under control. He's a magnificent specimen of a man, a pale Nordic god with broad shoulders, a narrow waist and strong thighs encased in tight breeches. My heart clenches with love and desire. I hate myself for it. I forbid myself to love him. He comes over to the table and falls on his knees before me. He clutches me around the waist with his head in my lap. "Katja," he moans, "You make me crazy. I only want to love you, I only want to be with you." He looks up at me, eyes frantic and desperate. "Why do you torment me like this?" He clutches me harder and buries his face in my skirts. I untie his ribbon and run my fingers through his silky blonde hair, such a contrast to my dark unruly curls. He'll never understand that I'm untamable. I can't be commanded, and that's exactly what he finds so irresistible. Our dance on the knife edge continues. We teeter between love and rage, desire and shame. I lift his head up and bend down to kiss him. He wants to consume me. I can sense the obsessive need in him. It repulses me. He's turned into one of those hungry ghosts my nana warned me about, whose bottomless hunger sucks the life right out of you. I pull back and sit straight up. Then I do something stupid and dangerous, something unforgivable. I laugh at him. "Vasily, such a little boy, begging for his mama's love." It's pathetic the way he clings me. I twist the knife. "What's the matter little boy, mama didn't love you enough?" He buries his head in my lap and groans, "Katja." I harden my heart, push him off me and stand up. "You disgust me," I say. His face contorts into a mask of pain and rage. He jumps to his feet and fastens his hands around my throat, crushing me between them. The last thing I see is the pain and rage in his eyes turning to love and regret.

I wake up this morning exhausted, feeling like I barely slept. I get to the office to find Timothy has inundated us with dozens of documents and a demand to present a preliminary brand brief in a week. I schedule a team meeting to figure out how to deliver a month's worth of work in six days. Five minutes later, Jessica shows up at my door. "Something's not right with Aquilo-Built," she says and plops down on my sofa. "What are you talking about?" I say. She's frowning, eyes narrowed. She crosses her legs and jiggles a foot up and down. "It doesn't make sense. Why would they give us the account? They should have gone with a big international agency." I haven't had time to think about it, but she's right. It is odd they chose our small regional agency. "And something's up with that Timothy guy," she says, rat-tat-tatting one perfectly manicured nail against her coffee cup. "He's definitely not happy about working with us." I think back on everything that happened in yesterday's meetings, and consider Timothy's snotty tone in a new light. She goes on, "He might be trying to sabotage us, setting us up to fail." I sigh. I can feel my shoulders and jaw tense up. "Why would he do want to do that?" I say. She stops tapping and jiggling and sits up straight. "I don't know, but I'm going to find out," she says in her don't-fuck-with-me tone. "Jessica, this is the biggest opportunity of both our careers. We cannot screw it up," I say. "We have to knock their socks off." My shoulders and jaw tense up even more. Jessica starts jiggling and rat-tat-tatting again. "Timothy is a bully. You're going to have to set some very firm boundaries with him." I sigh again and roll my eyes.

She gets up to leave, pauses at the door, hands on her hips, and says, "Don't look so freaked out. I'll get to the bottom of this. You just get to work on the brand brief." She grins at me and says, "Don't worry. We'll figure out how to handle Timothy. He's no match for the two of us!" After she flounces off, all my excitement about the account drains away. A vise grips my temples. Its jaws tighten as the pressure to perform clutches onto my fear of failure, squeezing the blood from my brain.

The week passes in a blur. We've worked like maniacs to pull something together for the presentation today. I've had lunch catered and the conference room looks fabulous, with flowers and mock-ups for Aquilo-Built brand images on display. I triple-check everything in a fit of anxiety. Ben walks the Aquilo team in, Timothy, Nico and his assistant, Valentina. Timothy is looking prim and proper in a double-breasted pin-striped suit, but Nico is casual again in a pair of jeans and a silky polo shirt. We all shake hands. Timothy's is cold and clammy and he grips so hard it hurts. Nico's hand sends a tingle up my arm and a flutter in my stomach. I chalk it up to nerves and nod at Roger to start the projection. I start the presentation and keep my focus on Nico. I try to ignore Timothy leaning back in his chair with his arms folded, looking like he's just caught a whiff of something foul in the air. I can tell we're on the right track when Nico leans forward, nodding his head and smiling. He exchanges an excited look with Valentina and she starts typing notes into her laptop. I'm on a roll, confident, in the zone, when Timothy interrupts me. "What makes you think any of this will work in the Chinese and Indian markets?" he says in a shitty-ass tone, his head cocked to one side and the corner of his lip curled up. Nico frowns. Valentina stops typing. Jessica rolls her eyes at me and turns to Timothy, all Southern sweetness. "Well, you make us think it'll work, Timothy," she says. "You sent us the inspiration." He scrunches his nose and forehead in confusion. "In the materials you sent over," she says. "It was so smart of you to commission that research." That shuts him up for a moment.

"Shelter is a universal human need and a universal human right," I say, "and beyond the need for shelter is the need for a home. People have powerful emotions and desires about their homes. Home is where we create a family, an identity, and a future. We can leverage the latest neuroscience to connect Aquilo-Built with those powerful emotions." Timothy scoffs. "That sounds like a bunch of ad-speak poppycock," he says. I bite back a snippy retort and take a breath to get my irritation under control. Valentina catches my eye and shrugs in apology. Nico looks surprised, then tight-lipped and annoyed. He shoots Timothy a frown and says, "Actually, Alexis is right on target. This is exactly why I wanted to go with them." He turns back to me and says, "You took a similar approach with that solar campaign, didn't you?"

"Yes, we did," I say. I don't know what's going on with Timothy, but I don't want to alienate him any further. He's tapping his pen against his pad, staring at me with his pale blues eyes frozen. "I can appreciate Timothy's healthy skepticism, but the science behind it is solid. Of course, there's an art to applying the research to a specific audience and brand. That's our aim with Aquilo-Built. However, we could take more time to conduct extensive market research if you want to delay the launch."

Nico holds up a hand and jumps in. "I'm not opposed to more market research, but I don't want any delays." He stands up to end the meeting. Timothy looks a bit miffed, like he wasn't quite done with me yet. "I'm impressed," Nico says. "This is just what I was looking for. Send over the slide deck and we'll review it." He turns and walks out of the conference room. God, he looks good walking away. Keep it together, Alexis! Valentina closes her laptop, stands up and gives me a big smile. "Great job," she says, then cuts her eyes towards Timothy. "You handled that well." Timothy stands up, turns his back on me and walks out of the conference room. Jessica shakes her head, rolls her eyes, then jumps up and goes after him. Ben comes over and puts his hand on my shoulder. "Don't worry about Timothy," he says. "You rocked it! He's just pissed Nico overruled him on the agency selection. You gave Nico what he wanted, so stay the course." Sure, stay the course — between a rock and a hard place. All I have to do is keep Timothy from tearing me apart and avoid getting caught in Nico's whirlpool. Sounds easy, right?

CHAPTER SEVEN

Sea Gypsy

When I get to the office this morning, there's an envelope on my desk with my name on it, made from a heavy, creamy paper. My name is hand-written on the front in a large clear script. Inside is a single sheet of the same thick paper folded in half. There's an engraved stamp of an eagle's head in lapis blue at the top, with the initials "NA." It's a note from Nico: "Alexis, I'd like to meet with you privately. Please join me for lunch. A car will pick you up at 1. Sorry about Timothy." A thrill of excitement skitters through my nervous system. I examine the note again, study the large open letters in what looks to be ink from a fountain pen. Who uses a fountain pen these days? I don't see any way to respond, no contact information. Does he just assume I'll drop everything and join him? Of course he does. He gave us the biggest account this agency has ever seen, and certainly the biggest account I've ever worked on. My phone rings. It's his assistant, Valentina, calling to confirm. I've got meetings all morning. No time to go home and change. I'll have to show up to lunch in jeans and a silk blouse. Oh well, nothing to be done. He was business casual yesterday, but I'd like to at least appear as though I can handle a major league account. My meetings run long, which is a blessing in a way. It leaves me no time to fret.

A black Tesla waits for me at the curb. The driver hops out and opens the back door. "Good afternoon, Ms. Rykof," he says, "My name is Jackson. Mr. Aquilo sent me to pick you up. He's waiting for you at the marina." Lunch at Marina Del Rey sounds good to me. It's a beautiful spring day and we get there in about twenty minutes. But Jackson doesn't pull up at any of the restaurants or hotels. Instead, he pulls up by a dock and escorts me through the locked gates where a powerful speedboat waits, engines idling. "Sonny will take you to the yacht, Ms. Rykof," he says, "Enjoy your lunch. I'll be here to take you back to your office when you return." He hands me down into the boat, makes sure I'm seated comfortably and casts off. Lunch on a yacht? Gotta hand it to Nico, he sure has style. Once we clear the harbor, the engines rev and we race straight out to sea. We pull up behind a huge yacht about two hundred feet long, all sleek modern lines, with "Sea Gypsy" painted on the back. A steward waits to greet me at the platform. "Welcome aboard, Ms. Rykof," he says, "My name is Jimmy. Follow me please." He leads me up to an outdoor dining deck where Nico's waiting.

Nico stands up to greet me with a kiss on each cheek. So much for yesterday's formality of a handshake. "Welcome, Alexis," he says with big smile. "I hope you don't mind me shanghai-ing you out to sea for our lunch."

There's no pretending I'm not impressed. I've never been on a boat like this before. "Not at all, Nico. Your boat is stunning." We sit down to a beautifully set table. A steward pours fresh-made lemonade. Nico looks relaxed in jeans and a white polo shirt. As lunch is served, he gushes about the boat's eco-friendly design features. "I love being on the ocean," he says, "and I wanted a fast ocean-going yacht, but they're environmental nightmares. I refused to compromise my principles, so I designed this with the Italian shipyard. It's the first of its kind." Nico gazes at his creation like a proud papa. "I admire your commitment," I say, "Was it a difficult process?" He shrugs. "It took a bit to convince the shipbuilders," he says, "but I had a world-renowned naval architect and an engineering team from our company working on it. I'll give you a tour later if you like." His eyes crinkle and he breaks into a big smile. "I think you'll agree no comfort or convenience was sacrificed to achieve net zero energy consumption." I study him as we dig into our delicious lunch, sea bass locally caught and vegetables organically grown in the ship's vertical solar-powered gardens. I hadn't noticed his eyes yesterday. In the bright light reflecting off the water, they're a brilliant, emerald green. With his dark, curly hair, his strong features, and his muscular athlete's body just beginning to thicken, he really is quite the hunk. I think back to my Google research, trying to remember if his age was stated anywhere. He looks to be somewhere in his early forties. My pussy-meter starts purring. I tell it to shut up. This man is off-limits, do you hear me? There's no way I can risk this career opportunity by getting involved with my client, no matter how gorgeous, charming and impressive he may be. It's time to act professional and get down to business.

"Nico, forgive me if I'm being too direct, but I'm curious," I say. "Of all the agencies in the world to choose from, why did you pick us?" I hold my breath. He laughs. "Not too direct at all, Alexis," he says. "It's a fair question. I brought this project to your agency because of you." Ben had told me as much, but I still don't know the reason why. "That's very flattering Nico, but we've never met before and we're just a regional agency. Why would you put the launch of your company in our hands? It's obvious that environmental concerns are a serious passion of yours, and your vision is global." Nico watches me with an amused smile. I smooth my napkin and go on. "Don't get me wrong — I'm thrilled to work on this. But I'd like to understand the reasons why you've entrusted us with so much responsibility." I hope I haven't been too blunt, but it just doesn't add up. Now it's his turn to study me. I try not to fidget, blush or look away. I make myself take slow, quiet breaths. He's looking at me with a steady, unwavering gaze. I get lost in his eyes. Something about them feels so familiar. Those eyes, those eyes, I know those eyes. The faces of the three men from my dreams last night appear superimposed over Nico's face, one after another. I gasp and shake my head to clear my vision. I take a sip of lemonade to break the spell. "Everything OK?" he says. The lemonade goes down wrong and I start choking. When I recover, he's leaning forward, looking at me with a concerned expression. "Alexis, are you alright?" he asks. "Excuse me," I say, "I'm fine now. Please go on." I try to push the memories out of my mind. I refuse to feel those women's emotions. It would only confuse the present situation. Now is not the time to consider the implications.

"Well, it's a little embarrassing, really," Nico says. He looks down. Fiddles with his fork. Adjusts his napkin. Takes a sip of lemonade. He's nervous. It's adorable. I wait silently. "I guess I don't have a rational explanation," he says. "I make a lot of my decisions based on intuition. I saw that campaign for the state solar initiative and I thought it was brilliant. Something about it captured the kind of tone I want. I did a little digging to find out who was behind it and looked at some of your other work. I know it sounds crazy, but I just knew you were the right person for the job." I don't know what to say to that. I wonder if he's also had dreams of our past lives together. Maybe there's some sort of homing device inside us. "I'm very intuitive, too," I say. "I'm sure you've learned to trust your intuition with all you've accomplished. I appreciate your trust and I hope I don't ever disappoint you." Nico smiles and reaches out for my hand. "I know you won't," he says, "We're going to be working very closely together. Normally I wouldn't be so involved, but I am passionate about transforming the built world. This new company is my baby." That gets the pussy-meter purring again. Or maybe it's his hand. I can't help it. I love his vision. It matches my own concerns, my own desires to do work with a far-reaching impact. I think of all that is possible, all we can achieve with his money and power behind us. Maybe it's more than that. Maybe it's his presence, the sheer physical reality of him. He's still holding my hand. Warm currents of energy stream up my arm, into my heart and down to my pussy. "Do not blow this," I warn myself. "Keep it professional. Friendly, but professional." I'd like to just sit here, holding hands, looking into those gorgeous green eyes, fantasizing about a romantic future, remembering our past lives. I pull myself together and gently disengage my hand from his.

"So, Nico, why am I here? What did you want to accomplish with our lunch today?" It's not like me to be so direct with a new client. Maybe I'm overcompensating for my attraction. I force myself to sit calmly, not to say anything else, just wait. I watch him gather into himself. He closes his eyes for a moment, takes a deep breath. I can feel his energy shift. He opens his eyes and begins to speak about his vision for the company and for the world. His focus is a laser, and the power that radiates off him is palpable. We adjourn to an office on the next deck down, and for the next three hours, we brainstorm on whiteboards, pore over diagrams and charts, make mind maps while his assistant Valentina takes notes. I wasn't prepared for any of this. I didn't even bring my laptop. The more he shares, the more he blows me away. He may be the most brilliant person I've ever met, and I've known some pretty brilliant people in my life. At one point, I just sit back and watch him as he paces up and down the room. The pussy-meter revs her engines. I ignore her and focus on the work at hand. Our creativity and thinking processes are very simpatico. We go back and forth, laying out different strategies, inspiring each other with off-the-wall ideas. It's like playing tennis with a top-ranked player. It elevates your game. I'm having a blast. After three hours, the walls of whiteboards are covered with our work. We take a break and sit back to look at it. His assistant, Valentina, a lovely and competent young Italian woman, asks if we'd like some refreshments. "Good idea," Nico says, "But have them serve it on the top deck." He turns back to me with a big grin, "I think we deserve a break, don't you? We've done enough for one afternoon." I wave my hand at the whiteboards, nod and smile back at him. "I agree," I say, "Any more and my circuits might short out." On the way up to the top deck, Nico says, "I know I promised you a tour, but it's a big boat. It will take us a while. Is it alright with you if we postpone it for next time?" There will be a next time. Be still my beating heart. "Yes, of course, Nico. I look forward to it."

Up on the top deck, the sky is beginning to color pink and orange with the approaching sunset. "How did it get to be so late?" I say. He stands beside me, gives my hand a quick squeeze. "Time flies when the work is fun," Nico says. "I hope our impromptu work session hasn't disrupted anything urgent on your schedule this afternoon." Hah! As though anything could be more important than working with Nico. "Not at all," I say. "I planned to work on pulling the team together and beginning research on the launch strategy. This was perfect. Even better." The deck is fitted out with comfortable built-in sofas and low tables. There's a wet bar, too. "I feel like we should celebrate the beginning of our partnership," Nico says. Then he looks at me with the most adorable expression on his face — wide-eyed, eager, mischievous, confident. "It is a partnership, isn't it, Alexis? That's what I want it to be." A blast of energy fills my heart. Hope. Excitement. Anticipation. I can't even consider the possibility of love, or whatever. I take a deep shaky breath. I need to give my heart a chance to expand enough to hold the energy. "I'd like that, Nico," I say, "With all we accomplished today, I think we can agree we're off to an excellent start." I see that look again from when we first met, like he's trying to figure out how we know each other. There's a brief flash of longing in his eyes before he turns away. I notice his shoulders stiffen. Keep it professional.

"Do you like champagne?" he asks me. Do I like champagne? Do fish like to swim? Do birds like to fly? Do horses like to run? "I like champagne very much," I say. He pulls a bottle of Louis Roederer Cristal Rosé from the wine cooler and two exquisite crystal champagne flutes from the cabinet. They look like Baccarat. He brings them to the table and shows me the bottle. It's a 2004. "I know Cristal has become the official champagne of the club scene, but this Rosé is really a favorite of mine." He opens the bottle with the skill of a master sommelier and pours the blush pink wine into our glasses. I stare at his hands. Large, strong, beautiful hands. Hands with the callouses and big knuckles of a fighter or an athlete. "Here's a little bit of champagne trivia," he says, eyes sparkling as he expounds on one of his enthusiasms. "Cristal was first made for Tsar Alexander II, who asked Louis Roederer to reserve his finest annual cuvée for him. It was bottled in a transparent, lead-crystal bottle, which was a new thing at the time. Thus the name — Cristal."

I'm back to a midnight dinner in St. Petersburg, my lover in black tails and white tie. I'm still revved up from my performance, my debut as Kitri in Don Quixote. He picks up his glass of the same pale pink champagne to toast to my success. Then he pulls a black jewelry box out of his breast pocket and presents me with a magnificent ruby and diamond necklace, walks around the table to hang it around my neck. He adjusts the plum-sized, heart-shaped ruby dangling from the center to settle between my breasts. "I'd like to make a toast," Nico says, and jolts me back into the present. I shake my head to clear the vision and pick up my glass. I keep my eyes on the glass. I don't want to look at him. I don't know what I'll see. "Here's to a long and happy partnership," he says, "and to changing the world." We clink glasses. "To changing the world," I echo back. I take a big swallow of the champagne. I need to calm my nerves. I take another sip, to let myself savor it this time. "This is the best champagne I've ever tasted," I say, "It's nectar of the gods." He smiles, happy to please me. "I'm so glad you like it. My friends tease me that I prefer champagne over whiskey, or other more macho spirits, but I love the finesse and complexity of fine champagne. Besides," he grins, "the bubbles make me happy." Could he be any cuter?

Jimmy the steward arrives with a platter of hors d'oeuvres, a mini-feast of Provençal delicacies. We linger over the champagne and appetizers as a majestic sunset rolls across the sky, chat about our childhoods and our mutual love of the water. I want to know everything about him, but I try to keep myself from turning our conversation into an interview, or worse, an interrogation. He's happy to talk to me anyway. I learn Nico grew up in Milan and spent summers at the family villa in Sardinia. He was a competitive skier and windsurfer in his teens, but he decided he wasn't willing to devote his life to competitive sports. Sailing is his life-long love, beginning with crewing for his grandfather in the races at the Yacht Club Costa Smeralda. The sun sets. The magical afternoon ends. Nico walks me down to the floating platform at the stern to see me off. He takes both my hands in his and looks down for a moment. Electric currents shoot from his hands up my arms into my heart. He lifts his head and looks into my eyes. Those eyes. I know those eyes. "Alexis, thank you for seeing my vision with me," Nico says, "I am so happy to be working together." Then he leans in and kisses me on each cheek and sends me back to the marina in the speedboat. Jackson is waiting dockside with the car. The Tesla cruises back to the office.

I wander my apartment aimlessly when I get back home. I don't know what to do with myself. My emotions ricochet around, bounce from balloon to cookie jar, from chopping block to sparkling water. I feel window shade, dust mote, completely unsettled. There's a *milonga* tonight. I could go dance. I haven't been dancing in almost two weeks. Somehow, the thought of being in a man's arms, a man who isn't Nico, feels all wrong. I draw a bath, then pull the plug. I pick up the phone to call Cheryl, then hang up before it rings. I flip through the bobby pins on the coffee table, and the images don't even register. Then I start cleaning, cleaning like a crazy person, like an OCD on crystal meth, like my life depends on removing every speck of dirt. It's 10 at night and I'm sitting in front of the kitchen cabinet, surrounded by cleaning products, sponges, folded paper bags and boxes of trash bags. I give the cabinet one more swipe and throw the sponge down. What the fuck am I doing? I shove everything back in the cabinet, peel off the gloves and throw them in. I wash the rubber smell off my hands and rub on hand lotion, then walk to my bedroom. My closet beckons. I turn on the light and start to sort through my wardrobe, pulling out everything I haven't worn for at least a year. The clothes pile up on the floor. I go back into the kitchen for garbage bags, stuff them all in and haul them out to the front door. It's almost midnight. "Jesus Christ, Alexis," I huff, "What is your fucking problem? Go to bed." But I know what my fucking problem is. Nico.

When I get to my office this morning, there's another heavy cream envelope on my desk with my name on the front in the same bold script. "Dear Alexis," it says, "Thank you for our productive and delightful afternoon. I'd like you to visit our manufacturing and design facilities. Valentina will be in touch with details. Ciao, Nico." I try to remember where in the world these facilities might be, but I only have a vague sense of somewhere in Italy. Before I can spin off into any fantasies about a couple's trip to Italy, people arrive for my first meeting. I'm forced to stay focused on the work at hand with back-to-back meetings all day long. Timothy has sent over another huge packet of materials. Valentina organized all our work from yesterday and sent those files over as well. With the core team assembled, I fill them in on the work so far and delegate like a madwoman. Ben, Jessica and I meet over lunch. I negotiate a new role for Jessica that elevates her to my second-in-command. I need her as my partner in this. Of all the people in our agency, I trust her the most. Ben wants to get more involved, but this account is going to consume our lives. When Jessica points out the danger to Ben and the company of putting all our eggs in the Aquilo Group basket, he backs off. It's not that I don't want Ben involved, or that I don't value his ideas and input, but something shifted in me yesterday. I feel responsible for communicating Nico's vision to the world. I want to protect it, to make sure we get it right. This realization triggers another avalanche of complicated emotions I have no time to process today. I know Nico won't want anyone else taking lead on the account.

It's late, almost 8:00 PM when I finally wrap up for the day. My cell phone rings. It's an unlisted number. Normally I never answer calls unless I know who it is, but what if it's Nico? "Hello," I say. "Good evening, Ms. Rykof, it's Valentina." It feels weird to be addressed so formally. "Valentina, please call me Alexis," I say. "You call Mr. Aquilo Nico, don't you?" She hesitates a moment. "Well, yes," she says, "but I want to be respectful. Nico has asked all of us to take special care of you and make sure you have everything you need." My heart gives a flutter. "I appreciate the respect, but call me Alexis when it's just us, OK?" I could get used to Nico taking special care of me. "D'accordo, Alexis," she says. "I'm calling to confirm arrangements to visit the design center and the manufacturing plant. Can you leave this Thursday?" I open my calendar to see another day of back-to-back meetings. "Of course. Where am I going and how long will I be gone?" I ask. "Your first stop is Milan. After that, it's up to Nico," she says. "I see," I say. My mind is racing. Milan! I've never even been to Italy. Do I need a visa? I try to remember the expiration date on my passport. "A car will pick you up at 7 in the morning, if that's not too early for you." I'm still trying to process what she means by, "after that, it's up to Nico." Will I be alone with him? What about the weekend? Surely he wouldn't fly me all the way to Italy just for one day? I don't trust myself alone with the man. I need some time to think this through. "I'd like to bring one of my team along," I say, "Would that be alright? I can let you know who in the morning." If I have the buffer of another person, I just might be able to keep this relationship on a professional footing. That's what I tell myself, anyway. The note from Nico sits propped up against my computer screen. The lapis blue eagle floats off the page and circles around my head. Then it spreads its wings and takes off around the office. "I'm sure that will be fine," Valentina says, "There's plenty of room on the plane." I hold out my hand and the eagle comes in for a landing just above my wrist. Its tiny talons dig into my skin. "I'm sorry, can you repeat that?" I ask. "I just said 'ciao,' and that we'll talk in the morning," she says. I bring my arm up to my face to get a closer look at the eagle. Its eyes are green, like Nico's. "Right, ciao, Valentina. Thank you for calling," I say on automatic. I glance down to hang up the cell phone. When I look up again, the eagle is gone. I reach for the note paper and pick it up. The lapis blue eagle is perched in the same position as before. I run my finger over the engraving.

Jessica's my first choice to accompany me, but I need her to hold down the fort, especially at this stage of the process. My second choice is my assistant Natalie, but there's no way both of us can be gone at the same time. I'll need her here to run interference and keep everything coordinated. Maybe I should bring Roger. He is the creative director, at least for now, and he should see the design center in person. Besides, if he's with me, I'm sure to behave myself. Milan is my last thought before I fall asleep. Milan! Milan! I'm going to Milan!

I walk over to Roger's office first thing in the morning, but he's not here yet. Surf must be up. I leave a post-it note to call me on his computer screen. His assistant, another surfer dude, strolls in with coffee as I'm walking out. "Tell Roger to call me as soon as he gets in," I say. "It's urgent." It's two hours before Roger knocks on my office door. I suppress my irritation and try not to judge his laid-back attitude. He does good work and the art department loves him. Besides, I have to use him. I have no other choice. "Roger, how'd you like to go to Milan with me and tour the Aquilo Group's design center?" I ask him. "Awesome," he says, "I would love to go. When do we leave?" he asks. "Tomorrow at 7:00 AM," I say. "Meet me at my place. A car will pick us up." Just to be on the safe side, I ask him, "You do have a current passport, right?" Roger grins and says, "You bet I do. I was in Costa Rica over Christmas this year." He shakes his head with a wistful look in his eyes. "The waves were killer, man." I roll my eyes and call Valentina to give her Roger's info. "Will the driver have the tickets and boarding passes?" I ask her. "Oh no, no boarding passes, Alexis," she says, "We're all flying over together in the company jet." The office is buzzing with activity this morning. Sunlight floods through the window onto the coffee table. It bounces off the two ceramic yellow pots of miniature daffodils, filling my office with a lemony glow. "Who's we? Who's flying over with us?" I ask. "Well, you, me, Roger, Nico, and Timothy for sure," she says. "There may be one or two others. Why?" A private jet? Holy shit! "No reason, just curious," I say. I've never flown on a private jet. And I'm going to Milan. With Nico. The others don't count. "OK, thanks Valentina," I say, "I'll see you in the morning." I immediately book a wax appointment for the late afternoon. I'll have to fit in a pedicure after that. And pack. After that vicious pruning in my closet, that part shouldn't be too hard.

CHAPTER EIGHT

Milan

I've packed light for the trip, just enough for a long weekend. At the last minute I throw in that old one-piece bathing suit, the one with the flattering fit. I've been a good girl. I packed only one sexy dress, the rest is casual business attire. My doorman rings up at 6:55 AM to let me know the car is waiting. I go downstairs. Roger isn't here. Damn that man! I text him, "The car is here. Where r u?" No reply. Jackson, the driver from the other day, loads my two carry-on bags into the trunk. I give Roger another five minutes, then tell Jackson to leave without him. "He can meet us at Van Nuys Airport," Jackson says. I text him again. No reply. At the airport, Nico's special agent on the ground ushers me onto the waiting jet. Valentina is there to welcome me. *"Buongiorno,* Alexis," she says, "Nico is on a conference call in the office. May I get you something to drink? Breakfast will be served after we take off." The plane is luxurious with built-in sofas, large reclining seats with tables and a kitchen. "Some Darjeeling tea if you have it," I say, "And Roger isn't here. He never made it to my apartment this morning. I have no idea what's happened to him. When do we take off?" The steward has come back to confer with Valentina on the final head count prior to closing the door. "We'll take off any minute now," she says, "I'm sorry, but we're not going to be able to wait for Roger." Just then, my phone chirps. It's a text from Roger. "Sorry, can't make it. Broke my ankle. Going into surgery." Well, there goes my chaperone. I text back, "Sorry to hear that. Good luck with the surgery." The doors close. We taxi out to the runway and take off. My first ride in a private jet!

It's a long trip to Milan from Los Angeles, twelve hours. Nico works through most of the flight. I sit in on some of his work sessions with Timothy, Valentina and Deming, the head of his material sciences company. I spend the rest of the time catching up on emails, dozing, reading or watching a movie. The steward keeps us well fed with a scrumptious breakfast and lunch. When we land, it's 5 AM local time. Two black Teslas wait on the tarmac when we come down the stairs. Nico asks me to join him in one car and everybody else takes off in the other. "I hope you don't mind," Nico says, "I've arranged for you to stay in my family home." My heart thrills. He wants me close. The car speeds through the early dawn streets. I feel rumpled and stiff from the flight. "I want you to see where I grew up, and it will be more comfortable than a hotel," he adds. We pull up to a gate set in a high wall. The gate opens and we drive into the courtyard of an imposing mansion. A man comes out the front door as we pull up. Two Italian greyhounds bound out behind him and go crazy when they see Nico. Nico introduces me to Giuseppe, his majordomo, and his two dogs, Sofia and Beppe. "Giuseppe will show you to your rooms," Nico says. "If you like, you can join me in my jet lag recovery protocol. It keeps me functional with all the flying I do across multiple time zones." I perk up. "What does that look like?" I ask. He goes into one of his enthusiastic geek outs again. "First a shower, then an IV drip of various antioxidants, vitamins and minerals my doctor devised while we get an acupuncture treatment to reset our biological clock. Then twenty minutes of laps in the pool followed by twenty minutes in the infrared sauna and a green juice power smoothie. I finish it off with a deep meditation or nap for thirty minutes. It takes about two hours total and I'm completely functional for the rest of the day." This man impresses me over and over again. "That sounds fantastic," I say. "Count me in!" I say. He beams. Sofia and Beppe circle me, wagging their tails and sniffing me out. I'm happy I meet their approval. "Giuseppe will show you where everything is. I'll meet you by the pool in fifteen minutes."

Giuseppe escorts me to a guest suite on the second floor. "Anna will unpack and iron for you, Ms. Rykof," he says in a charming Italian accent. He gestures to a uniformed maid hovering in the background with my two bags in hand. "There's a robe hanging in the bathroom," he says, "and pool slippers, too." He shows me into the enormous marble bathroom, then steps back in the bedroom and opens a set of French doors to the patio. "The pool house is just at the end of the garden," he points out. "Take the stairs down and follow the path. If you need anything, please let Anna know. She'll be looking after you." I'm a little overwhelmed by all this grandeur and attention. Anna gives me a shy smile and gestures to my bag. "Is OK?" she asks. She's short and round, somewhere in her early sixties, with dark hair pulled back in a bun. "Yes, Anna," I say, *"Grazie."* Anna brings my toiletries into the bathroom and sets them next to an array of high-end Italian bath and beauty products. Then she leaves and closes the door behind her. I don't want to keep Nico waiting. I strip down and hop in the shower. When I come out, my bathing suit is laid out on the bed with the pool slippers on the floor. There's no sign of Anna.

I walk over to the pool house through a lush, well-tended garden, accompanied by the burbling sound of water features. Nico reclines in a wide lounge chair with an IV tube attached to one arm while a woman inserts acupuncture needles into his ears. "Ah, Alexis, you're in for a treat. I've refined this protocol over the last few years and it works like magic," he says. "This is my doctor, Juliana." She quickly finishes up with Nico and sets me up with an IV. I feel much better after the treatment. Then we go for a swim. I wish I had a nicer, newer bathing suit, and decide to remedy the situation at the first opportunity. Nico wears a pair of fitted swim trunks. I try not to stare at his classic Adonis figure with broad shoulders tapering to a narrow waist. I do my best not to look at his package. Despite some thickening through the middle, he's still a prime specimen of hunky manhood.

He's a real Italian stallion. I suck in my stomach and dive in after him. Nico does two laps for every one of mine and I soon give up trying to keep up with him. He hauls himself out after twenty minutes. I finish the lap and arrive breathless at the edge. He reaches a hand down and lifts me up like I weigh nothing at all. Next is the infrared sauna. Nico explains that it penetrates deeper than a regular sauna and rattles off half a dozen health benefits. He puts on Japanese Zen flute music. "Please don't think me rude," he says, "But I like to use this time to quiet and rest my mind. It's one of my secrets to peak performance." I lay down on the bench and float away with the music. In what feels like no time at all, the timer goes off. I'm covered in sweat. "Now we hydrate," Nico says. There are two large glasses of fresh green juice waiting for us on the table between the lounge chairs. He finishes it in a few short gulps. "I'm going to my room for a short nap," Nico says, "I'll meet you in the garden for a light breakfast in an hour. Then we'll go to the design center, OK?"

I feel light and clean and a little drowsy from the sauna. I take another quick shower in my room to wash off the sweat, then I lay down on the bed and put my headphones on. The Tibetan singing bowl music sends me into a deep meditative state. Next thing I know, there's a knock on my door. It's Anna bearing a mug of Darjeeling tea, made just the way I like it. She gestures to my hair, still wet. She points to herself and asks, "Hair dry?" I feel like I'm in a modern-day episode of Downton Abbey, with my own personal lady's maid. "*Si, grazie,*" I say. She does a quick and expert job. My hair looks sexy and polished when she finishes. I quickly put on some makeup and get dressed. It's only 8:00 AM by the time I head back out to the garden. I feel like a new woman, refreshed, energized and clean, inside and out.

After another wonderful meal, we leave for the design center. This time, Nico takes the wheel. He maneuvers us through Milan's infamous traffic like he's the love child of Mario Andretti and Neo from the Matrix. I shriek at a near-miss and Nico grins at me like a naughty boy. After the first adrenalin rush of terror, I relax and enjoy the thrill ride. I might as well admit it — he's taken control, and I like it. I watch his big beautiful hands on the wheel and imagine them on my body. I study his profile, his strong nose, his full-lipped mouth. He does resemble an eagle, face calm and eyes intent, as he steers us around the crazy drivers. I marvel at his powers of concentration. The whole thing's kind of turning me on.

The design center is a revelation. Nico presents its treasures to me with his typical enthusiasm. It's cute. I can tell he's trying to impress me. I don't understand everything they're working on, but the prototypes and miniature models give me an excellent sense of the possibilities. Nico's passion is infectious. I love to see him geek out over one detail or another. We lunch in the company cafeteria, but this is Italy, and this is Nico's cafeteria. The food here would pass for a Michelin-rated restaurant.

After lunch, Nico leaves for other meetings. I meet with Valentina, Deming, and some of his lead designers to go over the different construction materials and 3-D animations. We discuss security procedures for the prototypes and compare the differences in international building codes. For the first time, I wish Roger were here to see all this. By the time we finish for the day, it's close to 5:00 PM. I'm astonished. I haven't gotten any sleep for over 24 hours (except for a couple of naps), but my energy has held up through this long, intense day. Damn if that jet lag protocol isn't magic after all. Valentina needs to make a couple of calls before we leave. I use the time to check email. I don't know who she's talking to, but it sounds like she's giving orders. "I just need to send a quick email to Nico," she says, "then we can go." She turns to me with a huge smile on her face. "Alexis, you are in for a treat tonight," she says. "But first — we must shop!" Valentina is one of the brightest, most efficient women I've ever met. She can't be more than thirty years old, but she has the poise and confidence of a woman at least ten years her senior. She's a beauty herself, with long, lovely dark hair, a wide easy smile and big brown eyes. She's slightly on the heavy side, but she's well-proportioned and she carries it well. "Why, where are we going?" I ask. She winks. "It's a surprise," she says. "I cannot say." A driver is waiting outside with another black Tesla. Nico must buy these things by the dozen! Valentina hesitates by the car. "Alexis, *Milano* traffic is awful," she says. "It will take us forever by car. Do you mind if we go by scooter?" Another street adventure? I gulp. When in Milan, do as the Milanese do. "Sure, Valentina," I say. My stomach butterflies. "Why not?" Valentina leads me to a row of electric scooters and puts our bags and laptops in the storage bin. She hands me a cute yellow helmet and we take off. After a nerve-wracking fifteen minutes, sure we'll be killed any moment, Valentina pulls into a narrow street of shops.

She leads me into a boutique full of fabulous clothes and begins a rapid-fire conversation in Italian with the sales clerk. We sit at a small couch and they serve us tiny cups of espresso. I rarely drink coffee, but I daren't refuse. Fortified with high-octane caffeine, we lounge as the sales clerk presents us with a bouquet of dresses. "But what are we doing here Valentina?" I ask, "What are we shopping for?" She winks at me again, smiles that generous smile of hers and says, "I've arranged a special evening for you. All I can say is that I must find you something that makes you feel beautiful, something you can move in freely." I surrender. Why on Earth would I resist buying a beautiful dress in Milan? One dress in particular catches my eye. It's a deep ruby red with a V-cut in the front, a deeper V-cut in the back, a fitted bodice and a skirt that swirls out, shorter in the front than the back. Something about it feels vaguely Flamenco or gypsyish to me. Black lace covers the bodice and the panels of the skirt. I try it on. The shoulders need to be pulled up, but otherwise it fits perfectly. I twirl around in the mirror, swirling the skirt to wrap around my hips and thighs. This would make an amazing tango dress. I turn and pose, check to see how it looks from all angles in the three-way mirror. "Valentina, I have to have this dress!" I say. "But it needs to be altered. What will I wear tonight?" More rapid-fire Italian ensues and the sales clerk goes off to make a phone call. We sit down for a little aperitivo of Prosecco and Campari. Ten minutes later, a little elderly Italian woman arrives with a sewing basket to pin up the shoulders of the dress. Valentina pays for it despite my protests and hustles me out of the shop.

We get back on the scooter for another death-defying ride to arrive at a shoe store, but not just any shoe store. This store specializes in tango shoes. "Girls' night out? Are we going tango dancing?" I ask Valentina. She puts her finger to her lips. I see a pair of red and black shoes that would go perfectly with my new dress. Fifteen minutes later, we're on the scooter headed back to the first store, shoes in tow. The little old seamstress has worked her magic. My dress is ready. I try it on again and slip into the new shoes. The ladies all crowd around exclaiming over my appearance. *"Bellissimo!"* *"Magnifico!"* *"Sfarvoso!"* Valentina's looking at me like I'm her daughter on prom night. "Alexis, you look absolutely gorgeous," Valentina says. The sales clerk holds up her hand, says, *"Aspetta, aspetta,"* and runs out of the dressing room. "What's the problem?" I ask Valentina. "I don't know," she says. The sales clerk comes back with a pair of black and red chandelier earrings that set the dress off to perfection. I love them! Valentina still refuses to let me pay. We leave the store with our purchases wrapped up in a bag. I sling it over my shoulder and hop back on the scooter. Valentina weaves in and out of traffic to pull up to Nico's gate, rings the bell and waves at the camera. The gates open and we pull into the courtyard. Giuseppe hurries out to help with the bags. The two of them whisper together like co-conspirators. "Valentina, that was so much fun! Thank you for the best shopping trip ever!" I give her a big hug. "It was my pleasure, Alexis." She gives me a kiss goodbye on each cheek. "Have a great time tonight!" she says and takes off with a jaunty wave. "Wait, what time are you picking me up?" I call after her.

"Be ready to leave for dinner at nine," Giuseppe tells me. That gives me just about an hour to get ready. Plenty of time. I decide to take a bath in the huge marble tub. Giuseppe hands my bags off to Anna. She oohs and ahhs as she unwraps the dress and shoes. I usher her out of my rooms as gently as I can. It's not that I don't love being pampered, but I need some alone time. I sniff all the different bath salts and oils, find one that smells like roses and pour a generous amount in the tub. I pin up my hair and take off my makeup. I want to use a face mask, but I can't read Italian, so I'm not sure what all the different products are for. I opt for the Moroccan clay mask I brought with me, light the row of candles around the edge of the tub and slide into the hot fragrant water. I lay back on the bath pillow, close my eyes and breathe. It's been a whirlwind — the flight, Nico's grand estate, then the design center and all the work going on there. It's a lot to process. No more time to think. I've got to get out of the tub and get dressed.

I sit at the vanity and put on my makeup. I decide to go for dark smoky eyes and a neutral lip. I walk out to the bedroom and see that Anna has laid out my dress and shoes. She's even left a fresh red rose attached to a hair clip. Really, Anna? That's a bit much. I put on the dress and shoes. Normally I would never wear tango shoes in the street, but oh well. I slip on the earrings and assess myself in the mirror. I twirl around. I look gorgeous, even if I do say so myself, hot, sultry and elegant. I pick up the rose and walk back to the vanity. As I pull back one side of my hair and pin it above my ear, I hear a warning voice: "Be careful. Don't let this man take over your life." She has a heavy Russian-sounding accent. I see another woman's face in the mirror, a striking young woman with dark hair and black eyes. It's the woman from my dream, the ballerina. Her name pops into my head. Katja. What is she talking about? I close my eyes, shake my head and take a deep breath. When I open them again, my face stares back at me.

Nico greets me at the front hall. "Good evening, Alexis. I guess Valentina made plans for us? You look spectacular in that dress." He's dashing in a perfectly tailored Italian suit of such a deep green it's almost black. His emerald silk tie makes the green of his eyes pop. "You look pretty good yourself," I say. "Valentina insisted I wear this suit," he says. I laugh. "She does seem to be in charge tonight," I say. The driver is waiting out front, but Nico dismisses him. He ushers me into the front seat and waits for me to adjust my skirt. Once he's behind the wheel I ask him where we're going. "I've been assigned to take you out to dinner and dancing, apparently," he says. The Tesla zooms silently out of the gate. "I didn't know you danced tango," I say. He smiles but says nothing as he negotiates through evening traffic. In a few minutes, we arrive at a small restaurant.

The owner greets Nico at the door with a huge smile and a rapid stream of Italian. He seats us immediately and claps his hands to summon the wait staff. There's flurry of activity at our table. Nico and the waiter confer in Italian and my menu gets whisked away before I even get to read it. He's ordered for us both. I feel a brief flash of annoyance. Is it mine or Katja's? I try to get things back under control and ask him about one of the prototypes I saw today. "No business talk tonight," Nico says, "We deserve a break, no?" He's got that mischievous look on his face again, the one I find so irresistible, green eyes twinkling with a lop-sided grin. A small saucer of balsamic vinegar makes a swirling pattern in its little sea of olive oil. "OK," I agree, "What should we talk about?" The restaurant is full on a Friday evening, a mix of families and couples dining in this elegant wood-paneled, flower-filled room. "Let's talk about music and food, two of my favorite subjects," he smiles and leans in. "What kind of music do you like?" He's looking straight at me, head tilted to one side. I feel like I'm on a first date. Shit, I guess this is our first date. I can't be dating him! "My tastes are pretty eclectic," I tell him, "I listen to a lot of chill lounge, electronica, reggae, world music, classic rock, soul, R&B. Everything except for country and opera. What about you?" Nico sits back. "My tastes are a bit more esoteric," he tells me, "I'm a big fan of post-tonal music and jazz, especially bebop and free jazz." I'm not entirely sure what he means, so he has to explain.

He launches into another one of his enthusiasms, the frontiers of modern music in the 20th century. He got into it while at graduate school in the States — dual master's degrees in material sciences and international business, at Stanford no less. I'm only half-listening as he goes on. I don't really give a shit about the subtle distinctions between the genres of cerebral jazz, but I love how much he's into it. I study his face and hands as he talks, the way he brushes back the curls that fall onto his forehead. After a while he comes to a stop, ducks his head down and gives me a kind of embarrassed look. "Alexis, forgive me," he says. "I'm boring you." I laugh and raise my glass to him. "Here's to passionate enthusiasms. May they keep us young forever." He laughs and clinks glasses with me, "To passionate enthusiasms." Our next course is served, an entire fish baked in a salt crust. I watch in fascination as Nico takes over from the waiter to filet it in a few deft movements. He slides half of it onto my plate and then asks me, "Speaking of passionate enthusiasms, tell me how you got into tango?" I take a sip of wine to buy some time and try not to squirm or blush. I can't tell him about the tangasms that got me hooked. "I've always loved to dance. When I moved to LA, I wanted a way to meet people. I used to do some salsa but I wanted something more elegant and sophisticated, so I took up tango," I tell him. "What about you?" I learn Nico got into tango to please a former girlfriend. "I don't get much time to dance these days," he says, "but I heard it's a hobby of yours so I thought I'd take you to my favorite *milonga*." He tilts his head to the side and looks at me, like he's hoping I'll approve. God, he's gorgeous. And so adorable.

There's already quite a crowd at the *milonga* when we arrive. The club is all modern Italian design, with sleek banquettes, metallic architectural details and colored light effects. Nico is a popular figure and it takes us a while to get to the table where his friends are sitting, as everyone stops to kiss him hello. The current *tanda* ends as soon as we sit down and Nico invites me to dance. "Be careful," I hear that Russian warning in my head again. He escorts me onto the dance floor. A traditional tango starts up and we step into the embrace. It's the first time we've touched, besides our hands or brief kisses on the cheek. The sensation of his hands on my body and his animal vitality send flickers of electricity all along my nerve endings. His scent intoxicates me — something totally unique, sandalwood and spice along with a leathery, tobacco smokiness. The pussy-meter revs into high gear. Uh-oh. I'm in big trouble. Nico leads me onto the dance with an easy tango walking warm-up. I force myself to concentrate on the steps and the music and the signals from his body. I command that little slut of a pussy-meter to shut the fuck up. But she won't shut up. He feels too damn good.

By the second song, Nico gauges my ability and escalates the difficulty. He leads me into running *corridas* mixed with *cortes*, off-axis *colgadas* and *volcados*, quick-flicking *ganchos* and *boleos*. I marvel at the way our bodies synchronize effortlessly, as though we've been dance partners for years. He wraps me in a cocoon of attentive, protective care. I've never felt so at home in a man's arms.

I sigh as he pivots me around and attune to him even more closely. By the third song of the *tanda*, we're enveloped in our own magical world. My feminine energy wells up inside me, blossoming open. I hear Nico breathe me in. He pulls me closer. I lay my cheek against his as we glide and swirl around the dance floor in our private enchanted bubble. I don't want to come back to Earth when the *tanda* ends. Nico escorts me back to the table in an altered state, giddy, high, happy, content. The conversation at the table, all Italian, washes over me. I sit in a daze until Nico catches my attention. "Would you like to dance with Vittorio?" he asks. I make an effort to focus on the words, on his mouth. Vittorio is one of Nico's tango friends, a stocky man in his fifties. He smiles at me and inclines his head toward the dance floor. Earth to Alexis, Earth to Alexis, come in please! I pull it together, smile back, and nod.

Vittorio leads me out onto the floor and we enjoy a lovely *tanda*. He has a courtly, old-world sort of lead. It's grounding, comfortable, just what I need after the enchantment of Nico. When the *tanda* ends, Nico introduces me to another friend, a handsome young hunk in his thirties. He's on the short side, dark skin and dark hair in a tight grey suit. "Alexis, please meet Lorenzo. He's a fantastic dancer and a highly-respected teacher here in Milan." A Nuevo Tango song comes on and Lorenzo invites me to dance. His lead is assured, confident but sensitive. In a few bars, he appraises my ability and leads me into a dynamic series of *sacadas*, *boleos* and off-axis moves. Something comes over me when the next song starts up. I feel Katja enter my body and take over the dance. The red and black lace-covered skirt of my dress swirls around my hips and thighs. Katja dances through my body with abandon, with all her reckless gypsy sensuality. I sense people looking at us. I see Nico's fierce green eyes as we circle past the table. I don't know him very well yet, but he looks angry. There's a quick flash of Vasily's frantic eyes in a St. Petersburg dining room. I hear Katja laugh. With a burst of determination, I force her back to wherever she came from. "This is my life, not yours. Now leave me alone!"

Lorenzo walks me back to the table at the end of the *tanda*. "Quite a *tanguera* you have here, Nico," Lorenzo says in his heavily-accented English. Nico composes his face into something resembling neutral. "Yes, she is," he says. "I had no idea." I turn to him panting and sweating. He's looking fierce again, like that eagle on his stationary. "I don't know what came over me," I say. "That was a bit..." I hesitate, looking for the right word. Nico swivels his head around to look at me. His ferocity transforms into something else I can't read. I'm caught by his eyes, those same eyes over and over again — in the face of my temple Master, in my Persian captain of the guards, in Vasily, my Russian prince. "Wild?" I finish. I sound like a typical California teenager, ending every sentence on a rising question mark. I excuse myself to go to the bathroom. I need to regroup and touch up the make-up I'm sweating off my face.

I wash my hands and blot the sweat off my face. I see Katja staring back at me with a smug grin and triumphant look in her eyes. "Listen, Katja, Nico is not your prince. You can't just invade my body like that. Now go away and let me conduct my own affairs." She laughs as she reapplies rouge to her cheeks and kohl to her eyes. "But he is exactly like my prince was in the beginning." She tucks a stray curl back into her elaborate up-do and pins it in. "You'll see. He's the same man. Always has to run the show. The little dictator." She pulls up the bodice of her dress and adjusts her boobs to display more cleavage. "And one day he'll strangle you, too." She stares me down, hands on her hips, as I touch up my eyeliner, reapply lip gloss, smooth my hair back and readjust the rose hair clip. It reminds me of Katja. I take it out, flip her the bird and dump it in the trash. I hear her laugh as the door closes behind me.

When I get back to the table, Nico is gone. I scan the dance floor and see him dancing with a beautiful young woman in a tight red dress that barely covers her butt. He doesn't come back to our table when the *tanda* ends. Instead, he dances the next two with other women. Vittorio comes to my rescue and invites me to dance again. It's a fast *milonga* set and I have to focus to keep up with his changing rhythms. When we get back to the table, Nico is there. "It's getting late, Alexis," he says, "Shall we go? You need to get some sleep." Is he asking me or telling me? Damn that Katja for casting a cloud over our wonderful evening.

Nico is silent on the way home. When he pulls up to the front door and turns off the car, I turn in my seat to face him. He stares out the windshield, his face like a stone mask. "Have I done something to upset you?" I ask. He takes a deep breath and turns to me. There's that eagle glare again. Then it softens. "No. You did nothing wrong," he says. "I have no right to feel jealous, but I do." I'm shocked into silence. I don't know what to say to that. I'm confused, but secretly thrilled. He wants me. He wants me to be his, and his alone. "I don't know what to say," I murmur. Then he leans over and kisses me, like it's perfectly natural, like I'm already his, like he knows my body, knows how to please me, how to get me hot and wet. He pulls back to look me in the eyes. I fall into those green depths. "Alexis," he whispers and kisses me again. I'm totally rattled. I can't resist him. I don't want to resist him. I want to open everything to him. I kiss him back, then he gently pulls away.

"This changes everything, I think," he says. We sit looking at each other, breathing heavily. We both turn and face forward again without saying a word. I hear gongs and bells tolling in my head. The air in the car shimmers and waves with iridescent energy. A window opens up and all our lifetimes converge. We grasp hands and sit there breathing, feeling the enormity of the moment. At last, Nico unbuckles his seat belt and gets out of the car. He walks around to open my door and takes my hand to help me out. We walk into the house. "Let's not talk anymore tonight," Nico says. "Sleep in late. Catch up on the time change. We'll do another jet lag protocol tomorrow." He stands in front of me and takes both my hands in his. "We leave for Rio in the evening," he says. "I want to show you the site and the plans for the favela project." He kisses me on the forehead and says goodnight. I walk back up to my rooms in a daze. What the fuck just happened? I take a quick shower to wash off the sweat and makeup. I brush and floss my teeth. I avoid looking in the mirror. I take a dose of melatonin, put in ear plugs and slide a sleep mask over my eyes. I refuse to think about anything. I focus on breathing slow, deep, soft breaths.

I wake up happy as a child. It's 1:00 PM. I've slept almost eleven hours and I'm absolutely famished. I pull back the curtains and walk out onto the patio. It's a gorgeous day, fresh and sunny. I think I'll go for a swim. I peek into my sitting room. A tray waits for me on the coffee table. There's a thermos of hot water, my favorite Darjeeling tea, a tiny pitcher of soy milk and a crystal jar of honey. Next to that sits a bowl of neatly hulled local strawberries, tender and sweet, and a bowl of thick creamy yogurt. How does Nico know what I like? Where does he get his information? I bring the tray out to the patio and enjoy my solitary breakfast watching the birds and butterflies flit among the flowers in the lush garden below me. Then I study my face in the mirror to see if I look any different. I feel different. I can't put my finger on how exactly, but something shifted last night and now I'm on the other side.

I need to process all that's happened since Nico came into my life. I wish there was time to talk with Cheryl. I need help to figure out what I'm doing. I give myself a stern talking-to instead. "First of all," I begin, ticking off all the reasons why this is a bad idea, "What about your working relationship? What about your career? You can't risk the biggest opportunity of your life by getting romantically involved with this guy. What if it doesn't work out? Second of all..." I trail off. I can't seem to come up with a second-of-all. My brain makes a limp offering — I don't really know him. As if that's stopped me in the past. Then again, look how those relationships turned out. Not so good. I review every moment of our time together. He's been a perfect gentleman, nothing inappropriate. In fact, he's taken care of everything, anticipated my every need and comfort, and all with effortless style.

I put on my bathing suit and robe and head out to the pool. Everything is laid out — towels on the big comfortable lounges, IV stands, a table with bags of IV solution, IV needles, acupuncture needles, cotton swabs, medical tape and a biohazard container. Two massage tables stand under two large patio umbrellas, already made up. There's no one around. I throw down my robe and walk over to the diving board. I jump up and down a while, going higher and higher each time until I scare myself. Then I do a perfect jackknife and swim to the end of the pool underwater. It feels soft and silky. There's no chlorine smell. I wonder what they use to keep it so clean. I swim a few laps at top speed then roll onto my back and slow down for a lazy backstroke looking up at the sky. It's a unique Tuscan blue, different from the skies at home. I do a few laps on my back, then I play around like a dolphin for a while. When I get out, Nico is sitting on a lounge chair, watching me.

"Hello," I say, "Isn't it a beautiful day?" Nico smiles and wraps me in one of the extra large towels. "A perfect day," he says. He kisses me on the forehead. That's interesting. Somehow, it feels more intimate than a kiss on the lips. "Today, I thought you might enjoy a massage after our IV cocktail and sauna. You like massages, yes?" he asks. "I love a good massage, especially if there's energy healing or hot stones involved," I say. Juliana walks out to the pool area. "Then you're in for a treat with Marina," Nico says. "You'll love her style." Juliana hooks us to the IV's. Instead of needles, she puts little tacks in our ears, tiny needles on a Band-Aid backing. "Keep these on for two or three days," Juliana tells me. "They'll continue to work and help your body adjust to the change in time zones and climate. If they hurt or bother you, remove them." I run my finger over the needles. "Can I shower and swim with them?" I ask her. "Yes, of course," Juliana tells me, "no problem." While the IV bags slowly empty, Nico does some work on his laptop and I lay back chatting with Juliana. After the treatment, we take a sauna, then lay down for our massages. Nico was right. Marina is truly gifted. I can barely move to turn over when she's done with my back. She starts the second side with a deep massage and energy treatment of my feet. I refuse to give up wearing high heels or dancing for hours in 3-inch tango shoes, so I love having my feet worked on. By the time she's finished, I'm tranced out.

The next thing I know, Nico is whispering in my ear, "Time to wake up." I yawn and stretch on the table. I feel absolutely marvelous. I get up and put my robe back on.

There's a large glass of fresh green juice waiting for me. "What time is it?" I ask him. "Late," he says, "Almost five." Wow, where did the day go? "I don't want to rush you, but we take off at seven," he tells me. "Take off?" I ask. Oh right, he told me last night. We're going to Rio. Wait, what? Rio? "I know it's a lot of flying, but I want you to see the site and the plans for the housing project. We could go look at the one in Mumbai, but it's monsoon season." Nico gets a phone call. I watch him talk in rapid Italian while I drink my green juice. We haven't spoken yet, not a word about what happened last night or the changed atmosphere between us. I hesitate to bring it up. I don't even know what I want to say. We'll be on his plane for at least twelve hours. I promise myself I'll find an opportunity to talk during the flight.

When I go back to my room, Anna is there with my bags open and ready to pack. She's laid out two choices of travel clothes, one of which I've never seen before. On the bed are a pair of stretchy blue and green pants and top in a paisley pattern, very Emilio Pucci. I hold them up. "These aren't mine," I say to Anna. They must be silk jersey, they feel so soft. "Mr. Nico had them delivered," Anna says, "for the flying?" There he goes presuming again, but in a way that's so sure to please me, to suit my tastes, to anticipate my needs that I don't feel like he's trying to control me, like Katja would. Instead, I feel cherished and cared for. Why resist? I sigh and try them on. They fit perfectly and they're quite flattering. They're super comfortable too. *"Bellisima!"* Anna says when I come out of the bathroom. *"D'accordio?"* she asks. *"Si, d'accordio*," I say. She smiles and claps her hands, then bustles about packing my things in her expert manner. I finish getting ready.

Anna carries my bags to the front door. Valentina waits with a soft brown leather messenger bag. "Ciao, Alexis," she says and kisses me on both cheeks. "Are you coming to Rio with us?" I ask. "No," she says, "I'm just here to give these to Nico. But I'll be in LA again soon. Have a good time in Rio without me," she says and winks at me. Nico walks out dressed in jeans and a soft knit shirt in heather green. It makes the green of his eyes pop and shows off the muscles in his shoulders and his chest. A black Tesla waits in the courtyard. The driver gets out and loads the bags in the trunk. Nico turns to me and says, "Forgive me Alexis, but do you mind sitting up front with Giorgio? Valentina and I need to go over some papers together." He opens the front passenger door for me. "Of course not," I say. When we get to the airport, his jet is waiting on the tarmac. He gives Valentina some last minute instructions and we get on board. I see the steward and the crew, but no one else. "Is it just us?" I ask Nico. "Yes, just us," he says. He's supposed to be all eco-conscious, so how does he justify the private jet? It's like he can read my mind. "I used to feel guilty about owning a private jet and flying all over the world to conduct my business, or even for pleasure," Nico says, "but I need that kind of freedom and control to run my business efficiently. So I try to compensate as best I can. We calculate the carbon cost of every flight, and put double that amount back into reforestation programs. I use more eco-friendly bio-fuels when I can, although it's not always available. It's just one of those difficult compromises I have to accept." He sighs and looks away, then catches the corner of his mouth between his teeth.

Once we're airborne, the steward asks when we'd like dinner. "I'm famished," I say, "Can we eat now?" Nico laughs. "I'm so glad you're not like those women who pretend they don't eat." Hah! Hardly. If it wasn't for my intense yoga practice, I'd be as big as a house. "Hey," I say, "I love to eat good food." Over dinner, another delectable meal, Nico asks me about my life and my daughter. I ask him about his ex-wife and relationship history. I know, not too subtle, but I have to be sure about him. "If you don't mind my asking," I say, "Why did you never have children?" He's silent for a long moment. His expression is unreadable. "I wanted a large family. There was only my sister growing up. Patrizia couldn't have children. We tried fertility treatments, but they failed. She refused to adopt."

"Is that why you divorced?" I ask. "I'm sorry. That was blunt." He reaches across the table to take my hand, strokes his thumb across my skin. He sends little ripples of electric charge up my arm. The pussy-meter clicks on. How does he have this effect on me, just holding my hand? He looks up into my eyes. I can see thoughts pass like clouds across his mind. Then there's nothing but love pouring out of those green depths, love and care and tenderness. Those eyes. I know those eyes. He seems to come to some decision, then takes a deep breath and says, "Alexis, I know we just met, but it feels like we've known

each other forever. Does that sound like a stupid line?" I
shake my head. "No, I feel the same way, too," I say.

"I have feelings for you that make no sense to me," he
says. "I'm confused." I hold my breath and wait. "Last
night for instance, when you were dancing with Lorenzo."
I blush, recalling the wild, sensual dancing with Katja
taking over. "I suddenly felt jealous and possessive. I
wanted to pull you away from him and, how do you say
it? Punch him out?" Keep your mouth shut and let him
talk, I tell myself. "Then, when we kissed in the car," he
continues, "I felt something shift, almost like a puzzle
piece slid into place, and it just felt completely right that
we should be together." He looks down again. Wait, is he
blushing? "Does that sound ridiculous?" he asks. He looks
so raw and vulnerable. I'm torn. Should I tell him about
the dreams? Should I tell him about my fears and doubts?
Should I tell him we need to keep this relationship
professional? No, that's ludicrous. We've already passed
that boundary. The horses are out of the barn. Should I
tell him I feel the same way, too?

"It doesn't sound ridiculous," I begin, "But we hardly
know each other. We're just in the opening days of a
business relationship. What exactly do you see happening
between us?" Seriously, Alexis? That's your comeback?
Nico sits back, pulls his hand away. Idiot! What the fuck
are you doing? Tell him how you really feel. Don't blow
this. He's thinking. "I honestly don't know," he says. "Like
I said, my feelings for you confuse me." Put on your big
girl panties and tell him the truth. Don't be stupid,
woman. "Remember on the boat?" Nico says, "When we

toasted to our partnership?" I nod. How could I forget that blast of energy through my heart? "Well, I meant it then and I feel it even more now. We could be partners in every sense of the word." Holy shit! There goes the pussy-meter again, and my heart with it. I have to tell him everything. It all spills out.

"Nico, I've been confused and conflicted, too. Of course I felt the energy between us shift last night, and it scares and excites me," I say. "I'm conflicted because I'm afraid to risk our business relationship. This is the biggest opportunity of my career so far. What if things don't work out between us? And maybe our relationship is already compromised anyway." I could go on about all my conflicts, but I make an effort to rein it in. I pause to gather my courage to tell him the rest. "Alexis, of course I understand," he says, "That's why I've tried to restrain myself with you. I didn't want to use the power of my position in any way that might compromise you. But the truth is, something made me seek you out. I can't explain it. When I first found out who was behind that campaign and I saw your photo, I knew I had to meet you." Now's the time. He just gave you the perfect opening. Tell him. Tell him! "I think I can explain it," I say. I tell him about the three dreams about our past lives together. And then I tell him about Katja on the dance floor, too. I'm terrified he's going to think I'm some crazy person or dismiss me as some air-headed new age space cadet, but that's not his reaction at all. He sits back considering all I've just told him. He looks down, closes his eyes. Then he looks up into my eyes again. I see wonder. I see comprehension. I see love. I see resolve. "It doesn't sound crazy at all," Nico says. "In fact, it makes perfect sense." He reaches out and takes my hand again. "Perhaps we were destined to meet again in this life. Perhaps we have another chance to be true partners in every respect, in a way that was never possible before."

It's too much for me. I'm overwhelmed with emotions, mine and three other women's. I start to cry. Nico immediately gets up and comes around to my seat. "*Caro,* why are you crying? Don't cry." He scoops me up in his arms and carries me to one of the built-in sofas. I cry harder. He holds me in his arms, strokes my hair, murmurs soothing words, "It's alright. Everything's going to be alright. Don't cry. We're together now. Everything is going to be fine." Finally, I'm all cried out. I sniffle. I need to blow my nose. His shirt is wet where I've been sobbing into him. He shifts position and reaches over to the table for a napkin. I sit up and blow my nose, then I turn to face him. I look into those eyes, the eyes of a soul I've loved for thousands of years. I take his face in my hands, lean forward and kiss him — soft and sweet, at first. Then more urgently. For the first time, he doesn't hold back. He pulls me on top of him and starts to kiss me deeply, passionately, exploring my mouth with his tongue. I kiss him back for all I'm worth. I can feel myself getting wet. I'm so turned on to him. I begin to rub myself on his thigh. I can feel him start to stiffen. I reach down to feel his hardness through his jeans. He groans. I open my mouth to him, suck on his tongue, run my hand up and down his erection.

He stops kissing me to whisper in my ear, "Alexis, *amore*, I don't want our first time to be on the sofa in my jet with the crew in earshot." First I'm embarrassed. I pull away and sit up. Then I find it hysterical. I crack up. "So you're not going to initiate me into the mile-high club tonight?" I say. "The mile-high club?" Nico asks. "Oh, right," he laughs, "I get it. You've really never had sex on an airplane?" he asks me. "Not that I can recall," I say, and we keep laughing. "Something to look forward to then," he says. He smiles at me, adjusts his position and pulls me back down to snuggle into him. I breathe in that distinctive scent of his, all sandalwood, spice and smoke. "Lie with me here for a while and let me hold you," he murmurs. I don't let myself think about anything except how good it feels to be in his arms.

CHAPTER NINE

Rio

It's before dawn when we land in Rio. A car and driver take us to a hillside villa Nico rents with high walls and guard dogs. The villa is gorgeous with sweeping ocean views from most of the rooms. Nico gives me the master bedroom and takes one of the other bedroom suites for himself. When I protest, he insists. "Let's take a swim and have some breakfast," he says. "There's a sauna, too. I have someone coming by with the IV cocktail at ten." My body is protesting from all the flying, even with his magic jet lag protocol. I need to do some serious yoga. The terrace overlooking the ocean is a perfect spot. "Do you think they have a yoga mat around here somewhere?" I ask. "I'm sure they do," he says, "There's a gym downstairs, let's take a look." The gym is set up for serious fight training. A body bag hangs from the ceiling and racks of staffs and swords lean against the wall. "Whoa, it looks like somebody's into marital arts," I say. Nico has been rummaging around inside a closet. He emerges with a rolled up yoga mat in hand. "I like to keep in shape," he says. Nico doesn't do anything halfway. "I assume you know how to use all this stuff," I say. He shrugs, "I can handle myself," he says, and walks out of the room. I decide to do my yoga practice first and go get changed. When I come back out to the terrace I see Nico in the pool swimming laps like an Olympian. I'm still in the middle of my yoga practice when he gets out and comes back up to the terrace. "I'm going to go workout for a while," he says, "The sauna is inside the cabana over there." He points to a building on the other side of the pool.

When I finish my yoga practice, I go back to the bedroom to change into a bathing suit. I'd love to swim naked, but I don't know if any servants or gardeners might be around. I haven't seen anyone but the guard at the gate. I'll check with Nico. I walk to the gym to ask, but really, I just want to see what kind of workout he's doing. It obviously takes more than IV drips and green juice to keep that fine Italian stallion physique in shape. Plus, I've never met anyone who has his vitality, focus and endurance. I've gotten way more sleep than he has these past four days. Even with the treatments and massage, the long flights across multiple time zones have taken a toll on me. I peek through the door to the gym. He and another man are fighting with staffs. Nico knocks his staff away and they switch to hands and feet. They're moving so fast I can't even follow the action. I close the door and back away.

I feel a little dizzy. The hallway starts to waver. I lean back against the wall and close my eyes. I take a deep breath. When I open them again, I'm in a large open courtyard enclosed within mud-brick walls. The sun is beating down. It's hot and dusty. I see my Persian captain, sword and shield in hand, practicing moves with one of his men. They're a well-matched pair and fight ferociously. I grip the amulet around my neck. I hate the way they practice with each other. It terrifies me. The guardsman delivers a mighty blow that drives my beloved to his knees, shield up over his head. I can't bear to watch anymore and turn to leave. I walk straight into the wall of the Brazilian villa. I hurry away to the pool, dive in and swim lap after lap underwater to clear the vision from my head. I get out and walk to the cabana. I see a headphone jack at the sauna with a cable. I plug in my iPhone and put on a fifteen-minute track of Tibetan bowl music.

I lay in the sauna and try not to think or feel anything, just let the reverberations of the bowls carry me into inner silence.

When the music is over I go back to my room, take a shower and get dressed. I'm hungry. I walk out to the living area. Breakfast is already set up on the terrace. Nico is reading something on his iPad. He looks up when I walk over. "How was your yoga practice?" he asks. "Feeling better?" I sit down. There's fresh papaya and mango, yogurt, a basket of breads, and granola. A pot of tea sits steeping. Nico has a smoothie in front of him. "It was good," I say, "How was your workout?" He looks at me with a concerned expression. "Has something happened?" he asks. I hesitate. I don't want him to think I was spying on him. "*Caro*, you must tell me if something has upset you. You can trust me." I serve myself some tea. Then I add a large helping of fruit to a bowl of yogurt. I decide I might as well tell him the whole thing. "It's nothing really. Just another bleed-through from one of those other lives. I came to ask if it would be okay to swim naked in the pool and I saw you fighting. It triggered a flashback to when you were my captain in Persia. It terrified me to watch you fight then." I take a sip of my tea. "It shook me up a little, that's all." We both notice my hand is shaking. Nico gets up and pulls me from my chair into his arms. He holds me close. "You're here with me now, and we're both perfectly safe. Nothing's going to happen. José and I know what we're doing." We sit back down. He reaches for my hand and smiles at me. "We have the entire day to ourselves," he says. "After breakfast we'll get our treatment. Then we can do whatever you like."

We spend a fun relaxing day together. We take scooters to the beach and do some shopping on the way. What better place to buy a bikini than Rio? On the way home, we pick up some fresh-caught fish for dinner. Tonight we cook dinner for ourselves. We enjoy our meal on the terrace. It's romantic at night with the lanterns lit, the sound of the ocean and samba jazz playing in the background. After dinner, Nico says, "I want to take you dancing again. There's a good *milonga* not far from here." The thought of dancing with him again sends a thrill all through my body. "But tonight, we only dance with each other," he says. Do I detect a note of command in his tone? I go to change clothes. I love that red dress, but I don't know if I'll ever be able to wear it again. Katja ruined it for me. I put on the one sexy dress I brought. It will work for tango. It's a classic little black dress, deceptively elegant and understated, yet oh so sexy in the way it hugs my curves. Fortunately, my new tango shoes will go with it. Tonight, I decide on a bright red lip and neutral eye shadow. I carefully draw a thin perfect cat eye with my eyeliner, apply two coats of mascara and give thanks again for the long thick eyelashes I inherited from my grandmother. When I come out, Nico whistles. "For sure tonight you dance only with me," he says, sweeps me off my feet and swirls me around. Outside, a driver is waiting.

The *milonga* takes place at an old dance hall. It's a mixed crowd with a surprising number of young people. There are some great dancers here. Nico is dressed more casually tonight, in a *guayabera* and loose slacks. With his dark coloring and dark curly hair, he could be a native. The DJ plays an interesting mix of traditional and Nuevo Tango music with some other Latin-flavored sets thrown in. This is the kind of music my body responds to best. We get drinks at the bar and watch for a while. Then a Nuevo Tango set comes on. He invites me to the dance floor. Everything has changed between us since we last stood together in a tango embrace. It seems like months ago. It's been two days. We step into a close embrace. We breathe together. We feel each other. His special scent fills my head. We begin to dance. Without any fancy moves or footwork we express the passion building between us, the desire we have yet to consummate. Nico's athleticism and natural rhythm take over. Our movements are dynamic, sensual, expressive. He leads me into slow pivots, long drawn-out slides punctuated by rapid walking and crosses, syncopated steps then pauses in perfect stillness, which I preserve from any embellishment. He plays with the accents and I follow him without hesitation. Our bodies are in perfect unison. I lay my face up against him and relax into the circle of his embrace. I feel at one with the music, completely present in the moment and the intimate connection between us. I feel free. My heart opens. My feminine energy wells up. Nico responds. His male presence intensifies, amplifies, radiates. My pussy throbs in reaction. Our electrons carry on their own cosmic dance, spinning vortexes, while melting molecules frolic in wild abandon. Heavenly choruses sing over a pulsing primal beat. It's exquisite torture, a holy communion of juicy sweaty bliss.

When the *tanda* ends, I don't move. I don't want to break the spell. The DJ plays a kind of hip-hop samba mash-up for the *cortina*. I look up into Nico's eyes. He gazes back at me, hypnotized. I fall into those eyes. We kiss. He leads me off the dance floor back to the bar. We don't speak. He keeps hold of my hand as we sit and sip our drinks. The next *tanda* is a fast *milonga*. We watch the dancers. Nico caresses my thigh and strokes my back. My pussy is so wet I'm afraid it will soak through my panties to my dress. We dance three more *tandas* before leaving the *milonga*. Nico holds me close on the way back to the villa, stroking my head and my arm. We don't speak.

The front door closes behind us. Nico takes me in his arms and kisses me like a man dying of thirst who has reached the oasis. My legs go weak. I cling to him. He picks me up and carries me to the master bedroom. Someone has dimmed the lights and turned down the bed. He lays me down and falls upon me, running his hands up and down my legs, squeezing my thighs, then over my hip and waist, up my ribs, molding to cup my breasts. I'm moaning and panting like a wild thing. He's kissing me and murmuring endearments, switching between English and Italian, *caro*, my beauty, *amore mio*. His cock is rock hard against my thigh. Then he slows down and pauses. He pulls back to look me in the eyes. We breathe and gaze into each other for a moment. Then he stands up and takes all his clothes off. I watch in fascination. I've seen him in bathing trunks, but this is different. He's so strong and beautiful, with his broad shoulders and hard-muscled chest. The slight thickening of his torso just makes me feel more attracted to him, makes him seem even more solid and powerful. He stands before me, a mighty, wild stallion in his prime. I let my eyes feast on him. He has the most beautiful penis I've ever seen. Long and thick, but not too thick, with a beautifully defined head. It's slighter darker than the rest of him, a pale bronze. I get up and turn my back to him so he can unzip my dress. We let it fall to my feet. He unhooks my bra, pulls it off my shoulders and turns me around. It drops to the floor. He takes my breasts in his hands and bends his head to kiss them all over. He sucks one nipple into his mouth, then the other. I gasp and my legs give way. We lay down on the bed again and begin to kiss. I wrap a thigh over him. He's gently squeezing and rubbing my breasts, pinching my nipples. He kisses me with a devastating combination of sensitivity and authority. I'm moaning again, rubbing myself up against his thigh. He reaches down to pull off my panties.

I'm suddenly aware of how sweaty I was on the dance floor. "Nico, darling," I whisper, "Let me go wash up a little. I want to be fresh for you after sweating so much on the dance floor." He just sits up, reaches down and rips my panties in half, tearing them apart at each hip. "I want you just the way you are," he growls. "I want all your natural womanliness." Then he grabs a pillow and lifts my hips up to slide it beneath my ass. He spreads my thighs apart and gazes at me for a long moment. I see wonder and admiration and desire in his eyes. I can feel my pussy swell and open like a flower beneath his gaze. Then he bends forward, puts his mouth on me and begins to kiss and lick and suck my pussy. I'm delirious with pleasure, moaning and rolling my hips around. He parts my lips, spreads me wide open. I grab hold of his head and arch into him. He makes love to me with his mouth and his hands, tracking my energy, seeking out my response, licking and sucking and stroking me into higher and higher spirals of ecstasy, worshipping at the altar, drinking the divine amrita of the Goddess, stoking my fires 'til my insides turn molten and everything dissolves into liquid light. The channels between my womb and my heart open. The nectar and honey come streaming down upon his head in rainbow waterfalls of bliss.

Nico eventually comes up for air. He wipes my juices off his face and climbs up over me to kiss me on the mouth again. He rears back on his knees and pulls my thighs up and around his waist. I reach down to take hold of his cock and position him. He rocks and rolls his way inside me in circular increments. I gasp and groan. My pussy waves and ripples, convulses up and down his length like she's trying to suck him inside her. He's inside me as deep as he can go. The head of his cock is right up against the mouth of my womb. He pulls my hips a little closer and rolls us over onto our sides. Now we're lying face to face, my legs wrapped around him, and his rhythm is driving me wild. He's looking into my eyes. We start to kiss again. The tip of his tongue strokes the roof of my mouth just behind my front teeth, then circles and plunges with the same rhythm he's fucking me. Everything opens to him. My mouth, my heart, my pussy, my inner most secret core. The veils begin to thin and part. I've opened a portal and he's driven us through it. We're journeying together, riding spiral electron waves into ever vaster bliss fields, sailing through luminous oceans of love, rocking and rolling into the next portal, him driving us on, me opening and parting the veils. Then we're through again to the next dimension, and still he's stroking me, driving us on and on and on and on. Eventually I just can't come anymore, can't hold the focus. He's tracking me so closely, feeling everything inside me, so he lets himself climax, bucking into me like a wild stallion, setting me off on one last spiral.

Today we're scheduled to visit the site for the favela project. José, his sparring partner in the gym yesterday, is in the courtyard waiting for us when we come out. There's another man too, both on motorcycles. Nico confers with them. A third motorcycle sits parked nearby with two helmets hanging off the bars. Nico gets on, starts it up, he hands me the other helmet. I guess we're going to the favela by motorcycle. "Who are these two men?" I ask. He introduces me to José and his partner, Inacio. They're both tough-looking, hard-muscled men in jeans and tee-shirts. "Extra security," Nico says. I wonder why we need extra security. José leads the way out of the gates with Inacio following behind us. When José leans forward to adjust something by his foot, I see a gun stuck in the back of his waistband. Nico would never put me in danger, would he?

Our first stop is a meeting with Amélia, the executive director of a community organization Nico's been funding. She's a petite woman in her fifties, well-spoken and passionate. After a couple of hours, we take off on the bikes to tour the proposed area and talk with some of the residents. Amélia rides behind José, and in about twenty minutes, we're climbing the steep narrow streets of a favela. A million-and-a-half people live in these communities. It smells like raw sewage. The site selected has some of the worst living conditions of all the favelas in the city. If Nico's multi-pronged plan can work here, it can work anywhere. Nico talks with a number of people as we walk through the area. He can speak a little Portuguese and Amélia translates as needed. The plan is to build small multi-home hubs, and each home will generate its own electricity with common waste treatment and water supply. After the tour we head back down the hill to another meeting in a small casual restaurant.

Nico, Amélia and I enter and sit down. José waits outside, leaning up against the wall. I don't see Inacio. We walk to a table in the back where a man named Carlito sits. He looks like an oversized toad, or maybe a giant pig. I take an instant dislike to his smug, porcine manner. He's gorging on the greasy food, talking with his mouth full. The conversation has something to do with bribes and corruption, with both police and public officials. I can't follow it all, but the gist is that Nico's project is a threat to certain powerful figures. If Nico and his partners succeed, their favela housing will have better water, power, sewage and other municipal services than the rest of Rio. It'll create an uproar. Carlito heaves himself up to go the bathroom and Nico turns to me. "I want you to plan a communication strategy to expose these people," he says. He's got a wicked gleam in his eyes, like he's ready to take down the whole system. "I also want your team to work with Amélia and other local organizations to create a campaign geared to the residents." A flood of ideas pop into my head. "We might be able to use citizen journalism in this situation," I say, "We could do the whole Arab-spring thing and start a community news network on social media platforms. It could even turn into another job-training and employment opportunity." Nico's eyes light up. "That's a great idea," he says. "I think you've found one solution to many problems." I know he's always going for two or three birds with one stone. I'm glad he likes it, but I can't wait to get out of here and away from Carlito. He's really starting to gross me out. I catch him leering at me as he comes back to the table. We get up to leave. José will take Amélia back to her office. I say goodbye and promise to be in touch. Nico and I go back to the villa.

It's late afternoon when we pull in through the gates. It's been an intense day. Nico excuses himself to go work in the home office for a few hours before dinner. I set up on the terrace overlooking the ocean, catch up on emails, then Skype with Jessica. "Where are you?" she asks. I see a whiteboard covered with notes behind her. I can hear our busy office in the background. It's like a splash of cold hard reality. I've been in an alternate universe these past few days. "I'm in Rio de Janeiro," I say. She leers at me. "Oh really? I hope you're having fun while we slave away here. By the way, poor Roger won't be able to surf for six weeks." We both laugh. "When are you coming back?" she says. I realize I don't exactly know. Nico has taken over my life. "It's been a whirlwind," I say. "I might fly back tomorrow or Wednesday. I should be in the office by the end of the week." I dread dealing with the jet lag without Nico's protocol. We cover a few status updates and review some possible candidates for the team. After we hang up, I jot down some ideas on the favela project, then go for a swim before dinner.

There's been no time all day to think about last night. It was late when he woke me this morning and I had to hurry to get ready to leave for our meeting with Amélia. I'm floating on my back, looking up at the sky turning colors with the approach of sunset, trying to sort my feelings out. I flashback on images and sensations from our lovemaking. My heart fills and expands. My pussy starts to tingle. Nico swims up beside me. He takes me in his arms and kisses me, soft and sweet at first, then with more urgency and passion. "Forgive me, I've been neglectful," he says.

"Why, what do you mean?" Birds chatter in the jungle of flowers planted all around the pool area.

"I haven't even thanked you properly for our night together. It's been non-stop all day." He dips his head back into the pool. The water droplets sparkle in the golden-pink light of the setting sun when he comes back up. He really does resemble an eagle with his strong nose, his dark hair wet and slicked back and his green eyes glowing. He kisses me again. "You make me very happy," he says.

"You can thank me by feeding me a proper dinner. I'm starved," I say. "And then take me to bed and make love to me again."

"Alright my love," he laughs. "At least we know your priorities."

Nico takes me to a romantic outdoor restaurant for dinner. It's set into a hillside with a series of terraced patios overlooking the city and the ocean beyond. The food is fantastic French-Brazilian fusion, served under flickering lights amid lush gardens. Dinner winds down. It's time to talk about us. I stare at the decapitated shrimp heads on my plate and try to think how to begin. "So what happens now?" I ask him. Nico looks at me over the candlelight. The night is balmy. A light breeze wafts the fragrance of night-blooming flowers over the patio. He takes my hand. "What do you want to happen?" he says. I watch the candle flames dance in the breeze. A drop of wax trickles down to join her sisters in the melt-pool below. "I don't know. It's complicated," I tell him. I don't tell him I'm afraid to fall in love with him. "What do you want, Nico?" His thumb stops stroking the back of my hand. His eyes become hooded. I feel him draw into himself. Then he looks up at me again. "I think what I want is you, Alexis," he says. I see naked need in those green depths. I don't know what to say. It's happening again, like the night we first kissed in the car. I feel everything shift, tectonic plates sliding one over the other, falling into place. The waiter comes to clear the table. Nico asks for the check. "Everything is happening so fast," I say, "I need time to process."

He brings my hand up to his mouth and kisses it, first the back, then the center of my palm. My pussy tingles.

"Let's go back to the villa," Nico says, "We can talk more there." He pays the bill and we leave the restaurant. The car winds up the hillside to our villa. I look out the window at the city lights. "What are we doing tomorrow?" I ask.

"I think tomorrow I put you on a plane for Los Angeles and I return to Milan," he says. My heart clutches. I'm not ready our magical idyll to end. I need more time with him.

We sit on the terrace among the lush plants back at the villa, lounging in the cushions on one of the outdoor sofas. We gaze at the city lights and the ocean below. A tray of after-dinner brandies and cognacs sits on the coffee table. Little crystal snifters glitter in the flicker of the candles. The moon has just risen. It casts a shining silver path on the ocean straight toward us. Nico puts his arm around me. I snuggle into my favorite spot up against his chest. I can hear his heart beating. We don't speak. I don't want to think about anything. I just want to absorb the moment. I sigh and look up at him gazing at the moon. He turns and looks down at me with a wide-eyed expression of wonder and vulnerability, mouth soft and relaxed. He tilts my face up to kiss me.

We get into a hot and heavy make-out session on the sofa. I decide to blow him right there out on the terrace. I push him back against the pillows and unzip his pants. He's already sporting a semi-hard-on. I pull his cock out of his briefs and stroke it up and down a few times. How is it possible I haven't sucked his cock before now? The stone floor hurts my knees so I pull one of the big pillows down. Then I bend over and start to kiss and lick up and down the shaft. He moans. Something comes over me. I want to take control, dominate the situation, give him something to remember. I look up at him. His eyes are half-closed, gleaming in the moonlight. I yank his pants down, toss them to the side and push him back down into the pillows. Then I torture him with my mouth and hands. Nico pants and groans under my ministrations. I suck the head, slide and twist my hands up and down the shaft at the same time, then suck him into my mouth and throat as far as I can take him. I lick and suck his balls, run my thumb along the underside of his shaft to stroke the sensitive spot under the head. He gasps and starts to come, but I won't let him. I stop moving and grip the base of his cock hard, press my thumb into his perineum. I look up at him again. He's panting, eyes closed. I rise up on my knees to kiss his mouth. He opens his eyes and looks at me. Then I start up again. I want to drive him crazy. I don't let him change the rhythm or control my movements in any way. I bring him to the point of climax a second time, but I stop before he can come. He's gasping and panting, "Unnhh, unnhh, Alexis. Oh God, oh God." I do it again, sucking and licking him until he's about to come, then hold him back before he can climax. Three times I bring him to the edge, but I won't let him come. I've made my point — I'm in charge. Now I want him inside me.

I stand up and pull off my panties, soaking wet. I pull up my skirt and straddle him. I lean over to kiss him, slip my tongue into his mouth. Then I brace my hands on his shoulders and lower my pussy onto his rock hard cock. I ride him like a bronco. I control the rhythm, I control the movements, rocking and rolling my hips around his big beautiful cock. I open my top and pull his head to my breasts. He obeys my lead and kisses them, massages and sucks them, pinches my nipples and takes them between his teeth. I ride him harder, alternate fast strokes with slow, deep thrusts, lift myself up 'til just the head is inside me, then plunge down on his upright shaft. "Oh God," I gasp, "I'm about to come!" I grab Nico's hands and plant them on my hips. He gets the message and pumps into me, still sucking and biting my breasts and nipples. "Yes, yes, fuck me. Fuck me harder," I command, panting and groaning. I start to come and it tips him over the edge. I lean forward and we kiss and moan and pant into each other's mouths as I come down all over him and he releases into me. I collapse onto him. We slide down onto our sides. I'm almost embarrassed by my wild aggressive behavior, but Nico nips that in the bud. He strokes my hair back and kisses me sweetly. "Alexis," he breathes, "that was incredible." The moon beams down, bathing us in silvery light. The warm breeze caresses my skin. "*Ti adoro*, my wild beautiful love."

CHAPTER TEN

Back In LA

It's 10:00 PM when I land at Van Nuys airport on Tuesday night. A car is waiting for me. I'm physically and emotionally exhausted. Nico put me on a chartered flight because he didn't want me to fly commercial. I protested at the extravagance, but he said it was worth it. "I need you back at work and functional. It's a justified, business expense," he told me as we stood on the tarmac, saying our goodbyes. I get home and immediately strip off my clothes and run a hot bath. My eyes feel dry and scratchy. My throat, too. "Do not get sick," I tell myself. I make a cup of mint tea and steep some chamomile tea bags to put on my eyes, then retreat to my bathroom, light all the candles, put on my Tibetan bowl music and pour extra rose oil in the tub. My nervous system is on overload. I don't know if I can handle any kind of relationship with Nico, business or romantic. "Don't think about it now," I tell myself, "you're in no state to think it through." I try to breathe and think of nothing, but images keep intruding, fragments of the past week flashing across my mind, jagged kaleidoscope slivers, shiny and bright. The water has cooled by the time I get out of the bath. I brush my teeth and avoid looking in the mirror. I take melatonin, turn off my phone, put in ear plugs and slide a mask over my eyes. Buried under the covers, those jagged slivers chase me from the deck of the Sea Gypsy back and forth across the Atlantic, over the Equator, up and down the hemispheres. When I finally fall asleep, my dreams are filled with tests and trials I'm unprepared for, unable to perform, and I fail miserably and publicly each time.

A buzzer keeps going off. I swim through the murk to semi-wakefulness. It's the door buzzer. My phone says it's 9:30 AM. Who the fuck is ringing my buzzer? I throw on a robe and stumble to the door, foggy and furious. I open it to a smiling woman in a lab coat, doctor's bag in hand, IV stand in the other. I stare down at her. She's like a tiny brown roly-poly. "Good morning, Ms. Rykof," she says, "I'm Dr. Mathilda Sanchez. Mr. Aquilo sent me to give you the jet lag treatment." I squint in the glare reflecting off her sparkly harlequin glasses. My mouth is dry as the Sahara. I feel like shit. Who does he think he is, ordering my life without asking? Like I'm another piece of property his staff has to keep in top running form? Even though I know the treatment will make me feel much better, I'm about to snarl at her to leave me the fuck alone. Then I reconsider. What do I have to lose?

An hour later, I'm semi-functional and dressed for the office. It's non-stop from the moment I walk in the door to the moment I walk out at 8:00 PM. The team has been busy. The kick-off announcement is scheduled for ten months away. The plan is for Nico to speak at the biggest green build conference of the year. Natalie, Jessica and I hole up to rough out a time line. It's going to be tight to have everything ready in time for the launch. We chunk out the work flow. It's a daunting prospect when I see it all laid out. Then there's the budget. We've got a week to deliver estimates to Timothy, Nico's martinet of a chief operating officer. I look at Natalie and Jessica's preliminary numbers and gasp at the enormity of what we've taken on. Natalie goes back to her desk, but I ask Jessica to stay. "So, how was your trip with our hunk of a client?" Jessica asks. "Exhausting, intense, inspiring," I say. Jessica raises one perfectly groomed eyebrow and waits for me to elaborate. "It's complicated," I say. I don't want to get into anything about our romantic adventures. "So you did fuck him," Jessica says. "How was it?" I suppose it was absurd to imagine I could keep it from Jessica, with her x-ray eyes and telepathic powers. "I can't talk about that now," I say. And what would I say anyway? That he rocked my world? That I may be falling in love with him? Is it possible we only had sex twice? "It's complicated," I say again. She laughs. "Is the care and feeding of a five-hundred-pound gorilla more than you bargained for?" As usual, Jessica sees right through to the crux of the matter. "You could say that. It's been a little overwhelming." Talk about understatement of the year. "Well, don't sashay all moony-eyed around the office. It won't help for people to know you're fucking the client." Shit! I'm sure there's already some jealousy and resentment about me being put in charge of this account.

All I need is for the rumor mill to start churning. The fact that I only fucked him after we got the account will be a moot point.

The rest of the week is filled with meetings and interviews. Ben, Jessica and I convene with our CFO to discuss the budgets. They're astronomical to me, tens of millions for the first year alone. "Ka-ching, ka-ching," Ben chortles behind his super-fashionable glasses. They're big, round and blue. They make him look like a Eurasian Mr. Magoo. He's giddy at the prospects of global expansion. I'm about to leave the office late Thursday afternoon when Roger comes hobbling in. "Welcome back, Alexis. How was the trip without me?" Roger says. "It's too bad you missed it," I say. "You would have loved the design center. Did you get a chance to look through all the photos and videos I sent?" Roger leans up against my desk. It feels like he's hulking over me. "I heard you went to Rio after Milan," he says, ignoring my question. What's this about? I'm not the one who broke my stupid foot. The way things turned out, I don't know if I'm happy Roger couldn't be my chaperone, but he sure can be a pain in the ass. "Yes," I reply, "We went to tour the project site and meet with the people from the community organization." I want to get out of here, but Roger's big blonde head is staring down at me. "Must be great to have a big client fly you around the world on his private jet," he says. I can't believe this asshole has the balls to leer at me. I swallow back a retort. Keep it professional. "Is there something I can help you with Roger?" He smiles, pushes off my desk and hobbles out, then pauses at the door. "Keep up the good work," he says. He actually winks and gives me a thumbs-up. Fucking dick.

Cheryl flies down Friday for more wedding dress fittings. I'm looking forward to our weekend. God knows I need help sorting out what to do about Nico. I haven't spoken to him since Rio. He's texted me a couple of times, but we've both been super busy all week. I take Cheryl to the spa where two Korean women in black underwear scrub off the top layers of our skin. Then we make the circuit between an herb steam room, an ice room, a salt bath, and a room of heated clay balls the size of marbles you lie down on. We finish off with a massage and I realize I'm famished. "Do you want to eat here or pick up Thai food on the way home?" I ask her. We're in the locker room getting ready. I'm drying my hair. Cheryl is standing naked by the bench rubbing in body lotion. I can't help but check her out in the mirror. She's a real hottie with her blonde hair, blue eyes and long legs. Being in love sure does agree with her. She looks like she's dropped a few pounds. We haven't talked about Nico once, nor Paul for that matter. The spa is crowded on a Friday night. You're supposed to be quiet in here. Cheryl looks around. "Let's eat at home," she says.

We settle in for a girls' night on the sofa with a banquet-sized order of Thai food and a DVD from Redox. "So tell me how things are going with Paul and the wedding?" I say. She grins, sighs, and admires the huge yellow diamond on her finger. "Paul had a little talk with the wedding planner and she's been behaving herself ever since." She takes a big bite of green curry. "That's not like the feisty Cheryl I know and love," I say. Cheryl shrugs and shakes her head. "Well, it was too late to fire her and Paul didn't want me to be stressed out. He let her know his accounting firm would be going through every charge with a fine-toothed comb." She laughs and flips her palms up, like there was nothing she could do to stop him. "He doesn't usually throw his weight around on something like this but the big wedding was his idea so he feels kind of responsible. I was fine with just the destination wedding in Vietnam." I wonder what kind of wedding Nico would want. A big society event? Or maybe something small and private on the Sea Gypsy? "I'm more invested in the actual ceremony than the huge formal affair after," Cheryl says. "I only want the people really close to us there so we can create something sacred and intimate." It warms my heart to see Cheryl so happy. "And how's the Maui house coming along?" I ask. She rolls her eyes. "I have two words," she says. "Island time." We crack up. "At this rate, we'll be lucky if it's ready by Christmas. I'd love it if you and Laura would come stay with us over the holidays. She can bring her boyfriend, too." This is life Cheryl leads now — Christmas in their custom-built estate on Maui with friends and family. It's a long way from the soccer moms we once were.

"Are you going to tell me what's going on with you?" Cheryl asks. The coffee table is littered with the detritus of our meal. We've almost finished the bottle of Riesling — not usually my favorite, but perfect with the spicy Thai food. I sigh. Then it all spills out. "My life was hit by a tsunami who goes by the name Nicolo Aquilo," I tell her.

"I feel like I've got a rocket between my legs. It's taken off and I'm just holding on for dear life." I shred my napkin to bits as I fill her in on the past two weeks. "The whole thing has been like a dream. It's happened so fast. I try and track it back, but it gets kind of blurry. I don't know if it's all the travel or some altered reality thing. We only had sex two times but it feels like way more." Cheryl looks at me with concern, drawing her perfectly groomed brows together. "I'm just so conflicted," I say. I sweep the shredded napkin into a pile. "On the one hand, it's the biggest account I've ever had and Nico put me in the lead. It's going to be a huge long-term engagement with a multi-year international roll-out. You know I was getting ready to leave and start my own agency right before this happened?" Cheryl nods. "So what's the problem?" she asks. I pick up another napkin and start working it. "Well, for one thing, fucking the client is not good for business or for team morale. Roger already hinted at that today."

"Fuck that asshole!" Cheryl spits. I love that Cheryl is always on my side. "But seriously," I say, "it's a problem. It sets up a funky power dynamic. It's risky. What if things don't work out between us and I lose the account? Plus, I don't want people to think I got the account by fucking him." Cheryl laughs. "It wouldn't be the first time, nor the last," she says. "Maybe not, but it's not how I want to be known in the industry." I'm halfway through my second napkin. Cheryl empties the wine bottle into our glasses. "There's got to be more to it than that," she says. "I'm overwhelmed by it all," I tell her, "professionally and personally. I don't know if I can handle lead on something this big. The budget for the first year alone is close to fifty million. I've never handled this much responsibility before. What if it's too much for me? I'm not even sure I want that much responsibility. Nico has a huge world-changing vision. What if I fail?" My dreams from the other night come back to me, that horrible sickening feeling of failure and public humiliation. "When I imagine us together, I begin to doubt whether I can deal with that life day in and day out. I don't know if I want a life that big. Sure, from the outside it's all 'Lifestyles of the Rich and Famous,' but would it become a burden? Would I start to feel oppressed and crushed by it? I had less than a week with him, and it was totally overwhelming."

Cheryl sips her wine while she considers my dilemma. Her giant canary diamond blazes as she twirls a strand of honey-blonde hair around her finger. I love to watch this woman's mind work. Now that I've said it all aloud, it hits me even stronger than before. I just don't know if I'm up to it all. "Alexis, you haven't said a single word of how you feel about Nico," Cheryl points out. She's right. How do I feel about him? "What's up with that?" she asks. Good question. "I'm not even sure," I say. "He's kind of swept in and taken over my life. On the one hand, he just assumes he knows what I want and makes plans without asking me. On the other hand, he's taken care of me like a princess and anticipated my needs and desires so well I can hardly complain, can I?" Cheryl passes me another napkin. I look down and realize that I've already annihilated the second one. "Is he bossy about it?" she asks. "That's just the thing," I say, "No, he's not. It's all done with this invisible effort. It appears in front of me, just the next thing that's happening. Arrangements have been made." I stop to drink my wine and sort out my feelings. "I mean, I find him enormously attractive. He has these gorgeous green eyes. They make me melt. And the sex..." I shake my head. I can't help but smile. "Yyeeeah, that part was great." Just thinking about it makes my face flush. "I admire and respect him," I tell her, "and he can be so adorable."

She cocks her head and tilts her palm up. "So what's the problem?" she asks me. "Well," I sigh, "now's when it gets a little weird." I tell her about the three past life dreams and what happened on the dance floor with Katja. "Curiouser and curiouser," she says. Cheryl gets up to clear the table. She puts on the kettle on and drops bags of Sencha green tea in mugs. "I want him, and I'm afraid to want him," I say. "It scares me how at home I feel with him." She brings the mugs of tea back to the living room. "Maybe you just need to slow things down and get to know each other," she says. "Keep your personal life out of the office. That shouldn't be too hard. I can't imagine he's going to be around much, anyway." Cheryl's advice grounds me as usual. I calm down. "Don't hide your feelings for Nico from yourself," says a quiet voice inside. I wonder whose it is.

Nico calls me Sunday morning. About fucking time! You don't just come into a girl's life, sweep her off her feet, fly her around the world, feed her like a queen, fuck her brains out and then go MIA. "*Ciao*, Alexis," he says. "How is my wild beauty today?" What, just because I took control last time, now I'm his "wild beauty?" Damn if that doesn't make my heart sing. I feel a flicker of embarrassment when I remember it was only our second time together. "I've missed you," he says. I'm sitting in my bedroom chaise with my morning tea, thinking about dragging Cheryl to yoga class with me. "Have you really? Even with your non-stop schedule?" I say, "That's good to hear."

A huge bird lands on the rail of my bedroom terrace and I jump, spilling my tea. It's an eagle. It turns its head and stares straight at me through the glass door. It flaps its wings a few times. The wingspan is at least seven feet. It begins to preen itself. Nico is saying something. "I'm sorry, what did you say?" I ask him, still eyeing the bird. The bird eyes me back. It struts up and down the rail, then flaps its wings again and takes off. "I said I'm coming to Los Angeles. I need to see you." What's an eagle doing in the middle of LA? Wait, did he just say he's coming to LA? To see me? "When are you coming?" I ask. The tea has stained my nightgown. The lilies on the side table have dusted the surface with rust-colored pollen. "I arrive Friday afternoon," he says. "Will you spend the weekend with me on the Sea Gypsy?" I'm still fixated on the eagle landing on my terrace. I need to think. "Who else is coming?" I ask. "No one," Nico says. "It will just be us — and the crew, of course. And no business, I promise. I thought we might cruise over to Catalina. We can dive, snorkel, go jet skiing, kayaking, whatever you like. We can even go up to Santa Barbara for brunch on Sunday and invite your daughter to join us." There's no way I can resist his offer, but I'm not sure about the brunch part. I'm not ready to introduce him to Laura so soon. "OK, Nico, yes. It sounds like fun," I say. "Great!" he says. "I'll pick you up on the way from the airport."

I hear a high pitched yelping cry. Then I'm soaring in a cloudless blue sky over desert. I see a man and woman on horseback below me, and in the distance, the shining ribbon of a river, and a city beside it.

"Alexis?" Nico says. The sound of his voice jolts me back into my body. I gasp. It takes a second to reorient. "Yes?"

"Thank you."

"For what?"

"For agreeing to spend the weekend together," he says. "Before, it was business. This is personal, just for us. No work. I promise."

I don't respond. He's done it again, endeared himself to me completely.

"I can't wait to be with you again," he says.

After we hang up, I go tell Cheryl. She's sitting at my desk in my office-slash-guestroom doing some wedding planning stuff. "Well, it does show solid motivation on his part," she says. "He's obviously quite taken with you." Then I tell her about the eagle. She narrows her eyes. "That's bizarre," she says. "What did you say Nico's last name was?" I tell her and she types something into her laptop. "Did you know 'aquilo' is the word for eagle in Italian?" I look at my cork board where I pinned the two notes he sent me. The embossed lapis eagles look alive, as though they could take off and fly around the room at any moment. I hear that distinctive yip again, high-pitched, almost a scream. I shiver. "You don't think he's some kind of sorcerer or something, sending his familiar to spy on me?" I ask her. Cheryl squinches her face at me. "Don't be ridiculous," she says. "You're just acting paranoid." I shake my head. "It was a golden eagle," I say, "just like the one he flew in the life we had in Persia." I flip back and forth. First I feel my heart soar. We're soulmates who have loved each other for thousands of years. Then I'm pissed off. I hate feeling powerless, with no control, no choice in the matter. I pace around the room, pick up a book and put it down. I fuss with the curtains. I straighten a picture frame.

"Alexis!" Cheryl says. "What?" I say. She's turned the chair around. She's looking at me with her arms folded across her chest. "Girl, what is your problem?" she says. Something Nico said on the flight to Rio comes back to me, about being destined for each other, true partners this time around. "I don't like feeling like I have no choice." She laughs. I grit my teeth. "It's not funny!" I say. Cheryl just keeps laughing. "It's absolutely hysterical, you silly woman," Cheryl says. She gets up and puts her arms around me, sheltering me in her motherly reassurance. Cheryl gives the best hugs. "Now you listen to me," she says, "Do not blow this. Take your time. You don't have to worry about other possible lives together. Just focus on this life. This is the one you're living now, and it's your life to live. Even if you've had past life experiences with other versions of him, you are none of those women. You're still you and you have the power to choose what you want." I can feel the tension drain from my shoulders and the pressure release in my chest. I sit down on her bed. "So what do you want?" she asks. My mind goes blank for a second. Then my pussy tingles and sends a jolt to my heart. "I want to be with him again. I want to explore our connection," I say. "Well, OK then," she says. "You'll get your chance next weekend. Now stop pacing around and let me finish these emails." I notice the time. Shit, we're going to be late. "You can't," I say, "I have to leave in five minutes for yoga class and you're coming with me."

The week passes by in a blur of work and anticipation. Time alternates between rushing by and dragging on like a racing snail. I've scheduled a bikini wax and a pedicure for Thursday after work. This time I pack enough to be gone for a week with an outfit for every eventuality, from hiking to fine dining. Nico calls from the plane, "I'll pick you up in an hour." I dash out of the office and zoom home, change clothes and pack my last-minute toiletries. I turn back at the door and grab a tube of lube from my bedside table and stuff it in the bag. Hey, you never know when you might need it. The buzzer rings. He's here. Why am I so nervous? Is it just excitement? I walk off the elevator pulling my bags behind me, and Nico is there waiting in the lobby. I'm immediately wrapped in his strong arms and lifted off the floor. Then he kisses me, once, twice, three times. I laugh. "I'm happy to see you, too," I say. Jackson waits with the Tesla in the driveway and off we go.

The Sea Gypsy dominates the dock. It's the largest private yacht in the marina by a good hundred feet.

Jimmy brings our bags aboard. "Everything set?" Nico asks. "Yes, Mr. Nico," Jimmy says, "We just finished loading everything." Nico turns to me. "Do you want to unpack first or have drinks up on deck?" I'm way too excited to be out on the Sea Gypsy again. I don't want to waste the remaining sunlight inside a stateroom. "Drinks up on deck please," I say. Nico nods. "Jimmy, tell the captain to cast off immediately," he says, "and ask Susan to come up." Susan? Who's Susan? He better not have invited anyone else, not after he promised. Nico leads the way to the top deck. "What would you like? Champagne, tequila, fresh pineapple juice, iced tea?" he asks. There's an ice bucket with a bottle of that exquisite Cristal Rosé. "What are you having?" I ask. "Pineapple juice for now," he says. "It really is fresh made, not from a can." I don't think I've ever had fresh pineapple juice. "OK, I'll have the same," I say. I sip on the most delicious juice I've ever drunk as we pull away from the dock and motor out of the marina.

The Sea Gypsy makes her way into the channel and Susan arrives, IV stand and doctor bag in hand. "Alexis, this is Susan," Nico says. "She's one of the stewards, but she doubles as the ship's nurse." Susan sets Nico up with his jet lag treatment. "Do you have someone to administer this treatment everywhere you fly?" I ask him. "Most of the time," he says. Susan inserts the needles into his ears. "My regular locations for sure. I can't afford to lose my edge because of jet lag. I travel so much and it's hard on the body, so I've worked out ways to compensate." Susan slides a needle into the web between his thumb and index finger. "Why suffer when you can avoid it?" He grins at me. "Don't you want me at peak performance this weekend?" He really is adorable with those green eyes and dark curly hair. "Yes, Nico, I certainly do." We laugh. "Why don't you get a treatment too?" he says. "It's a great energy boost." So I do.

As we head out into the open ocean, I tell myself, "Alexis Rykof, this is your life." It's a perfect June day. I'm sitting on the top deck of a superyacht, eco-friendly no less, the warm breeze blowing through my hair, sipping fresh pineapple juice, getting an energy boost IV, watching a pod of dolphins surf our wake with my rich Italian stallion at my side. "Enjoying yourself?" Nico asks. The early evening light has turned the ocean into a shimmering golden mass. We're lounging on the large built-in sofas under a shade awning in the shape of a bird's wing, pure genius. I think I recognize it from their Milan design center. "Absolutely," I say. "I'm loving it. Thanks for inviting me." The IV bags are empty. Susan removes the needles and tubes and packs everything up. "Thanks, Susan," he says, "And can you send the appetizers up now?" Nico gets up, does some stretches and a few rapid pushups. "OK, that should do it," he says. "Ready for some champagne?" I laugh. "Feeling like a new man?" He just grins as he fills two flutes with the pink champagne, hands me one and raises his glass in a toast. "To our first weekend together, just for us." We clink glasses and drink. "This really is my favorite champagne," he sighs, glancing at me over the rim of his glass. "It is rather extraordinary," I add.

Nico sits next to me and slides his arm around my shoulder, pulling me into his chest. I snuggle into his spicy, smoky, sandalwood and leather scent. My pussy-meter begins to purr. We sit and sip our champagne in silence. Then Jimmy comes up with a tray of fresh spring rolls, ceviche, and some sort of guacamole and chips dish — but to call this lighter-than-air creamy froth and the paper-thin crispy discs "guac-and-chips" would be like calling the Sea Gypsy a dinghy. That would just be wrong. You cannot fault this man his standards in food. Not one bit. Nico gets up after our culinary orgasm, stretches his arms, twists his back and yawns. "Would you excuse me please? It was a long flight and I want to take a shower before dinner. Do you want to settle in, unpack?"

He shows me to the master stateroom. He's done it again. He gave me the master and took the guest suite for himself. Well, we'll just have to see about that. I appreciate the gallantry, but I'm pretty sure he's sleeping in here with me tonight. My bags are already laid out in the closet. The master suite has one entire wall of glass with doors leading out to a private deck with a hot tub, sofa and lounge chairs. There's a giant soaking tub and separate shower in the master bath. Très sexy! Susan appears and asks if she can unpack for me, but I'd rather do it myself. Nico kisses me lightly. "Would you like to eat up on the top deck again?" he asks. "Wherever you like," I say. "Do you think you can find your way back up?" he asks. I nod. "I'll give you the full tour after dinner or whenever you like," he says, and comes over to give me another kiss. This one is a proper lover's kiss. "God, you feel good," he murmurs. We stand by the giant bed kissing. He wraps his arms around me, then slides his hands down to take hold of my ass, squeezing and massaging it. I open my mouth to him and we start making out. My pussy starts to pulse and throb. I can feel him hardening against my thigh. "You get me so hot," he whispers. I come up for air. "Go on, get out of here and take your shower," I say. I give him a little swat on the ass. He laughs, "OK, OK, I'm going." After he walks out, I fall back on the bed and stare up at the ceiling. The light reflects off the water in a shimmering dance of gold. "Row, row, row your boat, gently down the stream," I sing, "Merrily, merrily, merrily, merrily, life is but a dream..."

Sunset dinner on the deck is exactly what you'd imagine in some over-the-top romance movie — majestic skies with sweeps of pinks, reds, oranges and purples, magnificent food and wine served by invisible hands, flickering candle light, fragrant flowers, a soundtrack of soft jazz in the background and two lovers gazing at each other. We stroll around topside after dinner, touring the various decks. We've dropped anchor off the shore of the Descanso Beach Club and the lights from shore twinkle off the stern. Now that the sun has set, a coastal chill washes over us. Nico sees me shiver and brings the outside tour to an end. "You're cold," he says, "let's go inside." We continue our tour inside and Nico points out all the features that make this vessel the first of its kind. He's geeking out over the design and engineering specs that got them closer to net zero energy consumption. When he launches into the team's "revolutionary application of water and waste processing technologies" my eyes begin to glaze over. "Alexis, forgive me," he says. He leads us back to the main salon. "I get carried away." He wrinkles his nose and gives me an embarrassed grin. "Not at all, Nico. I love how excited you get, I just don't have the technical knowledge to follow it all." We settle into one of the sofas. Some variety of cerebral jazz is playing in the background. Not my preference and certainly not the right soundtrack for a cozy romantic evening. "Do you mind if I change the music?" I ask. We definitely do not see eye-to-eye when it comes to music. I grab my phone and sync it to his sound system. The sexy stylings of my favorite Neo-Soul oozes out of the invisible speakers.

"I'm so happy you agreed to join me this weekend," Nico says, "I've thought a lot about what you told me on the flight to Rio." Way to get my full attention, dude. Which part has he been thinking about? My conflict over our professional relationship? The past life dreams? What? "Have you given any thought to what I said? Maybe this time we can create a true and equal partnership in every aspect of our lives." I set down my glass and turn to face him. He's fidgeting with his glass, turning the stem around between his fingers. I can see the outline of his chest and shoulder muscles through his shirt. The Sea Gypsy croons and murmurs to the sea as she shifts about at anchor. "Nico, we barely know each other. Let's take our time. I think it's best if we keep our business and personal relationship separate, at least for now." After my talk with Cheryl I want to be mature and prudent about this. I want to really get to know the man beyond the lifestyle. Nico looks at me, his green eyes laser-focused, like he's trying to penetrate my mind. Then he softens, and there's that look of wonder and vulnerability again. And something else. Something that feels like love. I fall into those eyes that feel like home, like safety, like peace and contentment, like devotion. "We can try," he says, "but I don't think that will be possible for much longer." I don't want to think about all the complications, let alone talk about it. I just want to drink in the feelings and be close with him. There's one surefire way to get him to stop talking. "Don't you ever get tired of trying to manage the world?" I ask. I swing my body around to lay on top of him, press my breasts against him and position my pussy over his thigh. I place his hands on my ass and say, "Here, manage this for a while." Then I lean in and start kissing him all over his face, rubbing myself up against him like a big cat.

Nico takes charge. He gives my ass a firm smack and sits up higher to settle me over his lap. He kisses me deeply, taking over my mouth while he runs his hands from my ass to my boobs, massaging, squeezing, pinching. Next thing I know, my shirt is off, my bra unhooked and tossed aside as he feasts on my breasts. I reach down to feel the hard length of him through his pants. I squeeze the head and he groans. He flips me over onto my back and pulls my pants off. He strips his clothes off without taking his eyes off me lying there on the sofa, naked and thoroughly aroused. He bends over to kiss me, thrusts his tongue into my mouth, runs one hand up and down my thighs, cups the mound of my pussy then moves back up to my breasts to pinch and pull my nipples. I writhe and moan, open my mouth and legs to him, trying to pull him on top of me, but he doesn't let me. Instead, he pulls my legs up and apart and kneels on the sofa between them. He spreads my lips and bends down to lick my wet folds and suck on my clit. He's got his hands on my ass cheeks and inner thighs, his mouth on my pussy, spreading me wide, driving me wild. He flicks his tongue up and down the underside of my clit, puts two fingers inside me and sends me into a long orgasm. I'm screaming and wailing as he works it without mercy until it gets too sensitive and I can't take it anymore.

I lie there panting as the last spasms shake through me when he pulls me up into his arms. When he kisses me, I taste my juices all over his face. Mmm, mmm, mmm, that man sure knows how to bring the sugar out of me. His cock is upright between our bellies, at rigid attention. He turns me over onto my knees. My hands grip the back of the sofa with my butt up in the air. He bends over and plants a few kisses on each cheek, then bites my ass. He stands up behind me, smacks it and growls. "Now I'm going to ride that beautiful ass until you beg for mercy." He spreads me open wide again, brings the head of his cock right up to the mouth of my pussy, and drives into me in one long, steady thrust. He settles himself inside for a moment, rocking and levering himself even deeper. Then he does just what he promised. He rides me like the fine, powerful stallion he is. He strokes in and out with a driving rhythm, my pussy wet and open to him, the honey and nectar pouring down. When he reaches one hand around to rub my clit, it sends me over the edge. I rear back and buck into him, my hands splayed against the wall for leverage. He's pumping into me, rubbing my clit, smacking my ass, massaging my breasts, pinching my nipples. My entire body lights up. Electric sparks shoot off me in all directions and my pussy does the whirling dervish on his big, hard gorgeous cock. He's got me on one of those spiraling multiple orgasms and I'm crying out in ecstasy. "Beg for it," he demands. He smacks my ass again. "Yes, yes, fuck me," I babble. "Take me. I need you to. Please, fuck me. Fuck me harder!" Then he grabs both hips and pumps into me until he climaxes with a low roar.

I collapse onto the sofa pillows and he slides out of me. Nico lays down behind me and pulls me close to him so we're spooning. We lay there together, panting and stunned. The ship's clock chimes 10:00 PM. The playlist ends. A silence falls over the room. There's only the murmur and swoosh of the sea against our hull. He kisses the back of my neck, whispers in my ear, "Alexis, you are so beautiful." He moves down to my shoulders, growls, "You make so hot. You drive me wild." We make our way to the master cabin and take a bath together. Then we climb into bed and hold each other, looking into each other's eyes, kissing sweetly. He falls asleep before we can make love again. I guess the long flight finally caught up with him. That, or I wore him out. I fall asleep with a contented smile on my face. I dream of Persia, the same scenes over and over again. First we ride like the wind across the desert, away from the city. We cast our birds and race them. Then we're at our camp and I slide off my horse into his arms. He carries me into our tent where we make love on thick piles of rugs.

In the morning, we make love again, this time sweet and slow, lying on our sides, arms and legs wrapped around each other, looking into each other's eyes, kissing softly, deeply, gently, rocking and rolling into each other to make it last and last and last. I start to come. My heart and my body melt open to him. He feels it and holds me closer, trying to get as far up inside me as he can, rocks into me until he comes, too. It feels like an act of communion. The intimacy is so intense I almost can't handle it. We lie there together looking out into the water. The morning light suffuses the room in a lemony glow as the boat rocks us in a cocoon of love.

"Ready for some breakfast?" Nico asks. "I'm absolutely starved," I say. "That's my girl," Nico laughs. I pig out at breakfast and plow through a fontina cheese and wild mushroom omelet, two pieces of toast slathered with butter and apricot jam, and half a dozen pieces of turkey bacon. Nico eats his normal, human-sized portion and asks what I'd like to do with our day. "We can go jet skiing, we can hike the island trails, we can go snorkeling, we can hit the beach club and swim…" It all sounds like fun, but I figure I should work off that enormous breakfast with a hike.

The boat's tender takes us to shore. We pick up a permit and walk through town to the Hermit Gulch trailhead. It's a deep climb up to the ridge. I'm sweating by the time we get to the top. We're rewarded with expansive ocean views in every direction. We spend the morning hiking the Trans-Catalina Trail, stopping for a picnic lunch the chef packed us. "Thank you for taking me to Catalina," I say, "I haven't been here before. It's so beautiful." It's nice to do something normal with him, hiking and a picnic. I'm having the best time. "I love being with you like this," he says, "out in nature. It's fun to simply hang out together and relax." We head back to town after lunch and wander around a bit, but it's kind of touristy. Nico tells me there's great snorkeling and diving just south of town. "Isn't the water cold?" I ask. But Nico has already thought of that detail, as per usual. "I've got a wetsuit on-board for you," he says. The tender takes us back to the Sea Gypsy to change and pick up gear. We spend the late afternoon swimming around in the kelp forests and the rocky reefs. We've brought bread and peas to feed the fish. They swim right up and eat out of our hands.

I'm ready for a shower and a nap when we get back to the Sea Gypsy. Nico feels the same. We take a long shower together, getting kind of frisky, then snuggle down into the big bed. Nico falls asleep quickly. It's something he's trained himself to do, another technique he's mastered in his never-ending quest for peak performance. I watch him sleep, the dark curls damp on the pillow, the strong nose and the finely carved lips. My Italian stallion. I close my eyes and take slow deep breaths. The whirlwind days of our first week together seem like fantasy. Spending time out in nature and on the water, here and now, feels so normal, so real, so grounded. Sure, we're on a great big luxury yacht, but it feels natural and relaxed. It's been so easy between us all day, like I've always wanted it to feel. I could get used to this. We've had a lot of fun. His dry wit makes me laugh and he loves it when I'm silly with him. I drift off until Nico kisses me awake. "Mmm, why hello," I say and kiss him back. "Much nicer than an alarm." He laughs. "How would you like to cruise up to Santa Barbara tonight and anchor off the coast? We can have brunch at the Biltmore in the morning, jet ski in the afternoon, then cruise back to the Marina in the evening. What do you think?" I roll over on top of him and give him a big kiss. "I think it sounds great," I say. He smiles, happy to please me. "I'll go tell the captain. Meet me up top for drinks before dinner?" I smile back at him and nod.

I decide to go to dinner au naturel island-girl-style, and tie a sarong around my waist with a cute little top. I add some lip gloss and fluff my hair, but no makeup. I want to be real with Nico. I want him to see me as I am. I'm testing him, I guess, but I want to see how he responds. Nico's mixing us drinks when I get to the top deck. He turns and smiles. "Seeing you like that makes me want to take you to the tropics." He comes over and gives me a big kiss. "I've thought about it," he says. "Thought about what?" I ask. "Taking you to the tropics," he answers. He hands me a glass. "But I didn't want us traveling again." I take a sip of the drink. "This is delicious. What's in it?" I ask. "Tequila, lime juice, bitters, and ginger beer," he says. It's another gorgeous evening, the air still warm, almost balmy. I study the patterns of the mint leaves he put in my drink. "What do you mean you didn't you want us traveling again?"

A serious look comes across his face. He takes my hand and leads me to sit beside him on the sofa. He's looking very GQ casual tonight in a loose white short-sleeved shirt and a pair of faded jeans. The white sets off his green eyes and dark skin. He really is such a hunk. "I want us to have a real life together," he says. "I have to travel so often for business, but I don't want our relationship to be like that." My heart skips a beat. A hidden flower of hope and longing buried deep inside me begins to unfurl its petals. I don't say anything. I sip my drink and let myself explore this unfamiliar sensation. "Alexis, I'm serious."

Jimmy arrives with a tray of appetizers and saves me from having to say anything. I watch the crew weigh anchor and we get underway, cruising north up the coast with the setting sun. After another fantastic dinner, we go down to thank his chef, Remy, a small dark Haitian man. He grins from ear to ear as I rave about his food. Nico and I spend the evening hanging out in the salon, talking and playing backgammon. I really am going to have to do something about his musical tastes. He loves challenging and cerebral music, Bebop jazz and complex atonal modern compositions. Then for variety, he'll listen to heavy metal when he works out or wants to ramp up his energy. Ay-yi-yi. I put on one of my chill lounge mixes, which he thinks is mostly boring. It's still early, maybe 10:30 PM. I turn to him and say, "Let's go to bed." Tonight we take our time with each other. In his arms, that hidden flower blooms.

Sunday is another magical day. We blow off brunch at the Biltmore. Remy's food is far superior and I don't feel like getting dressed and putting on makeup. Instead, we spend the day on jet skis, zooming up and down the beaches of Santa Barbara. We turn back in the late afternoon and cruise down the coast. I doze in a lounge chair on the deck. When I wake up, Nico is gone. I go looking for him and find him in his office working. "Hey, I thought this weekend was just for us, no work. Isn't that what you promised?" I say. "I know, I know," he says, "I'll be done in a few minutes." He's staring into the screen, tapping away. I stand there invisible, gone from his mind. He glances up. "Something urgent came up in Milan," he says, "I have to deal with it." I stalk out of the room and back to our suite to take a shower. I try and talk myself out of, but I'm pissed off. So what, he got some work done while I napped. Big deal. I don't know why it bothers me so much, but it does. He's waiting for me when I come out. "I have to go back to Milan." I don't say anything. I get my bags out of the closet and start packing. "I planned to spend the next few weeks here in Los Angeles," he says. I keep packing. "I want us to spend more time together." I walk into the bathroom to gather up my toiletries. He follows me in and leans against the wall. "Will you come back to Milan with me?" he asks.

I whip my head around. "I can't just pack up and fly halfway across the planet at a moment's notice whenever you choose," I snap. "Of course not," he says, "That's not what I meant." I pack the toiletries into bags. "You put me on the Aquilo-Built account. You want a successful kick-off? I have responsibilities, a team, a boss to answer to." I zip up my case. "You can call the shots at work, at the agency, but not in my private life. And how is it going to look to the people I work with, people who need to respect my authority and competency? I can't go gallivanting around the world with you every other week." I turn around, hands on my hips, glaring at him. "They're not stupid. It's completely obvious we're fucking." Nico looks surprised. I turn around, grip the edge of the sink and lean over it, taking deep breaths. I'm so angry I could spit. I forgot my tweezers. I see them in a pool of water on the edge of the sink. "I'm sorry. I didn't mean to upset you," he says. His phone rings. He looks at the screen. "I have to take this," he says. He leaves the room.

Nico drops me off on the way to the Van Nuys airport where his jet is waiting. He's on the phone the entire drive here, speaking rapid Italian in a low urgent voice. He gets out of the car to kiss me goodbye, but I'm stiff and unresponsive in his arms. "Thank you for the weekend on your boat," says the polite little miss. "I'll call you tomorrow, *caro*," he says, "We can work this out." Then he's gone. The Tesla pulls silently away. I stand in front of the door with my bags at my feet and watch the tail lights until the car turns the corner.

That night I'm back in St. Petersburg again. Katja is fighting with her prince. They're in an over-decorated room full of upholstered furniture and gaudy fabrics. She screams at him, "Even the serfs were freed by the Tsar, but to you I'm still your property!" She storms around the room. "But Katja," he says, "We'll have the dacha to ourselves for the entire weekend." Katja gulps down her glass of champagne. "What about my performances?" she yells, "I have the solo Saturday night. Do you know how hard I've worked to get Le Maître to cast me in this role?" Her eyes glitter obsidian. She throws a Rococo figurine of a little pageboy at him. "You think you can control me, Vasya?" She snatches up a pink and white vase painted with a pretty frolicking shepherdess, takes aim, and this one connects. It wings his forehead and shatters on the wall behind him. "You try to buy me, but you will never own my heart." I wake up filled with her black rage.

Nico calls late Monday night, just after dawn on Tuesday in Milan. He sounds tired. "I'm so sorry I had to rush back to Milan. Please don't be angry with me. I don't want it to spoil your memories of our beautiful weekend together." By this point, I don't know who's pissing me off more, him or me. I should have known there was no way he'd take an entire weekend off. "I'm sorry," he says. "I promised you no work and I couldn't hold to it." I'm lying in bed, the book I was reading open in my lap. "Maybe it's a promise you should never make," I say, "because you'll never be able to keep it." He heaves a big sigh. "No, no, I meant what I said about us spending more time together." I'm still pissed. Those Katja bleed-throughs are no help either. She loves to pour gas on an open flame. "Maybe we should just keep it to business," I say. "Don't say that." Nico jumps in. "I know it's no excuse, but I had a crisis on my hands. I had to deal with it." I don't say anything. The tea on my nightstand has grown cold. I run my fingernail up and down the case of my phone. "This... us... it's all new to me," he says. "Be a little patient with me, please. We can make it work." My heart melts a little, but he's not getting off that easy. "Our lives are very different, Nico," I tell him. "I'm not used to flying all over the world at a moment's notice on a private plane. My work is important to me. Please respect that." I stare at an ink stain on my sheet.

"I do respect your work, Alexis. That's why I hired you. I believe in you. I trust you," he says. I'm never going to get that stain out. He sighs again. "I didn't mean to be insensitive. I wasn't thinking. I just want you with me." Another petal of that hidden flower of hope unfurls.

I throw myself into work for the next two weeks. Nico's British taskmaster, the ever-perturbable Timothy, has been riding our asses hard. He's rigid and reactive, constantly challenging our research, our strategic insights, our creative concepts, our campaign roll-out plans, everything. It's obvious he doesn't think we're up to the task, but I can't really fault him. This is going to be a major international account, and we're just a regional agency, well-regarded, yes, but small. We've done some notable work, but hardly the size and scope of Aquilo-Built. I hope we're not getting caught up in the middle of a power struggle. I call an internal meeting with Jessica and Ben to strategize. We have to find a way to handle him, and we've only got a week before a major presentation to their team. "Maybe we should go to Milan and do the presentation in person?" Ben suggests. Milan? No fucking way! Immediately I jump in, "No!" Ben looks a little taken aback. Jessica raises an eyebrow and smirks. "Calm the fuck down, Alexis," I tell myself, "be cool." I take a breath and pull myself together. "It's not a good power play to present on their home turf," I say, "Let's invite them here."

I review everything I've figured out about Timothy. I have an idea. "Jessica, he's the most responsive to you and your Southern debutante ways." She laughs. "He is a bit like an old Confederate general," she says. "Stiff and proud with a stick up his ass." I cackle. "I want you to take lead on the presentation," I say. "Run it like a Southern matriarch and charm him into submission. Our guys can stay in the background. They'll be our Queens' guard. He'll just get all alpha male with them. Get our biggest nerd on the research team to present his part and be sure he can rattle off numbers until their eyes glaze over. Ben, you can take the role of the éminence grise in the background." We discuss the details and another issue crops up. "What are we going to do about Roger?" I ask. Ben glances at me, a confused look on his face. He adjusts his glasses. "What do you mean?" he asks. Jessica and I exchange looks. "Well, his California surfer dude style is not exactly reassuring to a man like Timothy," I say. I'm trying to be tactful, politically correct. The truth is, I want him off the account, but he's creative director of the agency. "OK, as account lead and head of strategy, you do the presentation on the creative concepts," Ben says. "Roger isn't going to like it, but I'll handle him, I promise."

Jessica pulls me aside after Ben leaves. "I concede your point on the power play, but did you ever think the rest of us might have appreciated an all-expense paid trip to Milan?" I sag onto the sofa in my office. "I'm sorry, Jessica," I say, "I can't handle going to Milan again right now. Things are complicated enough with Nico." She settles in next to me and kicks off her heels, a pair of sky-high Jimmy Choo stilettos. "Why? What's happening on the romantic front?" she asks. I fill her in. "You're taking a big risk with him," she says. "You don't want to blow the account." I sigh. "I know. But it's hard to resist him," I tell her. I slip my shoes off and prop my feet up next to hers on the coffee table. We wiggle our toes. "I *might* be falling in love?" Jessica tsk-tsk-tsks. "If only you had grown up in the South. Your Mama would have taught you how to manage your man." She swings her feet back down, sits up straight and turns to me, wagging her index finger in my face. "Get your priorities straight, but while you're at it, remember — there's no need to sacrifice love for money.

CHAPTER ELEVEN

Pink Diamonds

Nico calls me three nights before the presentation. "I'm coming to LA," he tells me, "I'll be there with my team for your presentation." We've only spoken a few times since our weekend on the Sea Gypsy. We've both been focused on work — him putting out fires and forestalling a crisis, me pulling together the presentation. "I can't wait to see you again," he says, "I've missed you." Before I can think about it, I blurt out, "Would you like to stay with me?" I look around my bedroom and imagine him here with me. My apartment is nice enough, but it's not very big, maybe twelve hundred square feet. "I was going to stay on the Sea Gypsy, but I'd love to stay with you," he says. Now I've gone and done it. "OK, it will be great to have you here," I say. "But it's nothing fancy, not like you're used to." He jumps right in. "Please don't even think like that," he says. "It's your place and that's what matters." My room's a mess. There's a big pile of laundry on the floor by the closet. A black lace bra crowns the heap. "Nico," I start, then pause. My chaise is buried under clothes and books. My shoes are strewn about the room. "I still want to keep our private relationship private, so can we be discrete about it?" I realize I'm holding my breath when I hear Nico exhale. "Of course, *caro*, whatever you wish," Nico says. The quiet voice in my head laughs at me, "Hah, good luck with that!" I hang up and make a list of all the things I have to do before he gets here. Can I redecorate my apartment in 48 hours?

The next night, the night before the presentation, I'm late getting home from work. Nico waits for me in the lobby. He only has one small bag with him. "I'm so sorry I'm late," I say, rushing up to give him a kiss, "Have you been waiting long?" He pulls me in for a big hug. "Not at all. I stopped at the Sea Gypsy first for a treatment and a sauna." He holds me close. I can feel the contours of his powerful chest muscles against my face. God, he smells good! "I'm so happy to see you," he whispers in my ear. "Three weeks is much too long to be apart." I have to agree. I take a quick scan when we get inside my apartment — all clear. Thank God my housekeeper was able to change days and get in here to clean. I show Nico around and make room for him in my closet. It feels strange to have him here and totally natural at the same time. He wanders around looking at my family photos, books and art while I prepare a simple dinner of broiled salmon in ginger and soy sauce with a summer salad. For dessert, we have fresh raspberries in crème Chantilly with almond snaps. I don't have any $600 bottles of Cristal Rosé in stock, so I serve a nice crisp Californian Sauvignon Blanc instead.

I excuse myself to take a shower after dinner. It's been a long day at work. When I come out, Nico is sitting up in bed, working on his laptop. He looks up and holds up a finger. "I'll be done in just a minute," he says. I stand looking at him in my bed. He's on my side. I try to imagine what it would be like if we lived together, if this were our nightly routine. And where would we live? Milan? Some place here in LA? What kind of a life would we have together, with his non-stop work schedule, the incessant demands of his growing empire? I work hard, but I don't want work to consume my life. Nico finishes up and closes his laptop. He throws the covers back for me. I slide in beside him. He puts his arm around me and pulls me close. I snuggle into him and breathe in his scent.

"It's nice, being here like this," Nico says. I can hear his heart beating. "Are you comfortable?" I ask, "It's not what you're used to." He sits us up straighter. "Alexis, look at me," he says, serious all of a sudden. He fixes me in those fierce green eyes. "You need to understand something about me. This is very important." A wayward curl has fallen over his forehead again. He's freshly shaved and his olive skin gleams in the glow of my bedside lamp. "It's not about the money for me," Nico says, "Sure, I grew up with wealth. I like fine food and fine wine, but money and luxury are not what motivate me." I push myself up to sit higher against the headboard. OK, I'll bite. "What does motivate you, Nico?" I ask. He takes hold of my hand, runs his thumb over my knuckles, squares his shoulders. He takes a deep breath and lays it out. "At first it was the thrill of the challenge. I was young. I had so many ideas.

Business was a game to me. It wasn't a competition. It wasn't about beating the other guy. I was testing myself to see how far I could go, if my ideas could work. I didn't just want to play the game. I wanted to master it. That's what motivated me. Same thing when I was an athlete. I wanted to win, sure, but only to prove that I could push the boundaries." I think about the sheer force of will and personal power required to do what he's done. It totally turns me on. "And what about now?" I ask, "What motivates you now?" He shrugs. "I grew up. Now I have a different purpose. I want to change things, to do something that has an impact. I want to make an actual difference."

I settle back into the pillows and marvel at the fact of this extraordinary man next to me in my bed, a visionary empire-builder and a hunk to boot. "Nico, thank you for sharing that with me. It helps me understand you better." He takes my hand again and kisses it, then holds my palm against his heart. "It's important to me that you know who I am," he says. "If you don't mind me asking," I say, "where do I fit into this world-changing vision? You kinda work all the time." Nico sighs. He runs his finger over my knuckles again and chews the corner of his lip. "I honestly don't know, Alexis," he says. "Up until now, it hasn't been an issue." Up until now? Up until now! Up until me, you mean? "And in the beginning, with your ex-wife? How was it then?" Nico lets out a rueful chuckle, lips turned down. "Well," he exhales, "I was a bit of a bastard then. Patrizia was from an old, aristocratic family fallen on hard times. Typical story — titles and crumbling estates, but not much money. She wanted babies and a husband to pay for a royal lifestyle. We were different people with different values. When it turned out I couldn't give her a child, the marriage fell apart. I think I told you, she refused to adopt."

Nico is shirtless leaning back on the pillows. He still has my hand in his pressed against his heart. I can feel it beating under my palm. Then my brain catches up to my ears. "What do you mean, you couldn't give her a child?" I ask. His shoulders stiffen. I see his lips tense. "I caught the mumps when I was at Stanford getting my Master's degrees," he says. He rubs the hinge of his jaw. "It left me sterile. That's why I never had children." I can hear the catch in his voice. "Nico, I'm so sorry. I know you wanted children." This is not exactly foreplay conversation, but I need to know. "Why did you never get married again, adopt children and start a family with a different woman?" Nico's laptop sits closed on top of the covers. The bedside lamps are too bright. I should get up and light the candles, put on some sexy music, close the curtains. A glass of ice water sits on a coaster on my bedside table, sweating. Nico has hung his clothes in my closet in his thoughtful and meticulous way. I can see our reflection in the big gold mirror on the wall by my bed — Nico's muscular body, dark olive skin and strong Roman nose beside me in my bed.

"I've had women in my life, but I didn't want to marry any of them. My passion went into my business," he tells me. He sounds cold. He turns to me and smoothes my hair back. "Now that you're in my life, my priorities are shifting." I don't know what to say to that. I don't want him giving up his world-changing vision for me. "Alexis, please believe me when I tell you I want a full partnership, on every level. I wasn't ready before, but I'm ready now. I never once felt this intensity with anyone else. What I feel with you is..." he sighs, shakes his head. "I don't know, it's new to me. Do you know how important you are to me?"

Enough talking! I turn out the bedside lamps and light the candles on the nightstands. I snuggle into him again and we begin to kiss, long deep sweet kisses. Nico has one arm wrapped around me. His other hand cups my breasts, caressing them and lightly squeezing my nipples between his fingers. Then he runs that hand down my body, over and around my hip to grab hold of my ass. I reach down, take hold of his cock, slide my hand up and down the shaft and over the head. He groans and gets harder. We stoke the fire between us and something emerges. Our lovemaking is as beautiful as ever, but there's a new quality there, some ineffable poignancy, a raw honesty, a depth we haven't shared before. I stop trying to protect my heart and let myself open to him, let him inside. I don't hold back. I can feel Nico respond with his whole heart, and not just his heart, but his whole body, his hands, his mouth — even his cock connects with me in a deeper, more intimate way. Every part of his soul reaches out to mine, through his body, through his skin, through his hands, his arms, his lips, his penis. Liquid light streams out of my pores, out of my pussy. I'm crying and moaning.

Tears are running down my cheeks as Nico rocks and rolls us into a luminous sea of love.

I wake up a happy, contented, well-loved woman. Then I remember — it's the morning of the presentation. Nico is already awake and in the shower. I join him. "Good morning," he says and gives me a big kiss. "Good morning," I kiss him back. "Nico, can Jackson come get you and take you my office? We can't be seen walking in together." Nico frowns and huffs something in Italian. "I'm sorry if it's inconvenient, darling," I say, soaping his back, "but it won't help my case with Timothy to prove the rumor true." Nico doesn't drink coffee in the morning, so I make him a super smoothie instead, full of berries, greens, hemp seeds and protein powder. He's on his laptop in my bedroom chaise when I bring it to him. Nico, in my chaise! I could get used to this morning routine. "Thank you," he says. "Mmmm, this is good." I sit by his feet, sip my tea and watch the hummingbirds feed on the trumpet vines growing on the deck.

"Wait, Alexis, what did you mean about your case with Timothy?" he asks. It's a beautiful summer day. I can tell it's going to get hot. The male hummingbird shows off for his lady. Should I tell Nico about Timothy? I don't want to be a little tattletale. Besides, I'm a big girl. I can handle this myself. "Nothing really," I say. "He's looking out for the company. It's no secret he has doubts about our ability to handle your launch, and you can't fault him on that. We are just a small regional agency. Not exactly a likely choice for agency of record on a big account like this." Nico doesn't say anything, but I see his mouth tighten and a fierce look come over his eyes. "My darling, I must go," I say. "Here's a set of keys. Just lock up when you leave. I'll see you there." I kiss him goodbye and leave for the office.

What can I say about the presentation? Let's start with the positives. Jessica was a charming and adroit mistress of ceremonies who managed to keep us on track and focused. She appeared, dressed as the love child of Nancy Reagan and Scarlett O'Hara, only with a much better haircut, and flattered Timothy relentlessly until he blushed, turning his pasty complexion a vivid pink. Nico loved the simplicity and pow factor of the creative strategy and thought it would translate well to any international market. Let's see, I think there was something else positive. Oh right, now I remember. I neither smacked nor kicked Roger or Timothy, the two of whom got into a ridiculous pissing contest, with Timothy doing his best to poke holes into every creative concept I pitched while Roger none too tactfully implied Timothy was an out-of-touch dinosaur who knew jack shit about modern advertising. I brought it to an end by proposing we conduct a number of focus groups in key markets to test the concepts, which Timothy tried to poo-poo as a research method of questionable objectivity and therefore value, until our research analyst backed it up with statistical data and gave the example of how it was used in the successful campaign of the current prime minister of Great Britain. Roger managed to dive head first into politically incorrect waters with reference to the childlike tastes in color palettes of the population of the Indian sub-continent, hell the entire Southeast Asian region, which he had observed firsthand on a surfing safari. To top it off, there was an AV snafu in the middle of showing the very expensive video we had produced to demonstrate the concepts in action, which took almost thirty minutes to sort out. Way to look professional, team. We take them all out for drinks and dinner afterwards.

As per our hurried huddle in the ladies' room, we manage to seat Timothy between Jessica and Ben, relegating Roger to Siberia down at the opposite end of the table. I'm in between Deming, the Chinese scientist and engineer who heads up the material sciences division and Nico. Deming and Nico met at Stanford and have been friends ever since. Deming is shy, brilliant and has a very dry and quirky sense of humor. During dinner, I discover the father of one of his best friends is a director at a top ten real estate development company in China. He promises to put us in touch. I need to start testing our concepts with the people who really matter at the top of the construction food chain. Jessica weaves her magic spell on Timothy and proceeds to get him pink-faced and drunk. At one point, I overhear Timothy tell Ben, "You know, I never would have selected your little agency. I told Nico you'd be sure to cock it up, but you all surprised me." He leans into Ben, jerks his head toward Jessica, then me. "And these two lovely birds aren't the daft cows I took them for," he says, oblivious to how loud he is. Look at him, trying to be chummy. I glance over at Nico and see him tighten his mouth into a thin line and give Timothy that fierce look of his. Timothy is too drunk to notice.

Jessica turns towards me, rolls her eyes and makes a gagging motion, sticking her finger down her throat.

After dinner, Timothy gets it into his head to go to a club. I don't know how much more of this day I can take but Nico saves me by bowing out. Deming also declines. Timothy still wants to go. Some of the younger people on our team are game. Timothy asks Ben about "hot clubs and celebrity sightings." I catch Jessica's eye while he's turned away, and put my hands together in a prayer position and beg her with my eyes. She shakes her head and rolls her eyes again and mouths, "You owe me, big time." I nod my head in agreement. Ben pays the bill and we all get up to leave. I walk out to the valet stand with Nico, Timothy and Jessica right behind. "Do you know, Jessica," Timothy says in his posh British accent, "I do believe you got our business just because Nico wanted to bonk Alexis." I flinch. I can't believe he said that! Jessica laughs and says, "Now, Timothy, no need to get jealous. All us brilliant, beautiful career gals admire you, too." Which doesn't even really make sense as a comeback, but it makes Timothy smile and preen. I'm beginning to wonder if Jessica spiked his drinks, given his total lack of filters, or if our oh-so-correct martinet just can't handle alcohol. Nico is most definitely not amused. Timothy, Jessica and Ben drive off in Ben's car. Nico leans over and tells me in a low voice that he'll see me back at my place. He gets into his Tesla with Jackson behind the wheel and they take off.

Nico's waiting for me in the lobby when I get home. He's silent all the way up in the elevator. My head is pounding. Once we're inside I ask him, "Nico, darling, do you mind if I take a bath? I've got the most awful headache." He looks at me with narrowed eyes and tight lips. "Why would you ask me permission to take a bath?" he snaps. I have no energy to discuss or argue anything tonight. "Because you're a guest in my home," I sigh, "presumably here to spend time with me, and it seemed like the considerate thing to do if I'm going to disappear into the bath." I step out of my heels and walk into the bedroom, unzip my dress and let it drop, then take off my jewelry. Nico follows me in. He leans against the wall, shifting his weight back and forth, and biting the corner of his lip. "I'm sorry, Alexis, I didn't mean to take my irritation out on you."

I get my bath started and light the candles. I take a couple of aspirin. I pour a hefty amount of essential oils in the tub — my old standard, rose, plus some ylang-ylang and sandalwood. I put on a headband and tie up my hair. I step into the hot fragrant water and sink up to my neck. I rub some cleansing cream into my face, dip a washcloth in the water and cover my face. I lay there breathing through the scented steam of the washcloth and try to relax. Nico comes in. "Tough day?" he asks like he wasn't there for all of it. "You could say that," I reply. He finds some oil in the cabinet and begins to massage my neck and shoulders. The washcloth has cooled off. I dip it in the water and cover my face again. Nico stops rubbing my tense muscles. I sigh and lift the washcloth off my face to see what's happening. He's stripped down. "May I join you?" he asks. "Come on in," I say, "The water is fine." Nico steps into the tub and leans his back up against the opposite end. He takes my tired feet in his hands and gives me an expert foot massage. When he begins to suck my toes into his mouth, I giggle and splash him. My headache is gone and I'm feeling much better.

We go to bed, and that's where Nico gets right down to business on my pussy, just dives right up in there and gets real busy with his mouth and his hands, his fingers and his tongue. That boy climbs down in there as far as he can go, so far down he's climbing up now, but there's no bottom to hit. Instead petals open, then the veils behind the petals open, then more veils and petals open, membranes thin as a spider web open, webs stitching the galaxy together, opening, always opening, no end of the opening. Drive us on, my fine Italian stallion, drive us on, get us to the pearly gates, those mother of pearl gates, seashell pink gates, shining wetly in the dark. Drive us on, my wild stallion, 'til waterfalls of light shower down upon your head and fill it with stars, Milky Way trails across the night sky of your mind, of my womb. Say hello, dear boy, to the portal of all human life.

The alarm wakes me. I roll over to Nico's green eyes smiling at me. "Good morning, beautiful," he says, wraps me in his arms and kisses me. I snuggle in. "What time are you finished today?" he asks me. I sigh and pull the covers over my head. The thought of the unavoidable debrief of yesterday's presentation fills me with dread. It's sure to be contentious. If only I could get rid of Roger and hire a new creative director. Then there's Timothy. What the hell am I going to do about him? I can't help but take a little pleasure in the massive hangover he must be suffering right now. Serves the little prick right. "I'm not sure," I say, "Not too late I hope." I peek out from under the covers. "Why? What do you have in mind?" Nico kisses me on the tip of my nose. "I thought we could spend the weekend on the Sea Gypsy," he says. "We could go back to Catalina, up the coast again to Santa Barbara, or head south to Laguna Beach, even San Diego." Just to tease him, I pretend I have to think about his proposal even though he's already seen how much I love being out on the water. "That sounds like fun, but Catalina again?" I joke. "Why not Hawaii?" He actually takes me seriously. He frowns in concentration and bites the corner of his lip, running the calculations in his mind. "Why not?" he says, "The Sea Gypsy is fast. We can get there in about two days with good weather."

I laugh. He must be joking. "Nico, I can't just take off and vacation whenever I want. I've got work obligations, meetings, a campaign to plan, a company to launch..." It's going to be another July scorcher today. I have to remember to put water out for the hummingbirds. "You can work on board. The Sea Gypsy is also my floating office," he says, "Everything's state-of-the-art — internet, video streaming, teleconferencing, everything you need." I sit up in bed to look at him. Is he completely oblivious? I can see from his matter-of-fact expression he really doesn't get it. "Are you crazy?" I say. He gives me a questioning look. "And what do I tell Ben, my team? 'Oh, sorry I won't be able to make the meeting in person. I'll be out of the office on our client's superyacht, cruising to Hawaii and getting my brains fucked out, but don't worry, I can video conference into the meeting.'" I shake my head at him. "Yeah, that'll go over real well." I slip out of bed and go take a shower. He really has no idea how the other half lives. After my shower, I make some Darjeeling tea for me and a green power smoothie for him. Nico's on his laptop when I come back in to get dressed. "So, what's your answer about this weekend?" he asks again, "Are you free to join me?" I hand him his smoothie. "I'd love to spend the weekend on the Sea Gypsy," I say. "I may have fallen in love with her. But unlike you, I live in the real world, so let's stick to local waters and get me back to the marina by Sunday night. Now, I really have to hurry or I'll be late." I bend over to give him a juicy kiss.

It's 4 PM and I'm still sitting on the sofa in my office. I'm exhausted. Frustrated. Overwhelmed. My brain cells are fried from the three-hour marathon debriefing in the morning, followed by another two hours holed up with Ben and Jessica after lunch. Part of the problem, I realize, is the agency business model and internal processes. It's inefficient and too hierarchical for my taste. These are the same issues that fueled my dreams of starting my own agency. I doodle circles and patterns on my legal pad, thinking about alternate organizational structures and workflow processes. Nico texts me, "Meet me at the boat when you're done." Fuck it. I'm not going to get any more work done today. I pack up my stuff and peek into Jessica's office on the way out. She's leaning back in her chair, feet up on her desk, sweetly informing the poor soul at the other end of the phone that she will personally show up at his office, hogtie him, hoist him to the ceiling and let him swing in the wind if he doesn't do right by her. She winks at me. "Well sugar pie, it's your choice of course, but it'll be terribly embarrassing for you." She motions to her sofa. I stand at the door and wait. "Harvey, do not test me. I am not in the mood," She's all business now, her voice cold and steely. "If those edits aren't on my desk Monday morning, I'll be there with my ropes and pulleys Monday afternoon." She switches back to Southern treacle. "Y'all have a great weekend now, y'hear? Bye-bye," she trills and hangs up.

"What was that all about?" I ask. She shakes her head. "You do not want to know." She looks me up and down. "Honey chile, you look a bit peaked." Jessica is still in full on Southern belle mode. She checks her watch. "Where are you off to?" she asks. I look up and down the hall to make sure no one's coming. I step into the office. I put my finger to my lips, "Shhh. Weekend on Nico's yacht." Jessica puts her feet down and sits up in her chair. "Alexis, far be it from me to discourage a girl from having fun, but like my Daddy always said, never shit where you eat. You do not want to mess with that Timothy. I bet he's a vindictive little prick. He's already figured out why we got the account and he is not happy about being over-ruled." I know it's beside the point, but I still have to say it for the record, "Nico gave us the account before we ever met," I say. "I never even laid eyes on him before he showed up here with his team." Jessica raises an eyebrow and cocks her head at me, like I've lost my right mind, as she would put it. She's not wrong, but it's too late. I might as well admit it to myself. I'm falling for him. "See you Monday," I say, "have a good weekend." I meant to tell her about my ideas, but oh well. It can wait. "I'll try my best," Jessica snarks, "but it won't be as good as yours."

By the time I get home, pack, and drive over to the marina, it's already 6:30 PM. I am not in the best mood. I find Nico on the bridge conferring with the captain. He smiles when he sees me and walks over to give me a hug and a kiss. "Can we please get the hell out of here as soon as possible?" I say. He pulls back and searches my face. Jessica's warnings struck a nerve, but I don't want to think about business anymore, especially Nico's business. "Hard day?" he asks. I nod. He puts his arm around me. "Would you like to take a hot tub before dinner?" he asks. "We can soak and have drinks on the master deck." That sounds perfect. Just what the doctor ordered. I nod again. "Go on down," he says, "I'll meet you there in a minute." When I get to our stateroom, I see one of the stewards has already unpacked for me. Even that service, a matter of routine for Nico, irritates me in my pissy mood. I tear off my clothes and grab a big fluffy robe and towel from the bathroom, pin up my hair and slide the doors open to deck. The deck hands have cast off and we're nosing our way out of the marina. I wrestle with the cover on the tub and shove it off to the side. Nico comes out and lifts it out of the way for me. "Perhaps you'd rather to go to the gym and do some work with the punching bag?" he grins. I punch him in the arm instead, then drop my robe and step into the tub.

Jimmy comes out with a tray of drinks and appetizers. I duck under the water and cover my breasts. I don't know if I'll ever get used to all these servants around. We head out of the channel and into the open ocean. My mood improves immediately once the Sea Gypsy picks up speed to plow through the waves. With the ocean breeze in my face, the horizon stretching before us, and Nico passing me appetizers, I relax and let the stress of the day blow away. I hang over the edge of the hot tub to pull Nico in for a juicy kiss. "Sorry for being pissy," I say. "I'm feeling much better now." Here I am, naked in a hot tub on a superyacht, enjoying cocktails and scrumptious tidbits under a majestic sunset. It's hard not to feel like I'm in an episode of Lifestyles of the Rich and Famous. I sweep my arm across our deck scene. "Attitude adjustment successful," I laugh. I rise up to rub my wet breasts against his chest, getting his shirt soaked in the process. Nico laughs and smacks my ass.

I pull off his wet shirt and unzip his pants, sink down into the tub and pull his cock out of his briefs. I lean forward and kiss the head. He swells and hardens in my hand. I begin to suck him off, pausing to pull his pants and briefs down. He steps out of them and stands before me naked and erect. I take him into my mouth again and suck his cock, swirling my tongue around the ridge and the sensitive skin under the head while caressing his balls. I take him into my mouth and down my throat as far as I can. I drive him wild and he starts to pump into me. I can feel he's close to coming, but he has other plans. He pulls out of my mouth and lifts me up out of the tub. I wrap my arms around his neck and kiss him. He reaches down and takes hold of my ass. I jump up into his arms, locking my feet behind his back, kissing him all over his face and neck. He carries me into the stateroom and throws me onto the bed, stands back and looks at me. I lay there and look back at him. His green eyes are shining, gazing at me with adoration. I adjust my position, moving up to lean back on the pillows. I display my body to him, running my hands over my breasts, mounding them together, spreading my thighs, opening the folds of my pussy to reveal the pink mouth at the center. "Do you have any idea how gorgeous you are?" he asks in a husky growl.

He crawls onto the bed and kisses and caresses my body, starting with my feet, working his way up to my face, until I'm moaning and writhing, begging him to fuck me. And that's just what he does, my obedient monster. He throws my legs over his shoulders and rears back onto his haunches to penetrate me. I grab his ass and pull him into me as deep as he can go, slap his ass to make him ride me harder, urge him on, "Yes, yes, yes, fuck me harder!" until I start to wail and come. He slows down, tips us onto our sides, shifts the energy. He gazes into my eyes, grabs hold of my ass to rock into me with a long rolling rhythm. I stroke his face and tip my head up to kiss him, run the tip of my tongue up along the roof of his mouth. We build the energy between us, circle it around like a particle accelerator, spiral it up the central channel until it overflows in a shower of rainbow light, rolling bliss-waves up and down my pussy and all over his cock, sending him over the edge. He releases into me, crying out, "Ahhh, ahhh, ahhh, Alexis, I love you!" It's the first time he's said it straight out.

I wake up early and full of energy the next morning. We're anchored off the coast of Catalina Island. I slip out of bed as quiet as I can to leave my sleeping prince undisturbed. His face is so beautiful in the morning light. I'm tempted to kiss him. I put on yoga clothes, grab my mat and head up to the wide covered aft deck. I pass Susan on the way there. "Can I bring you some tea and fruit, Ms. Rykof?" she asks. "Yes, please," I say, "Darjeeling would be great. I'm going to do some yoga, so maybe in about 45 minutes?" It's already warm at this hour and I'm glad for the shade. I work up a sweat with a vigorous flow sequence and plenty of arm balances. I enjoy my solitary breakfast, looking out at the ocean and listening to the sound of the waves against the hull and the seagulls overhead. I go back to our room to take a shower. Nico is just waking up when I come out.

"Good morning, handsome," I say. "How did you sleep?" I walk over to kiss him good morning. "What time is it?" he yawns. "Eight," I say. He stretches like a big cat. "I can't remember the last time I've slept so long," he says. "That's what good loving will do for you," I say. I kiss him again. He pulls me into bed with him and I tumble into his arms. "Nico, my darling, we can't spend all our time in bed," I laugh. He pulls me closer. "Why not?" he says. "I don't want you to get bored of me," I tell him and tickle him to get loose from his grip. He growls and pulls me in closer, bites me on the neck. I push his head away and tickle him again.

He turns serious again. "I could never get bored of you, Alexis." I laugh and reach to tickle him again, but he catches my hands and holds them to his heart. "Look at me," he commands. Those eyes peer into mine like he's trying to read my mind. A fresh morning breeze blows through the half-open doors to the deck. "I mean it. I've never felt this way with any woman before." His face softens. "I told you I love you last night," he says. "That wasn't some heat-of-the-moment sex thing." I don't say anything. I just keep looking into those eyes. They glow in the lemony morning light. I study the patterns of green and gold in his irises. "Alexis Rykof, I love you, body, heart and soul." My chest is going to burst. The love wells up inside me and overflows. I can't help myself. I start to cry. "I love you too, Nico," I murmur. We lie there holding each other in his silky sheets as the Sea Gypsy rocks us and the ocean breeze kisses our skin. I feel giddy, delirious, awed at the enormity of what just happened between us. He loves me, he loves me, he loves me. And I love him. Nico's stomach growls. Really loud. It sounds like a cement mixer. We both laugh. "Have you eaten yet?" he asks. "Yes, darling. I got up early and did yoga on the deck. Susan served me breakfast after." Nico picks up the bedside phone and calls the galley to order a monster breakfast.

We spend a glorious day on the water, exploring little coves, snorkeling, picnicking on an empty beach, racing around on jet skis. I'm happy as a kid at summer camp. After a shower and a nap, I wander up to the top deck. Nico is sitting on the sofa, working on his laptop as usual.

He looks up. "Sorry, *caro*, I'll be finished in a minute," he says. "Take your time," I tell him. I don't want him to worry. I'm not going to trip out on him again. I just stand at the rail looking out at the island and the ocean. He finishes up, closes his laptop, and walks over to stand behind me. He wraps his arms around me, kisses the top of my head and nuzzles his face into my neck. "Ready for some champagne?" Someday I'm sure I'll tire of his favorite champagne. Just not yet. "Yes, please," I say. He serves me a flute of the pink elixir.

"Come, sit here next to me," Nico says, "I have something I want to say." The early evening light is warm and golden. It hits the facets of my crystal champagne flute and splinters into a thousand sparkling rainbow fragments. The light dances off the tiny bubbles in my glass. A breeze kisses my face on its way out to sea. Nico faces me on the sofa and takes both my hands in his. "Alexis," he says. "I've thought a lot about the situation I've put you in. I didn't fully understand the difficulties until the presentation Thursday. Please forgive me for my stupidity and insensitivity." He looks down, shakes his head, pushes his curls off his forehead. I sigh. "Thank you for saying that, Nico, but let's not talk about any of that now," I say. "I don't want to spoil our beautiful weekend." I lean in to give him a kiss, then try to pull my hands away to stand up, but he holds me there. "I'm not finished," he says. He's got a determined look on his face. "This is important." I settle in again. I never really noticed before, but his ears kind of stick out. There's a tiny dimple in his right earlobe where a piercing has closed up. "I love you Alexis. I want us to be together," he says, "and I will not allow anything to get in the way of that." I swoon to feel his powerful protective instincts. Katja bristles at his commanding tone, but I love it. His strength and power turn me on. "We've only known each other for a short time, but I already know you are the love of my life. Body and soul."

My mind shuts off. I can't process what he's saying. I notice the grey just creeping into the curls at his temple. My heart tries to escape my chest. He lets go of my hands, reaches into the sofa cushions and pulls out a small black velvet box. "Alexis, will you marry me?" He opens the box. There's a diamond ring inside, a large rosy pink oval set between emerald-cut sapphires. It's enormous — big, but not vulgar. I don't know how many carats it is, but it's over half an inch long, minimum six or seven carats, probably more. I stare at it. The ring glitters and winks at me in its velvet cushion. Nico's fingernails are buffed and smooth. His hand is shaking just a little. His skin, tanned a deep olive brown, contrasts with the white of his linen pants. Gulls swoop and dive off the bow, screeching to each other. My brain is frozen. Nico takes the ring out of the box and slides it onto my limp finger. I can't take my eyes off it.

"Alexis, say something," he says. A thousand thoughts race around my head. It's all happening too fast. I've found the love of my life, but we don't even know each other. What kind of wedding would we have? Where will we live? I have to tell Cheryl. My heart bounces around my chest. I can't breathe. There's something wrong with my ears. The cries of the gulls sound muffled, then way too screechy-loud. "I don't know what to say," I whisper. "Say yes," Nico says. "Say that you love me." I look up again. His face looks so open and vulnerable. His eyes are wide and soft. "I do love you, Nico, but this is so fast," I tell him. "I think I'm in shock." Nico starts making his case in a low urgent voice. "Maybe it's a little sooner than I planned, but I knew almost from the beginning that I wanted to be with you. Can't you feel that we're meant for each other? You're the only woman for me, and I know I'm the man for you." My heart stops. Then jumps. Then stops again. My chest is too small to hold all this love. "Thursday's debacle just sped up my timeline," he says. He frowns, his face looks fierce and grim. "I hate the situation I've put you in. I won't tolerate anyone disrespecting you. I just won't. And I refuse to skulk around like secret lovers anymore. I'm proud to be loved by you, and I don't care who knows it." I look down at my hand again. It's shaking.

"I don't know, Nico," I say, "I need time to think about it." I reach for my glass and take a sip of my champagne. Nico gets up and starts pacing around the deck. "If we're married, no one will disrespect you or question your authority. You won't be fucking the client and you won't be fucking your boss. You'll be fucking your husband." I take a deep breath and try to get my mind in gear again. I imagine Timothy and Roger's reactions to the news. "Are you insane? Don't you see that marrying you will only prove my critics right?" It's incredible. He actually believes he can legislate people's attitudes by fiat. "Everyone will think I slept my way into the account." I can see I've surprised him. He really does live in a bubble. He sits back down and rubs the stubble on his jawline. "I hadn't thought of it like that," he says in a quiet voice. I lean back and sip my champagne, holding my hand out to study the ring. A circle of sapphires surrounds the large pink stone in the center. I glance over at Nico. He's looking off into the distance, brows furrowed, eyes narrowed in concentration. Then he jumps up all excited like he's found the solution. "What if I make you my partner in the Aquilo Group?" he says. "They'll have to respect you then." The man has gone crazy. He's pacing back and forth now, almost leaning forward, his words tumbling out in a rush. "It's privately held and I'm the majority shareholder. I do what I want. It's my company. You can take any role you want. You can be the Chief Marketing Officer of the entire Aquilo Group. Bring Jessica on board. Build an in-house agency. Hire outside agencies. Whatever you want. You'll be in charge." I don't say anything. He comes over and takes my hands again. "Let me crown you as my queen at my side. Half my kingdom."

I know Nico means well. It's sweet, really, but it's completely naive. I look back at him and watch as his face morphs, first into Vasily, then into my Persian captain, then my master in ancient Egypt. I've got three women's emotions swirling around, bleeding into mine. Katja is furious. "There he goes again, thinking he can buy you and command his way with everyone," she hisses. I can feel the hope and longing of the other two women taking wing inside my heart. To them, it's their last chance to have the relationship they've always dreamed of. Get a grip, Alexis! I blink hard. I take a deep breath to clear my vision. I push them all back to wherever they came from and try to focus in the here and now. "Nico, I know you like to find one solution to many problems, but you have to see this just won't work the way you think it will. And a business proposition disguised as a marriage proposal, just for the sake of expediency? It's hardly the way to a girl's heart." He looks stricken. "No no no, that's not what I meant." I hold my hand up to stop him going on. "Listen to me. First of all, you can't just give me half your company, even if I wanted it. I know you think it will make people respect me more, but it will have the opposite effect." He looks confused now. "Don't you get it? Do you honestly believe that rushing into marriage and making me your partner will stop people thinking I slept my way to the top? That they'll respect me more?" I shake my head. "Second of all, I would never marry you as some sort of contract or business deal. That's not what love is." I set my champagne glass down. I watch the bubbles make a break for the surface. I adjust my seat. "You really don't understand women, do you?" He bites the corner of his lip and frowns.

Jimmy arrives with appetizers and Nico waves him away. "Don't serve dinner until I call down," he says in an abrupt tone. I hear Katja harrumphing in the background. "I told you so," she says. I wait until Jimmy is out of earshot. "If you're making me a business proposition, that's one thing, but that's not what I want in my lover and husband. That's not how love works."

"I only know I adore you and want us to make our lives together," he says. "It's not a business proposition." He takes my hand, weighted down by that giant pink diamond, and kisses it three times. Then he turns it over, kisses the center of my palm and places my palm over his heart. He holds it there. He looks at me with so much love and naked need I can hardly stand it. Then the grown-up, rational part of me takes over.

"That's another thing," I say, "*How* will we make our lives together? How will that work? I mean, even if only from the practical standpoint. For instance, how many days a year are you traveling? Besides Milan and the Sea Gypsy, where else do spend most of your time? Do you foresee us getting a place here in LA? How will we manage my travel schedule when we start rolling out the international markets?" I can tell none of this is what Nico expected when he pulled that velvet box out of the sofa cushions.

"All good questions," Nico says, "We'll figure out the answers together, but you have to tell me how you want it be. What do you want in a life with me?" I look out at the horizon line. There's a magnificent sunset, the sky all pink and red and purple. I can't believe we're having this conversation. "I don't know. Not entirely, not for sure. I'd have to think about it," I tell him. "I do know one thing though."

"What's that?" Nico asks.

"I don't want us living our lives separately. I don't want to spend more time apart from each other than we are together," I tell him, "And I know one other thing, too."

"Tell me," he says.

"I want us to make a home together," I say, "A real home where we both feel completely comfortable, our own personal sanctuary of peace and beauty, and I want us to spend time there together." I don't recall ever thinking about this before, but out it pops. It's only when I hear myself say it that I realize how much I want a home and life together. "And I want to have Laura come with her boyfriend, and her family someday, if there are grandchildren, and to welcome our closest friends, and serve them fabulous food and have wonderful times. And I want us to spend time on the Sea Gypsy, and take her cruising around the Caribbean and the Mediterranean."

Nico laughs. He looks relieved. "For someone who doesn't quite know what she wants, you sure are specific." He takes my hands again and looks into my eyes. "Here's how it is. Right now, my life is not set up to align with all that. It's just been me. It will take a little time to make adjustments, change things around. But we can start figuring it out together from here on out. Some of it will depend on how you want to handle the business part of our lives. Do you still want your own agency? You could always create an in-house agency and run it the way you want."

The logical part of my brain shuts down. "I don't know," I say. "I can't think about this business stuff right now. It's all so complicated." I look out at the sunset over the ocean, at the vast possibilities stretching out in all directions beyond what my eyes can see. Then I get scared. Do I want a life as big as Nico's? It's a lot of pressure and responsibility. Maybe I want a quieter, simpler life. He wants to change the world and he's throwing all his resources behind the effort. His work and travel schedule are non-stop. It's overwhelming. Then again, I'm head over heels in love with him. I've loved this soul throughout the centuries.

Nico puts his hands on my shoulders. He looks me straight in the eyes again. "*Caro*, there are only two questions that matter. Do you love me? And do you want us to be together? The rest is just details and logistics." When he puts it like that, it all sounds so simple. "Yes, Nico, I do love you. And I do want us to be together. I'm just not sure how to make it work so we don't destroy our relationship." He smiles and pulls me to him for a hug. "How about this? You don't have to decide now." He kisses my left hand again. "Keep it as a promise ring," he says. "Wear it as a symbol of my commitment to you. Think it over, take your time. But I'm all in. I know we can make it work." My nervous system is on overload. My heart is about to jump out of my chest. I can't think straight. Time slows down. I can hear Nico's heart beating. It feels like ages between each heartbeat. I sit up and face him. "Nico, my darling, I can't say yes right now. We need to slow down and get to know each other first. And there's a lot to figure out. I'm not making any promises, but I'll wear the ring as a symbol of our love." I lean forward and press my lips softly up to his. I look down at my gorgeous pink diamond ring. It's the exact same shade of the Cristal Rosé he loves so much. I gaze out to the sun sitting on the edge of horizon. There's a brief flash of green light as it disappears beneath the ocean. I take Nico's hand. He puts his arm around me and I snuggle into my spot. I relax into the safety of his embrace, the broad wall of his chest under my cheek. I listen to his heart beating and breathe in his special smoky sandalwood. The sky edges into violet and indigo. The ocean laps against our hull as the Sea Gypsy rocks us gently home.

ACKNOWLEDGEMENTS

This book owes its existence to Barbara Deutsch, who challenged me to put myself in a self-imposed writing boot camp and just finish it. So I did, with the insane goal of 2000 words a day. Whew! Thanks to Derek Stettler, who was with me the entire period of that boot camp, providing comic relief and unwavering love and emotional support. Also to Kate McCallum and Ed Lantz for the safe shelter during that period.

Whatever writing technique I have, I owe to Jack Grapes, founder of the Los Angeles Poets and Writers Collective, and writing teacher extraordinaire. Jack, thank you for your generosity, humor, brilliance and support. My gifted editor, Joshua Grapes, made the book better and was a delight to work with, a joyful collaboration.

Cathy Hamilton, my sister from another mother and loving coach, helped me overcome fear and doubt to empower and free myself to launch the book into the world. Thanks to my early readers, whose enthusiastic response kept me going: Elena Kontorer, Melanie Wachsman, Tiffany Lundgren, and Cathy Hamilton. My dear friend, Ilona Glinarsky, introduced me to tango and guided me all along the way. Thank you for your love, support and generosity.

ABOUT THE AUTHOR

An interdisciplinary artist, writer and producer, Mikhaila explores the themes of creativity, consciousness, sexuality and female empowerment in a variety of media and performance arts.

For monthly updates and subscriber-only freshness, please join the mailing list at http://www.mikhailastettler.com

45140102R00169

Made in the USA
San Bernardino, CA
01 February 2017